They were *guardians?*

As she stared at him, inconsequential thoughts filtered through Roz's shock. He'd cut his dark blond hair short; it didn't touch his collar anymore. She recalled the only other time she'd seen him in a suit.

At their wedding.

"Where's Daddy?" little Cassie asked, peeking at Jack through half-closed lashes from where she sat on Roz's lap, and turning another page of the book with chubby fingers.

Dazed, Roz switched on the table lamp and began reading to the child again. "The seagulls thought Pinky was also a brave adventurer, and he was, but only in his imagination."

Out of the corner of her eye she saw Jack straighten his shoulders.

They were guardians.

Somewhere in the dread, a dangerous joy flickered into life.

Dear Reader,

Four books on and it's still such a thrill to write "Dear Reader." Thank you for reading *Second-Chance Family*.

I didn't set out to write a romance with a backstory of death, grief and divorce—in fact, I originally intended this book to be a light "fish out of water" story about two people suddenly finding themselves responsible for three challenging children.

But all my characters, including the kids, wanted to be more "real" than that. And my experiences with grief—my own and other people's—colored the book with dark as well as light. In times of grief there is also laughter, and I believe (as does the hero eventually) that love transcends loss. And that's a very uplifting thought.

In the initial draft, the kids ran away with the story and I ended up deleting some scenes that were a lot of fun but didn't serve the story's purpose, which was Roz and Jack getting back together. These scenes are posted on my Web site, www.karinabliss.com. For those of you who enjoyed meeting Luke Carter in this book, he's the hero of a previous book—*Mr. Unforgettable*. Right now I'm working on another Harlequin Superromance novel about a former rock star looking for a quiet life and a librarian who can't commit. The catalyst for these two misfits to come together is the son the heroine adopted out when she was very young. Again, more details are on my Web site.

All the very best,

Karina Bliss

SECOND-CHANCE FAMILY
Karina Bliss

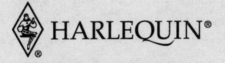

HARLEQUIN®

TORONTO • NEW YORK • LONDON
AMSTERDAM • PARIS • SYDNEY • HAMBURG
STOCKHOLM • ATHENS • TOKYO • MILAN • MADRID
PRAGUE • WARSAW • BUDAPEST • AUCKLAND

ISBN-13: 978-0-373-71524-4
ISBN-10: 0-373-71524-2

SECOND-CHANCE FAMILY

ABOUT THE AUTHOR

Karina Bliss figured she was meant to be a writer when at age twelve she began writing character sketches of her classmates. But a scary birthday milestone had to pass before she understood that achieving a childhood dream required more commitment than "when I grow up I'm going to be." It took this New Zealand journalist—a Golden Heart and Clendon Award winner—five years of "seriously writing" to get a book contract, a process she says helped put childbirth into perspective.

She lives with her partner and their son north of Auckland. Visit her on the Web at www.karinabliss.com.

Books by Karina Bliss

HARLEQUIN SUPERROMANCE

1373—MR. IMPERFECT
1426—MR. IRRESISTIBLE
1475—MR. UNFORGETTABLE

I'd like to dedicate this book to two wonderful women who saw promise in an unpublished writer and took her on board—my editor, Victoria Curran, and my agent, Karen Solem. Heartfelt thanks for everything you're teaching me about writing and publishing.

Acknowledgments

Thanks to Nancy Kashdin,
who suggested the name Julia Evans, in a
"Name a character" contest I ran through my Web site.

And also thanks to my niece Cassie,
and all my other nieces and nephews whose antics
over the years provide inspiration for the kids
in my books—the good ones, of course. ☺

CHAPTER ONE

"Jack...we weren't expecting you in today.... Oh, Jack, I'm so sorry."

His secretary's eyes welled up as she opened her plump arms.

Jack forced himself to squeeze her shoulder as he sidestepped her embrace. "Thanks for your support, Heather. Has Mr. Yoshida arrived?"

Her mouth dropped along with her arms. "Why, yes, but surely you're not... I mean, Dave is covering for you...."

Jack dumped his briefcase on his desk and turned impatiently.

"They're in the boardroom," she finished.

"There's a lawyer called Grimble arriving in thirty minutes. Look after him until I'm free, will you? I'll be leaving after that." He pulled a crumpled list out of his pocket. "Meantime, ring the *New Zealand Herald* with the funeral notice."

Heather's eyes filled again. "Of course. Is there anything else I can do?"

His cell phone vibrated. Jack removed it from the breast pocket of his suit, checked the caller ID, then handed it over. "Yeah. Keep people off my back."

He hadn't meant to sound so harsh, but he had too much still to do to commiserate with second-tier friends and relatives. "I'm sorry." Taking a deep breath, Jack started again. "If you could accept condolences and give everyone the funeral details?"

With a sympathetic nod, Heather took the call. "Jack Galloway's phone. Can I help you?"

He'd forgotten how busy the aftermath of tragedy was. Getting the bodies shipped home, making the important phone calls and initiating funeral arrangements left no time to mourn.

Jack buttoned his suit jacket and straightened his tie, then strode down the corridor to the boardroom. Not that he had tears in him anymore. Grief had hollowed him out six years ago; there was nothing left now, except the echo of it.

And anger.

"I'm afraid I don't know any details of Friday night's accident," he heard Heather say behind him, and his fingers tightened convulsively around the boardroom's ornate door handle.

All these well-meaning people had a right to know, but to Jack they felt like rats gnawing at the corpses. He wanted to beat them off with sticks, then shake his brother's body until Anthony's teeth rattled. *You've had your joke, Ants. Now get up.*

Steeling himself, he pulled the heavy door open and entered the boardroom.

Half a dozen men looked up from one end of an enormous oval table, but Jack focused on only one. "Yoshida-san, my apologies for not being here to greet you."

The man returned his handshake warmly. "It is good to see you again, Galloway-san." They were old friends, but only in karaoke bars, belting out eighties hits at three in the morning, did they call each other by their first names.

Jack's vice president gaped at him. "I was just about to tell Mr. Yoshida and his associates that—"

"No need," Jack interrupted, "I'm here. Let's get down to business so these gentlemen can get to the airport in good time." He shook hands with the rest of the Japanese delegation. "What kind of weather will you be going back to in Tokyo?"

After exchanging pleasantries, they brought out the joint venture contracts that would take Jack's construction company into the big time—a multimillion-dollar residential subdivision in outer Auckland. He signed the papers and felt nothing.

As their lawyers tidied paperwork, he and Hiro Yoshida strolled to the floor-to-ceiling window. Twenty-five stories up, it normally offered panoramic views of Auckland's harbor, but on this early November day blinding torrents of spring rain lashed the pane. Jack could feel the last chill of a persistent winter seeping through the thick glass.

Patting his pockets, he retrieved the lighter and ten-pack of Marlboros he'd bought en route to the office. He offered one to Hiro.

One of the lawyers glanced up from the papers and cleared his throat. "I'm afraid New Zealand workplace laws prohibit—"

Hiro leaned forward so Jack could light his cigarette. "I think today," he said gravely, "we make an exception."

So he knew. Jack drew deeply, welcoming the once-familiar burn in his lungs, then exhaled. It felt like the first time he'd breathed in two-and-a-half days.

Hiro did the same, watching him through the fragrant smoke. "You should be sitting with your brother's body, my friend," he said simply, and Jack remembered the Japanese mourned their dead through wakes.

He delayed his answer by tapping his ash into a nearby pot containing a rubber plant. "He and his wife died while they were on holiday in New Caledonia. They…their remains are being flown home today."

"But you have other family, do you not?"

"No immediate family." *Not anymore.*

Hiro's black brows creased in surprise. "Your secretary said they had children."

Jack's sanity over the last horrific forty-eight hours had depended on not thinking too much about the children. "Yes, of course." He lifted the cigarette, saw his fingers were trembling, and dropped his hand. "They flew back early this morning with one of my sister-in-law's relatives. I'll see them this afternoon."

The older man took Jack's cigarette and said gently, "Go now, my friend."

Jack bowed. *"Hai,"* he said simply, then obediently left the room and headed straight back to his office. The kids needed familiar faces around them now, not some strange uncle they saw only a few times a year. He'd delegated the personal stuff to people who knew the family's day-to-day routines.

Others had gone to the house and turned on power and hot water, others had organized groceries and done the airport run to pick up the kids and their maternal aunt this morning.

But at 3:00 a.m., after lying in bed, staring at the ceiling, Jack had got up and driven to the house. He'd picked up Anthony's running shoes, still lying inside the front door, and taken Julia's apron from the hook in the kitchen. Methodically removed every sign that might suggest to their children they could be coming back at any moment.

He knew how much these things hurt.

Entering his office now, Jack saw a bald man pacing the plush carpet. He'd forgotten the lawyer. Their eyes met and Grimble immediately adopted a sympathetic expression.

Jack waved away his condolences. "Let's skip the formalities, shall we?" He gestured for the man to take a seat, but remained standing himself. "You said on the phone yesterday that I was the executor of the will…no, don't start reading the whole thing. Give me the guts of it."

Slightly flustered, Grimble cleared his throat. "The mortgage will be paid off by compulsory insurance, but your brother and his wife had no other policies."

"Teacher's salary, and Julia didn't work," Jack murmured. "It's what I expected…. So the sale of the house is the only money the children will have?" The deal he'd just signed started to mean something again. "I'll organize fiscal support through the guardian." This, he knew, Ants and Julia would have covered. "Who is it?"

"Why, you." Grimble seemed surprised he didn't know that.

Feeling as though he'd just taken a hit to the solar plexus, Jack sat down hard on the corner of his desk. "Me!"

The lawyer nodded as he checked his notes, then delivered the knockout punch. "You and somebody called Rosalind Valentine."

ROZ SAT ON HER best friend's couch in suburban Auckland, reading a story to Julia's just-orphaned three-year-old daughter. It was hard to lose yourself in a story you'd read twelve times since breakfast, but she tried.

"'The dump,'" she began, "'isn't a place most animals would choose to live, but Pinky the mouse wasn't one of them.'" On her lap, Cassie stared fixedly at the picture of the jaunty rodent, her small fingers absently pulling at a loose thread on the well-worn couch.

"Turn the page for me, honey," Roz said, to distract her, but Cassie was a multitasker and managed to keep her grip on the thread. What the hell, the foam was already showing through, anyway. It was that kind of house, unpretentious and restful, reflective of the people who—who *had*—lived here. Roz picked up her glass of water from the coffee table and sipped, trying to loosen her throat. She'd had to do it a lot since the airport run this morning. Be brave for the children.

Snatches of conversation drifted across the hall from the kitchen, where the latest bunch of well-wishers was dropping off casseroles and condolences. "I can't look at those poor kids without crying," said a neighbor.

Roz read louder. "'Pinky loved the growwwwl of the bulldozers...'" she paused for Cassie to growl "'...as they pushed the rubbish into neat piles.'" The house still felt cold from being shut up for two weeks, so she did up the buttons of the toddler's rainbow cardigan.

"I don't think," said another female voice, "that the baby understands."

Cassie growled again, with a deep, carrying ferocity that startled the unseen speakers into silence, and Roz gave her an approving squeeze. "This mini madam," Julia had always said fondly of her youngest, "is going to be an opera diva or a trade union activist."

Julia. The words on the page suddenly blurred.

"Read faster," Cassie ordered. The doorbell rang and Roz put the book aside. More flowers or offers of help.

"I'll get it." Julia's sister, Fiona Evans, bustled through the living room, pausing to pry loose the thread from Cassie's grip. "No, darling, that's naughty." A youthful forty-two, the petite salon-blonde had a refined English accent reminiscent of boarding school matrons. "Here, have one of these instead." She thrust the chocolate box on the table toward her niece.

"It's pretty close to dinnertime," Roz ventured, but cautiously, because Fee had been staking territory since she'd landed in New Zealand this morning. By 10:00 a.m. everyone had got the message—she was in charge. She was obviously using superefficiency to manage her grief. The sisters and their families had been on holiday together, and poor Fee had had to identify the bodies. But her behavior was exhausting the kids. And Roz was pretty sure that Julia would hate to see her daughter being stuffed with candy.

"Special circumstances," Fee insisted. She handed Cassie two chocolates and carried on to the door.

Roz waited until she was out of earshot. "Can I have one of those?"

Cassie popped the one she'd just licked into her godmother's mouth.

Somewhere Julia would be laughing. "'The seagulls,'" Roz read, trying not to think about the soggy mess melting on her tongue, "'were rough and cheeky, but they had placed webbed feet on foreign shores, and in Pinky's eyes, that made them gods.'"

Jack came through the door. Roz gagged, then forced herself to swallow the chocolate. She'd thought she was ready for this.

Cassie cupped Roz's hot face with small, sticky hands and fixed her with a glare from eyes the same nut-brown as her hair. "Read...the...book," she said in a pitch-perfect impersonation of her Auntie Fee.

"'They liked being thought gods instead of scavenging bandits, so they often visited his cardboard box home at the far end of the dump.'"

"Hey, Cassandra." Roz pinned her gaze to the page as Jack crouched down in front of them and offered Cassie a badly wrapped present. "I'm your uncle Jack, remember? I've bought you candy."

Cassie grabbed her blankie, scrunched her eyes shut and turned her head away. It was an old trick, but Jack immediately withdrew a couple of paces.

Roz fought the urge to follow her goddaughter's lead as she felt his attention swing to her. For a moment longer she stared at the mouse in the yellow-checkered waistcoat, standing proudly outside his ramshackle box.

How do you greet a man who once saw you lying on the carpet in a hysterical heap, begging him to stay? Lifting her chin, Roz eyeballed his left cheekbone and said coolly, "Hello, Jack."

A man who'd just lost the last of his generation of family? Through a throat raw from crying, she added hoarsely, "I'm sorry we have to meet under such circumstances."

"We got guardianship. Is that your doing?" demanded her ex-husband.

Startled, Roz met river-green eyes and saw the same boarded-up expression that used to throw her into gut-wrenching despair. Her control snapped. "And *bloody* sorry that we have to meet at all." Then the import of his words struck her, and she cried, "What?" simultaneously with Fiona, who'd come up behind him.

Cassie was peeking at Jack through half-closed lashes. "Where's Daddy?" she asked suddenly. The adults froze. "Oh, I forgot." She turned another page of the book with chubby fingers. "He's dead."

With a sob, Fiona fled to the kitchen. Roz gulped water, ridding herself of the chocolate's residual sweetness so she wouldn't throw up. Jack turned his back and walked to the window. Even slumped, his broad shoulders blocked out the anemic light of an overcast afternoon. "Oh, God," he muttered brokenly, "what a mess."

As she stared at him, inconsequential thoughts filtered through Roz's shock. He'd cut his dark blond hair short; it didn't touch his collar anymore. She recalled the only other time she'd seen him in a suit.

At their wedding.

Cassie growled, and automatically Roz began reading again, but her mind was elsewhere. They were *guardians?* "It's too dark," complained the little girl.

Dazed, Roz switched on the table lamp, and the mahogany coffee table gleamed in the spill of light.

Once, it had been hers and Jack's. Covered with papers, usually, because most nights he'd prepared building quotes while Roz did the books. But she'd always made him phone the slow payers. "You're a softie," he'd teased her, then bent to kiss her pregnant belly. "Except here."

They were guardians?

"'The seagulls thought Pinky was also a brave adventurer,'" Roz croaked, "'and he was, but only in his imagination.'" Needing order, she gathered loose strands of her limp hair into a tidier ponytail. "'You see, he'd lost the tip of his mousy little finger in an accident with some rusty roofing iron.'"

Out of the corner of her eye, she saw Jack straighten his shoulders. "I'll go see the other kids, then you, Fiona and I need to talk." The grimness was back in his tone.

Without looking up, Roz nodded. "'But Pinky *told* everyone he'd been in a real house, seen cheese in a mousetrap and coolly decided it was worth losing a finger for.'"

They were guardians!

Somewhere in the fear, a dangerous joy flickered to life.

CHAPTER TWO

JACK FOLLOWED FIONA INTO the kitchen and stopped abruptly. She was weeping on the shoulder of one woman, and was surrounded by others similarly afflicted. He spun on his heel, but it was too late.

"Oh, Jack," she sobbed, mascara trails bracketing her aquiline nose. "I still can't believe it. Why would they leave guardianship to you and Roz? It doesn't make sense."

He scanned the other faces and recognized nobody. "First I need to see Sam and Liam. Where are they?"

Fiona's eyes went blank and he frowned. Damn it, it was her job to know. She was the kids' rock now. It was a shame her husband, Roger, couldn't be here to add his customary steadiness.

"Liam popped next door with a neighbor," said a brunette. "Sam headed out to the garage for something."

Jack strode back through the living room, ignoring Roz. But he couldn't escape her voice. Every huskily delivered word drew blood.

"'Sometimes Pinky added a fat, black, hissing cat to his story, and everyone believed that, as well, because of his unusual roof.'"

The door wouldn't open; Jack broke into a sweat.

"'It was the rust-spotted lid of a biscuit tin with a picture of five kittens sitting in a basket….' The opening mechanism's faulty," she told him. "Hold the faceplate as you turn the handle."

Ants had always been hopeless at DIY.

"'For a mouse to choose to live under a picture of his worst enemies was considered a very brave thing to do—'"

Slamming the door shut behind him, Jack paused on the doorstep to suck in fresh air, chill with light rain. Ruthlessly, he rebuilt his self-control, until it was impregnable.

Drizzle dampened his face as he made his way to the garage. It was empty, and Jack despised himself for the involuntary spike of relief.

Of the three kids, fifteen-year-old Sam Evans, Julia's son by a previous marriage, was the one Jack knew best. And dreaded seeing most.

When at twenty-two, his baby brother had said he was marrying a woman who was not only five years his senior, but had a seven-year-old son, Jack had done his best to dissuade Anthony. Then he'd met Julia and Sam, and had shut up.

About to retrace his steps, Jack heard a cough to his right. "Sammy?" The old endearment came instinctively. For a moment there was silence.

"Over here." His nephew's voice had broken in the three months since Jack had last seen him.

Rounding the corner of the garage, he found the teenager sitting on the back doorstep, his long hands overhanging gangly knees. The hood of his dark sweatshirt was pulled over a baseball cap, hiding his lank, dark hair.

What Jack could see of his face was sunburned and peeling.

At least they'd had the holiday first.

Skirting the sagging clothesline and its load of rain-soaked beach towels, Jack sat on the wet step beside the boy. Sam's face was moist; from the shower or tears, Jack couldn't tell, and knew not to ask.

The acrid smell of tobacco hung in the air, and a mashed cigarette still smoldered by his nephew's feet. Seeing the direction of Jack's gaze, Sam covered the butt with his trainer.

"You got another one of those?"

Sam shot him a startled glance from bloodshot hazel eyes, then handed over a ten-pack of Marlboros and a box of matches. Jack lit two and handed him one.

"After the funeral," he said, returning the packet, "we give these up."

Sam's fingers trembled as he dragged on the cigarette. "I don't want to go to the funeral."

"Neither do I, but I think we're too old to get out of it."

"Auntie Fee says I have to be a pallbearer for Mum's coffin."

"You don't," Jack said harshly.

For five minutes, they sat in silence, smoking. His nephew's shoulder, where it touched his, held a terrible tension. But they didn't have the sort of relationship that would make a hug natural, and the last thing Jack wanted to do was make Sam uncomfortable.

"You need to talk?" Because talking, Jack thought bleakly, solved everything. *Yeah, right.*

His nephew shook his head, then drew a deep, shuddering breath. "If I don't have to carry one of the coffins, I'll go."

"Whatever you want, mate."

Again there was silence. Daylight was fading quickly, but Sam seemed equally reluctant to return to the house. And there was a comfort in sitting shoulder to shoulder on the step, even in the cold and the drizzle. Jack watched the cigarette burn to ash in his hand.

Yes, he still had the capacity to grieve. With one contemptuous glance, Roz had evoked emotions that he'd thought would never affect him again.

"So I guess," Sam ventured, "I stay an Evans now?"

Oh, hell. The teenager had asked Anthony to adopt him, and his brother had been over the moon. "I'll ask, but…probably." No point in raising false hopes.

"Do we have to go live with Auntie Fee and Uncle Roger? I mean, I like them but…" His voice trailed off.

Jack didn't want to hear apprehension, so he screened it out. "They seem the obvious choice."

"But not straightaway, right? I mean, we won't be going home with Auntie Fee next week or anything?"

"I'm sure she'll stay on in New Zealand for a month or so." The lower step was soft…rotten, probably, and some of the spouting looked rusty. Jack would put a crew onto it next week, get the place shipshape before it was listed for sale. The kids needed top dollar.

"No, she has to get back—I heard her tell Roz." The boy's voice rose. "I don't want to live in England."

"Hey, mate, let's calm down. Nothing's been decided yet."

"So we could live with you?" Sam absorbed Jack's

expression and immediately changed tack. "At least I could. Auntie Fee could take the small ones."

"You need to stay together. And with Fiona and Roger you'd get to live with your cousins." Jack suddenly realized he had no idea if they wanted them, and panic hit.

"They're dorks," said Sam flatly. "They were no fun on holiday."

It took Jack a second to focus. "Who? Your cous—"

"I'm not going anywhere before the end of the rugby season." Sam shoved himself off the step, eyes wild.

A light snapped on, the laundry door behind them opened and Fiona appeared. She'd repaired her makeup and her red mouth made a perfect O of shock. "Sam, are you *smoking?*"

Jack palmed his cigarette and took Sam's. "He was holding it for me while I tied my shoelace. Thanks, buddy."

"I mean it, Jack," Sam said hysterically. "I'll go live with Dad's family."

Instinctively, Jack dropped the cigarettes and caught him in a bear hug. Despite Sam's lankiness, the frame under all those baggy bro clothes was still that of a young boy. A lump caught in Jack's throat, cutting off a reassurance.

For a moment Sam let himself be held, then, with a sob, he pulled free. Furiously wiping his sleeve across his eyes, he pushed past Fiona and loped into the house.

"What's he talking about?" Her voice rose in panic. "Of course he's not living with those lowlifes—"

"Stop," said Jack sharply. "Send someone he knows well to see that he's okay. Then we'll talk this through in the study. Bring Roz."

Her shoulders squared, but her bright mouth trembled. "I want those children, Jack."

Relief washed over him, easing the ache that had begun when he'd seen Roz with Cassie. "Then I don't foresee any problem."

HE WAS GOING TO OFFLOAD the kids on Fiona.

Roz knew it as soon as she walked into Anthony's study and saw them sitting side by side on the ancient leather sofa, drinking tea. Jack hated tea.

Smiling, Fee picked up the teapot. "Roz, let me pour you a cup," she offered. "Milk, no sugar, isn't it?"

Barely knowing this woman, and without consulting Roz as coguardian, Jack was going to ship them off to a foreign country. Because he couldn't handle rejoining the human race.

Fury combusted in Roz's chest, making it hard to breathe, but she welcomed it. Angry, she could deal with him. "You son of a bitch. You're going to completely disregard what Anthony and Julia want, aren't you?"

Fee gasped and the tea she was pouring splashed into the saucer, but Jack didn't even blink. He picked up a paper napkin and began mopping up the spill.

Her color high, Fee got her breath back. "How can you talk to him like—"

"She's grieving," interrupted Jack. "We all are." He took the teapot from Fee and finished pouring with a steady hand. "Which makes it even more important to keep emotion out of this discussion."

Roz narrowed her eyes. "You'd like that, wouldn't you?" Dear God, she'd spent the last five-and-a-half years schooling herself to accept and forgive, and already she wanted to hurt him. She took the chair opposite the couch. "What about the kids…are you even going to ask them?"

His face impassive, Jack held out a cup of tea. "The children are too young to make a decision."

She made no move to take it. "Liam and Cassie might be. What about Sam?"

A flicker of emotion appeared in the green depths of his eyes and was gone. "Sam will come around." He plonked the cup in front of her. "And let's get one thing very clear before we go any further. You and I were appointed guardians. There was nothing specified about custody." Jack turned to Fee. "In New Zealand, the two roles aren't automatically synonymous."

So *that's* how he justified it to his conscience. "Of course they meant custody, as well," Roz declared.

His attention swung back to her like a club. "What makes you so sure?"

She swallowed. "It was over six years ago right after Liam was born. We were expecting Thomas and I only agreed…" Frightened by the blaze in his eyes, she rushed to get the words out. "…because we were just named as backup to your mother." Except Joyce Galloway had passed away two months ago. "For God's sake, Jack, what were the odds?"

"I knew you were behind it," he said bitterly.

"What I don't understand—" Fee adjusted her position so that her shoulder closed Roz out "—is why Julia chose you, and not me and Roger? I remember her saying you don't like spending time with the children."

Obviously, Ju had never said why. Jack's face froze and Roz intervened. "Actually, he spent a lot of time with Sam and Liam before…" His gaze flicked briefly to hers, and her throat closed.

"Before?" Fee prompted. Silver bangles jangled on her wrist as she picked up her cup…jangled on Roz's blistered nerves. If Fee didn't have the sensitivity to make the connection then Roz wasn't going to make it for her.

"Nothing." Roz sipped her tea, moistened dry lips.

Jack got up and started pacing the room. "I'm happy to take fiscal responsibility, but custody isn't even an issue." His lawyerlike detachment raised her hackles again. "Roz and I are divorced, and neither of our lifestyles are conducive to looking after child—"

"Speak for your lifestyle, not mine!" He'd become a hard-partying serial dater within days of leaving her.

"Why?" The grit was back in his voice. "Have you settled down with a third husband?"

Roz smiled at him. "No, Jack. I've finally learned that if you want loyalty you get a dog. Though my second husband was a huge improvement on my first. After the divorce, we even managed to stay friends."

His mouth tightened. "These kids need what they've lost, which is a mother and a father and a stable home."

"Which Roger and I can offer them," said Fee.

Roz turned back to Fee and impulsively reached for her hands. "On the other side of the world, away from their friends, their community. I know it's not your fault—" she said, as Fee's cold fingers spasmed under hers "—but they hardly know you."

"We just spent twelve lovely days together, and I owe her—" Fee stopped. Carefully, she removed her hands from Roz's. "They're my sister's children…my

blood. And their grandmother's in the U.K." Julia and
Fee's elderly mother lived in a nursing home and was
too infirm to travel. "You might know the children best,
Rosalind, but you no longer have a relationship with
them that would be recognized by law."

"All I'm asking is that we don't rush into a decision
about their future three days after their parents' death."

"We need to!" Fee's cup clattered into the saucer. "I
have to get back to the U.K. to my own two boys. It
makes sense to take the children with me now."

As delicately as she could, Roz raised the issue that
had been bothering her. "Can you really cope with
raising five children?"

Julia had always described her sister as a multitask-
ing perfectionist in need of an intervention. "I bought
that because it reminded me of Fee," she'd said once,
gesturing to a fridge magnet. It showed a sixties house-
wife with wide eyes and a toothy smile, and a caption
reading, "It's been lovely but I have to scream now."

Under her foundation, red mottled Fiona's cheeks.
"What are you implying?"

"Only that it's a huge responsibility. You need time
to think this through."

"I know my duty." Fee's English accent grew even
more clipped. "And as far as I'm concerned, if Jack's
happy, that's it."

"I'm sorry," said Roz firmly, "but as a guardian, I
have to be happy, too." She had no idea if that was true
or not, but someone had to put these kids' interests first.

"Oh, for God's sake, Roz, get real." Jack was suddenly towering over her. "Who's going to look after
them in the meantime? I've just signed a big construc-

tion contract, and you have a career. We both live in the city, miles from their schools. And employing some stranger as a nanny isn't going to help the kids."

"I'll take a leave of absence from my job and move in here for a couple of months." Roz listened to her declaration with the same astonishment as the other two. Her heart jumped into her throat, but she wouldn't renege. "They need to stay in their own home and stick to their normal routines—at least until the first shock passes. Finish the school year."

"And after Christmas they come to us," said Fee.

Roz tried to read Jack's expression, and found it impossible. "And after Christmas we make a final decision," she countered.

"No." He shook his head. "Their parents are dead. To pretend that life's ever going to get back to normal is cruel. Long term, they'll deal better with the changes if they're all made at once."

He'd done that to her, leaving her soon after the tragedy that had shattered their lives and their marriage. The clean break that had left jagged, painful scars. Roz wouldn't let him do that to Julie and Anthony's children.

"You're so wrong," she said passionately. "Right now, these kids need the nurturing only their friends and community can give them." *All the help that you and I turned down.* "Then they'll be equipped to face whatever changes are necessary—"

Jack was shaking his head again; Roz swiveled back to Fee. "And if they end up with you, well, then you've had time to make preparations." She could see the other woman was considering the idea, but then Fee glanced up at Jack for approval.

"No," he said again.

Roz grabbed the cuff of his jacket and hauled him to the other side of the room. "We can help them through this," she said in a low voice. "I know we can."

His mouth twisted. "Because we're so well-adjusted?"

"Because we know what it's like to lose the person you love most."

A muscle tightened in his square jaw. "Which is why," he said harshly, "I can't let you use these kids as surrogates."

But she'd already questioned her motives. "I can understand why you'd think that, but that's not what I'm doing."

"You'll get hurt, Roz." There was the trace of a plea in his voice.

"I know," she admitted. "But the kids' needs come first."

"Damn it, if you won't protect yourself, I will. No!"

And she knew she'd have to say the unsayable, the one thing that would rip out what was left of Jack's heart, the one thing that would kill whatever hope she'd ever had of making her peace with this man.

"You owe me." She didn't have to explain; it was always between them. The thing that had driven them apart, the thing she'd always sworn to him she didn't believe.

For a long moment, they hung on the gallows of the past.

"I always knew you blamed me," he said conversationally, but his eyes were so bleak Roz had to bite her tongue to stop herself taking back her words. If guilt would buy time for the kids, she had to use it.

"Okay." He moved away, closer to Fee. "I'll apply for temporary custody for two months. Then we reassess."

Roz relaxed her jaw and released her tongue, tasted the iron tang of blood. "Thank you."

"I need to go," said her ex-husband, the man who'd cried with her over their baby's tiny coffin. He brushed past her to get to the door. "I'll be able to give them up when the time comes," he said coldly. "Make sure you can."

CHAPTER THREE

LIAM GALLOWAY SAT in the narrow hall, his back against the study door, kicking the skirting board with the heel of his orange sneakers—same color as his hair—and getting a mutinous satisfaction from the dirty scuff marks.

Sam had said he couldn't go to Mum and Dad's funeral, and he wanted Auntie Roz and Auntie Fee to tell Sam he wasn't the boss. Except he didn't want to knock, because he could hear Uncle Jack's raised voice, and Liam was a tiny bit scared of his uncle.

It wasn't that he was so big…Dad was big, too. But Uncle Jack never smiled, at least not at Liam. He'd seen him stroke Cassie's hair once when Mum had left the room for a moment and Cassie had been asleep on the couch, but Uncle Jack hadn't looked happy doing it. Cassie probably had food in her hair. She usually did. Uncle Roger was much nicer—

The door jerked open and Liam tumbled backward, crying out in pain as his head connected with Uncle Jack's shin.

"What the hell are you doing, sitting there?"

Liam couldn't help it; he started to cry. His head throbbed, he'd had a fright and Uncle Jack sounded mad at him. He felt himself lifted in strong arms, cradled. "Mate, I'm so sorry, I didn't see you. Where does it hurt?"

But Liam didn't want a cuddle from Uncle Jack. He squirmed out of his uncle's grasp, running toward Auntie Roz—and was intercepted by Auntie Fee.

"Oh, sweetie." Liam found himself held in an embrace he couldn't shift, and gave in, resting his head against her breast and succumbing to hiccuping sobs.

"I want Mum," he wailed, even though he knew she was in heaven. Couldn't she just sneak down behind God's back?

Someone was vigorously rubbing at the sore spot on his head, just like Mum did, and Liam blinked away his tears. It was Roz, he discovered. Still, the pain went away and he felt better.

Wiping his nose on his sleeve, he sat up and shot a look at Uncle Jack, embarrassed for crying in front of him.

Uncle Jack's jaw was clenched, so Liam figured he was still mad, and ducked his head. The glimpse of his sneakers reminded him of his question.

"Sam says I'm not allowed to go to the funeral and that Cassie and me are getting a babysitter. But I can go, can't I?"

He'd asked Roz, but Auntie Fee, who was straightening the collar of his Spider-Man sweatshirt, answered. "Absolutely not."

Liam opened his mouth to protest.

"That reminds me," interrupted Uncle Jack from the other side of the room. "Sam had some crazy idea, Fiona, that you were going to force him to be a pallbearer. Don't worry, I cleared up that misunderstanding."

"Oh," said Auntie Fee faintly. "Good."

"I'll do it," volunteered Liam, though he had no idea what a pallbearer was.

"You're not going," said Auntie Fee and Auntie Roz together.

Liam stuck out his chin. "Mum and Dad would want me to go." Over the past three days, using their names had settled any argument. Sleeping in Sam's room, getting Coke instead of juice, letting Froggie out in the lounge when they'd picked the tank up from the neighbors who'd been minding him.

Auntie Roz took his hand. "Honey, funerals are very sad and you've never been to one before. Auntie Fee and I think you should stay home."

Liam scrunched up his face and tried to cry. It was strange how he kept crying when he didn't want to, but couldn't when he did.

"If Liam wants to go, he should be allowed to," said Uncle Jack.

Liam was so surprised he unscrunched his face.

"Jack, no," said Auntie Roz.

"He's too young," said Auntie Fee.

Liam went to Uncle Jack. "I'm six and everyone's been saying how brave I am. An' I have to say goodbye properly."

The tears threatened, but somehow Liam knew now was not the time to look like a baby. Uncle Jack hunkered down and put a hand on his shoulder, and Liam tried not to squirm under its weight. "You know they'll be in coffins," he said in a very serious voice, "which will be buried in the ground?"

Liam nodded and tried to listen carefully to everything Uncle Jack told him about what happened at funerals. He started to get nervous, but then something distracted him. He waited until Uncle Jack had finished before he mentioned the funny thing.

"Your eyes are the same color as James Zombie Maisy's are."

Uncle Jack blinked.

"That's our cat," Liam said helpfully. "Me and Cassie and Sam all got to choose a name. Mine's James the red engine, Sam chose Zombie because he's a Goth, and Cassie chose Maisy, which is some dumb mouse. We told her the cat is a boy," he added darkly, "but she won't change it."

He waited for Uncle Jack to say something, but he only blinked again. "Okay, I'm going to go tell Mum and Dad I'm coming to their funeral."

Uncle Jack's hold tightened painfully on his shoulder. "But, Liam—"

"I write them letters and an angel takes them every night, just like Auntie Fee said." Slowly, his uncle's gaze lifted to Auntie Fee's and Liam got a teeny bit scared of him again. "I mean, I know they're already watching us from heaven…." Liam didn't want Uncle Jack to think he was stupid or anything. "But the clouds must get in the way sometimes, right? So I have to write to them."

"Right," said Roz, when Uncle Jack opened his mouth to speak. She pulled him free of his uncle's grip and gave him a gentle push toward the door. "Give them my love, honey."

Behind him, Uncle Jack made a rude noise, but Liam found himself in the hall with the door closed before he could ask any further questions.

He heard Roz say, "Just because you don't believe

in anything anymore, Jack Galloway, is no…" Her voice faded out as she moved away from the door.

Liam considered putting his ear to the keyhole, but then thought of what Sam's face would look like when Liam told him he was—so there!—going to the funeral, and ran off to find his brother.

JACK DELIVERED his brother's eulogy with a hangover.

With every sentence, his stomach roiled and his head hammered. Cold sweat beaded on his brow and trickled into his eyes, stinging and blurring the words on the page. Fortunately, he knew them by heart.

It was a good speech, but his delivery sucked because his entire concentration was focused on not throwing up. Somewhere, his father was calling him an irresponsible loser.

His relief when he finished without barfing was so intense he swayed under a wave of dizziness and had to grip the podium.

The congregation came back into focus. Roz, dressed in a scarlet coat, because Julia had once joked that she wanted clown colors at her funeral.

Above it her face was pale, and there were dark shadows under her kingfisher-blue eyes. She looked like he felt—ragged, weary, battle-worn—though she managed a smile for Cassie, who sat next to her with the pastor's wife, happily playing with a string of shiny beads.

Once Jack had given Liam permission to attend the funeral, the adults had decided Cassie should come, too. She was too young to know what was going on.

"But," Roz said, "when she's older, she'll be glad to have been included."

In keeping with the theme, the little girl wore a garish pink fairy dress with gauzy wings, over purple-and-green stockings and pink sheepskin boots. On her head, a golden crown sat askew on a red Santa hat.

As though sensing Jack's scrutiny, she looked up. "McDonald's now?" she called hopefully. Laughter rippled through the congregation, momentarily lightening the sadness.

Even Jack smiled—until he shook his sore head. "Not yet, sweetheart." He caught Fiona's disapproving frown and straightened his lollipop tie, then made his way back to the front pew, where she sat with the boys, dressed in a severe black suit because she considered flouting tradition disrespectful. Jack was in Fiona's bad books, a situation he was keen to change.

In the last couple of days he'd made some serious errors of judgment.

The first had been to say yes to temporary custody with Roz, after she'd blindsided him with her "You owe me" comment.

The second had been getting drunk last night. There'd been too many suppressed emotions threatening to swamp him. He'd needed to release some of the terrible pressure; instead, Jack had simply passed out.

But the third mistake—the one he most regretted—had been letting Liam come to his parents' funeral.

The boy had started the service in high excitement, his eyes bright. Standing at the church door in his Sunday best, he'd handed out programs, conscious of being the center of attention, though not sure why.

Now his shoulders slumped and he leaned, bewildered, against his older brother. They made an incongruous sight. Sam, in his customary black, had painted his fingernails bright green as a concession to his mother. Liam, his short carrot-colored hair ruthlessly combed by Fiona, wore a suit and tie and looked like a miniature of his dad. *Oh, Ants.*

Roz leaned across Sam and whispered something to Liam.

"No, I wanna stay!" His petulant cry cut through the hymn, being sung tremulously by Anthony's high school class.

Jack edged past Fiona to stand next to the boy. "It's okay if you want to leave."

Vigorously shaking his head, Liam slid closer to his brother. Jack met Roz's accusing stare and turned to the front. Damn it, he'd tried. But he closed his eyes on a rush of self-disgust that had nothing to do with his hangover.

The hymn finished and there was a collective shuffling as those with seats sat down. Okay, a fourth bloody mistake—not booking a bigger chapel than the small one on-site at the cemetery.

How the hell was Jack supposed to know that Ants and Julia belonged to every social, community and sporting group in suburbia? Mourners spilled into the vestibule, where they listened to the service through hastily erected speakers.

Only the immediate family's long pew was half-empty.

This was ridiculous.

Before the minister resumed the service, Jack stepped back out into the aisle. "Listen, there's at least eight seats up here. Please use them."

People trickled to the front. An elderly lady, her hat smelling of mothballs, gave him a quick hug. "Bless you."

So help him, if one more stranger touched him… He needed a cigarette, he needed a Tylenol, he needed an escape from the neediness closing around him like a trap.

The service resumed; Cassie soon got restless and was taken outside to play. The minister invited Roz to speak.

As she passed, Jack concentrated on rereading his notes in the program's margin, but her scent, faintly floral, clutched at his memory. He hadn't seen her for five-and-a-half years, and she still felt like his wife.

He reminded himself that she'd remarried within a month of their divorce; reminded himself that she'd emotionally blackmailed him now into taking temporary custody of the kids. The feeling went away.

"We're here to mourn, yes," she began in a husky voice, "but also to celebrate the lives of two very special people and to be thankful they were in *our* lives."

Fiona nudged him. "Tell Sam to uncover his head while we're in church," she whispered.

Jack leaned across Liam, wincing as the child shrank back. "It's okay, mate. Sam…your aunt wants you to lower your hoodie."

The teenager lifted his head and Jack froze. Under the hood, his nephew was crying, helplessly and silently. Instinctively, Jack pulled his sunglasses out of the breast pocket of his suit. "Forget it. Here."

Gratefully, Sam disappeared behind Jack's aviators.

Liam took one look at the tears trickling under Sam's mirrored shades, and burst into noisy sobs that ripped at Jack's conscience. One mistake he *could* fix.

Grasping the boy's clammy hand, he tugged gently. "Let's go."

"No!" Liam struggled to free himself. "I wanna stay with Mum and Dad." As Jack tried to quiet him, the child tipped into hysteria. "I want them back."

His whole body breaking into a sweat, Jack picked him up. "It's okay, son." At the podium, Roz stopped midsentence, looking stricken.

Fiona started to rise. "Stay," he barked. "I'll take care of it."

Holding the struggling child tight, he strode down the aisle, the boy screaming in impotent rage. "You bring them back. Right now! I want them now!"

His small hands pummeled Jack's face and chest, his thin legs kicked wildly, but Jack held on, ignoring the sharp nails being raked across his cheek, oblivious to the shocked faces. His tone soothing, he repeated over and over, "You're going to be okay, mate. It's going to be okay."

Outside, the gray clouds that had shrouded the city for days had lifted, and sunlight streamed over the sodden trees and gardens surrounding the chapel. Mist lifted off the dewy grass, as well as the dark earth around the newly dug graves that lay beyond a stand of trees to their left.

Jack walked away from the building to the fountain in front of it, then shakily put the shrieking child on his feet, holding Liam's arms to his sides. Eyes clenched tightly, the boy kept hollering, hoarser now, but unrelenting.

"You buggerhead, you bring back my mum and dad. You bring them back right now!"

No reassurances Jack made got through to him.

A familiar voice behind him said, "Let me take him."

Abruptly, Liam stopped his screaming and opened tear-swollen eyes. "Uncle Luke!" Wrenching free of Jack's grip, he flung himself at the other man, clutching his legs. "D-d-don't let him take me," he managed to gulp between the sobs now shaking his entire body. "D-d-don't let him t-t-take me away!"

Aghast, Jack stepped back. Luke Carter crouched down and caught Liam's face in his large hands. "Liam, look at me," he said sharply. "Stop this yelling now," he ordered. "You hear me? No more."

For a moment the little boy looked up at him, bewildered, then with a wail threw himself into the big man's arms.

"It's okay, son, we're all here for you." His gray eyes met Jack's. "It's going to be okay." They were the same words Jack had used on Liam.

He didn't believe them, either.

Jack went around the corner of the building and vomited in the flower beds, amid the yellow daylilies and purple pansies. Then he slid down the chapel's redbrick wall, warm against his back, and closed his eyes.

A few minutes later, a shadow blocked the spring sun.

"You did the right thing, bringing him out," said Luke. "Give him a couple of days and he'll forgive you."

Jack looked up at the foster brother he hadn't seen in seventeen years. Still an imposing bastard, with swimmer's shoulders and an all-too-familiar scowl.

Luke added, "What jackass let him come to the funeral in the first place?"

"Me."

"Oh." His scowl softened.

But Jack didn't want sympathy. "Where is he?"

"Liz…my wife is looking after him. He knows her. He'll be fine."

"Pull me up," said Jack. "That's the last hymn and we're pallbearers."

Luke hauled him to his feet, but didn't release his hand. Instead, he gripped it hard. "Jack."

There was such a wealth of understanding in his voice that Jack's eyes burned. How ironic that the bitter enemy of his youth was the only one who understood his loss.

And shared it.

He returned Luke's pressure. "You didn't come to the family pew."

"I wasn't sure you'd want me there."

"He was your brother, too."

Luke and Anthony had been close as kids. It was one of the many things Jack had been jealous of, once. He'd needed maturity to understand that his rival had also suffered through being bought up by Frank Galloway, who'd neglected his own sons to coach his foster one to Olympic swimming gold. Eventually, Luke had suffered Jack's earlier fate and been disinherited when he rebelled—in Luke's case by throwing away his swimming career, the reason he'd originally been fostered. But then, it had always been Frank's way or the highway.

Luke said gruffly, "Thank you, that means a lot to me." He released Jack's hand.

Their foster brother had reestablished contact with Anthony after marrying Liz, but Jack had resisted a meeting—too busy. Still, Ants and Luke had been spending a lot of time together.

Through the chapel's open window, Jack recognized

the last chorus of "Amazing Grace" and swallowed. "It's time."

Luke started walking; Jack couldn't move. His foster brother came back and put a supporting arm around his shoulders. Wordlessly, the two men made their way back into the church to carry their brother to his final resting place.

Jack could almost envy Ants the peace.

CHAPTER FOUR

"WHAT DO YOU MEAN, you can't do it?"

Hearing the rising alarm in Roz's voice, Fiona struggled to pull herself together. Using her balled handkerchief, she dabbed at the tears streaming down her face, but they came faster than she could wipe them away.

Her gaze fell on the coffins and an image of her sister emerged—lying pale and small and still on a slab in a foreign morgue. Sweat popped out on Fiona's brow and she jammed the hanky against her mouth while she forced herself to swallow rising bile.

"Fee?" Roz whispered fiercely. "We're already one short if Jack doesn't come back with Liam."

But how could she find the strength to carry Julia, when the burden was already so heavy she could barely raise her head? If only Roger and the boys were here…but she'd insisted her husband take their shocked sons straight home from New Caledonia. That would also free her to concentrate on comforting Julia's traumatized children. Fiona was always doing things "for the best" and regretting them.

Oh, so bitterly regretting them.

The tears became heaving, silent sobs. Fiona lifted the hanky from her mouth and pressed it against her swollen eyes. "I'm s-s-sorry, but I just c-c-can't."

Roz slid along the bench and started pleading. "But yesterday you were adamant about carrying Julia's casket. Remember?"

Helplessly, Fiona shook her head.

"Take a minute," the younger woman soothed. "You'll be fine." But the jerky pats on her back told Fiona she thought otherwise.

Fee stiffened. How dare Roz disapprove of her? "Find someone else!"

"Because anyone will do?" Roz's tight laugh held a touch of hysteria. "Dear God—" Her voice caught. "Do you think this is easy for any of us?"

But Fiona wasn't listening. She was staring at the pallbearers making their way to the front, and her brief spurt of anger became a terror so real she nearly ran screaming out of the church after Liam. Nothing could make her touch her sister's coffin at that moment. Because in this sacred place God would surely strike her dead—if there was any justice.

She started to whimper. "Please don't make me."

A tentative hand touched her forearm. "I'll do it, Auntie."

Some part of Fiona knew she should say no, but she was past rationality now. "Oh, Sam…" She sagged against the pew in relief. "Would you?" Raising her head, Fiona flinched as Roz's eyes blazed into hers.

"He's been through enough. Pull yourself together, *now!*"

"Roz," said Sam, "I want to do it."

SOME QUALITY IN Sam's voice cut through Roz's panic. She closed her eyes and took a deep, deep breath. *You can keep it together,* she told herself, *You have to.* Opening her eyes, she looked at Sam. "Take off those sunglasses."

Green nail polish glinted in the light streaming through the stained-glass windows as he removed the shades. Roz barely knew him these days; he spent most of his time holed up in his room with his computer. His mother had worried about his antisocial behavior. Hazel eyes met hers now, red-rimmed but steady. "I want to do it," he said again.

"Okay."

"Don't give Auntie Fee a hard time."

She made herself do the right thing. "Fee…I'm sorry." But Roz couldn't feel pity for Julia's sister. Sam's interests should have come first.

Fiona nodded stiffly. The woman looked a mess, more human than Roz had ever seen her, and suddenly pity did come. She handed over a wad of tissues, which was accepted without thanks.

Fine, thought Roz wearily. She needed her energy for other things now.

As she and Sam stood next to the caskets, waiting for the last pallbearers to join them, he surprised her by lowering his hoodie. His hair was a flattened mess, but it didn't matter. Emotion rose up and choked her. "Your parents," she managed to say in a low voice, "would be so proud of you."

He made no sign he'd heard her, but his Adam's apple bobbed convulsively as he stared down at his boots.

Jack came down the aisle with Luke Carter, the foster brother she'd only met since the divorce. But Roz didn't have time to wonder at the men's obvious rapport, because Jack had caught sight of Sam and was looking thunderous. She forestalled him by catching his hand, so warmly familiar that her heart lurched. "It's okay," she murmured, "he offered."

Jack glanced down at their joined hands and Roz broke contact. But he recaptured her icy fingers and scanned her face. "Are *you* up to this?"

His concern, so unexpected, so poignant, nearly broke the last of her control. Seeing her reaction, all emotion left his face, and a sharp, familiar pain steadied Roz. *Some things never change,* she thought bitterly, and pulled free.

"I'm fine." Furious that he could still make her feel something after so many years, she took her position alongside Julia's casket, her eyes boring into her ex-husband's back as he went to stand next to Anthony's coffin.

The minister gave the signal and Roz closed her eyes briefly to refocus—*I don't want to carry you mad, Ju*—then reached for the ornate handle. Across the polished mahogany lid, her gaze met Sam's.

Silently, she transmitted what mental strength she had left, and saw him take a deep breath. *Yes. Breathe, Sam, even when it hurts.*

Roz followed his example, then lifted her share of her best friend's slight weight and, tears spilling down her cheeks, followed the pallbearers carrying Anthony's coffin. *I promise you, Ju, that I'll do my best for your kids.*

As the procession passed the front pew, Fiona mouthed, "I'm sorry." But Roz couldn't return her tentative smile. When it had really mattered, Julia's sister had dropped the ball.

Roz fixed her blurred gaze on Jack's unyielding back. *I don't know how the hell this is going to work,* she told him silently, *but we're keeping them.*

Whether you like it or not.

AFTER THE BURIAL, Roz wandered away from the crowds to a bench under a mature oak where Luke Carter's wife sat, supervising Liam and Cassie. Roz needed a respite, and this near-stranger seemed to understand, because other than a welcoming smile, Liz made no overtures.

A young man disengaged from the mourners and loped to a low-slung Nissan Skyline—Dirk Evans, Julia's brother-in-law from her first marriage. Like Sam, he was dressed tough, but unlike her nephew his persona was real.

Sam's father, Lee Evans, had been the white sheep from a very black flock of third-generation petty criminals. A cop, he'd been killed in the line of duty while policing his old neighborhood. Dirk was attending the funeral as the family's representative, but Roz suspected he really wanted to find out if Sam was inheriting any money.

She'd let Jack handle him.

The engine throbbed to life, blue smoke pumping from the oversize muffler. Hip-hop blared through the stereo as the car accelerated and sped out of sight. Jack had obviously made it clear that Sam's interests were being protected.

Relieved, Roz watched Liam chase Cassie around some camellias. Aging petals, once white, now the color of tea, fell to the saturated ground as the kids tore past the manicured trees. Cassie had kicked off her boots and the soggy feet of her kaleidoscope stockings flicked water in her wake.

I wish I had that kind of resilience, Roz thought, then realized she'd spoken the words aloud when Liz said gently, "It will come back."

She sounded like she was speaking from experience, but before Roz could ask, there was a wail somewhere behind them. Liz looked at her watch. "Right on cue."

Rising from the bench, she walked over to a baby carriage that had been partially obscured by the tree trunk.

Roz's throat went dry and her heart started pounding. "I didn't know you had a baby." She collected her scattered wits. "How old is…?"

"Joe is two months." Liz sat down again, flicking her ash-blond hair over her shoulder as she calmed the infant. She obviously had no idea of her companion's history, and Roz was grateful.

"We had him a year earlier than we'd planned," Liz confided. "He makes the last year of my mayoralty very challenging…don't you, darling?" She dropped a kiss on the downy black hair. "I figured at thirty-five we should start trying early in case it took a while, but I got pregnant first time." Her smile faltered as she addressed someone behind Roz. "What have I said, honey?"

Roz peeled her eyes off the baby and turned to see Luke staring at her with a mix of concern and apology— the usual reaction.

"It's okay," she assured him. "Really." She turned back to a baffled Liz. "May I hold him?" She took the infant, careful to support his neck. "He's beautiful."

It had taken a couple of years of therapy to be able

to do this, but she'd always loved babies and she wasn't going to pass up the joy of holding them. Cassie had been her first success.

Yes, she was resilient.

Bubbles formed on the baby's mouth as he cooed at her, and Roz smiled. "Oh, you're a flirt."

"Hmm," said Liz. "Wonder where he gets that from?"

"His mother," Luke replied, and Liz laughed. Beyond him, Roz noticed Jack watching them—a still figure in the moving crowd—and her breath hitched painfully. He was too far away for her to read his expression, but his whole bearing was one of yearning. She lifted a hand to wave him over, but he'd already turned away.

Fortunately, because Roz already regretted the impulse.

"I TOLD YOU Liam shouldn't have come to the funeral."

Needing a distraction, Jack turned to Fiona. "You were right. I should have listened to you."

Her expression softened. "You meant well, I know. But let's face it, Jack, you haven't got my experience."

Neither had Roz, and she'd also made the right call. But he appreciated Fiona's restraint. In her place, he wouldn't have been so understanding. "No." Six weeks as a parent didn't amount to expertise. He passed a hand over his eyes, trying to erase the picture of Roz with the Carters' baby.

"I just hope—" Fiona looked at his face. "Never mind, it's not like I did so well today, either. Shall we walk?" Tucking her arm through his, she led him through the gardens. "Smell those magnolias."

"You just hope…?"

"That Liam doesn't have nightmares about this."

Jack glanced across the garden to where the boy swung upside down from a tree branch. He was happy again now, but kids expressed grief differently from adults, passing in and out of intense feelings. Jack had done some quick research, and it scared the hell out of him.

"I could still take them now," Fiona said hopefully.

He resisted the temptation. "We were awarded an interim parenting order this morning, and anyway, Sam won't go. I've already told him he can play out the rugby season. No, I won't split up the kids," he added before she could suggest it. On that point, he agreed with Roz.

"Jack, I need some reassurance before I leave tomorrow."

"What kind of reassurance?"

Her hand tightened on his sleeve. "Your guarantee that the children will come to me and Roger."

He hesitated, strangely unwilling to commit to the decision he'd already made privately. He wasn't in a fit state today.

Across the park, Liam swung out of the tree, landing in a crouch next to Cassie. "I'm a big bad lion and I'm going to eat you up," he growled, and his little sister squealed delightedly and took off.

Liam caught Jack's eye and terror tightened his expression. Scrambling to his feet, he pelted as fast as he could after her.

Fiona was watching, too. "Promise me, Jack," she said softly.

He wasn't fit to care for children.

"You have my word," he said.

CHAPTER FIVE

"Miss Valentine is in the toilet," said Liam in his best telephone manner.

In the middle of flushing away the accident in Cassie's discarded panties, Roz gasped. A mistake. Holding her breath, she called nasally, "Liam, take a message," then went back to shallow inhalations.

"No, you don't have to ring back, I'm taking the phone in to her... Hello?" His puzzled face appeared around the bathroom door. "They hung up."

"No kidding." Gingerly holding Cassie's offending panties between forefinger and thumb, Roz walked to the back door, tossed them into the black rubbish bag outside, then pulled the drawstring tight and tied it in a triple knot.

"You're s'posed to wash them," Liam pointed out.

"And you're *not* supposed to answer my mobile. How many times do I have to..." His face fell and she bit her tongue. "Try and remember next time, hey?"

He followed her back to the bathroom and watched as she lathered up to her elbows. "You wash your hands a lot."

But she had other things on her mind. "Any idea who was on the phone?" *Please make it Jack.* He'd left for a four-day business trip to Tokyo immediately after the funeral. Was he calling in on the way home from the airport? She needed to know so she could have the house clean and the kids cute and cheerful.

"Your boss lady," said Liam.

Bloody hell. Roz was at a critical stage in several projects and had confidently assured her immediate superior she'd put in three or four hours a day at home. That had been a condition of her leave of absence.

Except Liam was home from school with a tummy ache that had miraculously cleared up at 9:10 a.m., and Cassie wouldn't nap when she was supposed to.... Wait a minute. "Cass, where have you got to? Come and get your bottom washed, sweetie."

No answer. Uh-oh. After living with Cassandra Galloway for a week, Roz knew silence meant mischief. Hurriedly rinsing her hands, she turned off the faucet. Which turned and turned. Another thing to add to her growing repair list.

"Cass, honey?" she called again, reaching for a towel. "Wait, how did *this* get here?" Freshly laundered this morning, it had a long smear of clay-colored mud across the white terry cloth.

"The model train Uncle Roger bought me in Noumea needed a wash." Liam caught her eye and obviously thought it politic to look sick again. "Are you mad at me, Auntie Roz?"

"No." She unclenched her jaw and gave him a hug. "Next time, use a rag, okay?" "Next time" had become her catchphrase.

"Next time don't put Froggie in the sink with the dishes."

"Next time put your crayons where Cassie can't find them."

"Next time tell me when you need the potty."

Cassie had regressed in her toilet training—normal under the circumstances, the doctor said. Roz had been to see him three times this week, always resisting his offer of sleeping pills to tackle her insomnia. What if one of the kids woke in the night and she didn't hear?

Sam spent all his time either in his room or with friends. Friends she knew nothing about. And he was surly when she asked about them. The boy needed a strong male to keep him in line, and whatever his faults, Jack was both that and a natural leader. He didn't suffer fools gladly, but he had endless patience with those he cared about.

Or at least he used to.

That thought was too painful, so Roz turned her mind to more practical matters. *I'll soften him up with dinner. Beef casserole with herb dumplings always used to work.* On all kinds of levels.

She caught herself checking her appearance in the mirror, and winced. The morning was already half-gone and she hadn't even brushed her hair yet. Cassie had thrust a book under Roz's nose at 5:00 a.m., and things had gone downhill from there. She promised herself a few minutes of grooming after she cleaned up madam. "Cass! Now's not the time for hide-and-seek. Come out now, darling!"

The longer the silence, the worse the damage. "Oh, hell." Roz flew out of the bathroom.

"I'll catch her with my lasso." An excited Liam disappeared into the playroom.

The home telephone started ringing, then stopped.

From upstairs, Roz heard Cassie say, "No, you can't," then the clunk of the receiver.

"Gotcha!" Taking the stairs two at a time, Roz came to an abrupt halt in the doorway of the guest bedroom— now hers. Wearing Roz's Versace sunglasses, a bare-bottomed Cassie sat on top of a heritage quilt, flicking through *Responding to Children's Grief*.

The sunglasses slid down the button nose as she lifted her head. "There's no pictures in your books," she complained. Already tossed across the carpet were *Seven Habits of Highly Effective Families* and *Toddler Taming*. Roz moaned. All the discarded library books had faint brown fingerprints on them.

She opened her mouth to gasp, "Don't move!" but Cassie had already slid across the quilt.

When she jumped off the bed holding Blankie, the diamanté lettering on her pink T-shirt sparkled: It's Not My Fault.

"You can wipe my bottom now," she said generously.

ROZ URGENTLY NEEDED to call her boss and grovel, but it took her another thirty minutes to strip the bed and get Cassie cleaned up. By that time both kids said they were starving.

Startled, she looked at the kitchen clock. It was already noon and she hadn't called a single client. "What would you like?" This wouldn't take long, and then she could storm into damage control.

"Salami mayonnaise tomato sandwich." Liam swung off the back of a dining chair. "And an apple to keep me healthy." His class had been learning about basic nutrition, and he insisted on five "palm-size" servings of fruit or vegetables a day. It didn't matter how many times Roz explained that the size thing was a guide—if the fruit didn't fit in the palm of Liam's hand, it had to be reshaped.

Knowing this health obsession was a result of his new fear of death, she tempered her impatience and pared down a large apple.

Cassie held out her small fist. "Me, too."

With another glance at the clock, Roz repeated the procedure, then made sandwiches. But the little girl growled when Roz handed hers over.

"Noodles."

Roz pushed it back. "Not today," she said firmly. She had let Cass dictate terms while she'd settled in, but noodles for both lunch and dinner had to stop.

The phone rang; Roz and Liam both dived for it. She got there first. "Rosalind Valentine speaking."

"It's Jack. I'm calling from the plane. Listen, I'm exhausted. How about we reschedule our meeting for tomorrow?"

You think you're tired! She bit back the retort and said patiently, "It's not a meeting, Jack. You're visiting your niece and nephews." Silence. "They'll be really disappointed if you don't show."

"I doubt that," he said drily. "It's not like we spend a lot of time together."

And that's about to change. But she didn't want to scare him away, so she dangled a carrot.

"We could discuss renovations." She knew her ex-husband was keen to get the house ready for sale. Roz had no intention of letting tradesmen in while the kids were still living here, but he didn't know that. Yet.

"I'll be there at seven-thirty, but I can't stay long."

She hung up, feeling more cheerful. Jack would spend time with the kids; he would bond with them. He would want to keep the kids. All she had to do was to show him how easy they were to look after.

"Noodles." There was a warning in Cassie's tone.

Preempting a strike, Roz removed the plate, dumped the sandwich in the trash and mashed up some banana with yogurt. "Yummy, yum, yum. I wish *I* was having this."

Cass took one look and closed her eyes tight.

"She's a terrible eater." Munching his sandwiches, Liam watched the battle complacently from his seat at the dining room table. "Dad said he was going bald because Cassie made him tear his hair out."

"Your sister was born to collect scalps." But the unexpected mention of Anthony brought a lump to Roz's throat; she busied herself clearing plates.

"Can we look at the family photo albums again tonight?"

"Absolutely."

Cassie opened her eyes and said with great sincerity, "Daddy lets me have cookies for lunch."

Kissing the top of her goddaughter's head, Roz lifted her down from the table. "Nice try, sweetheart, but how about we wait until you really *are* hungry?"

Cassie growled; Roz smiled serenely. Her job was people management for a multinational human resources company. No way could she be bested by a three-year-old. Nor, for that matter, a thirty-four-year-old ex-husband.

She settled the kids with some toys and was picking

up the phone to call her boss when Sam strolled in the back door. "What time is it?" she said, startled.

"Teachers' meeting, so we got off early. Anything to eat?"

"Sure." Roz handed over the sandwich she'd made for herself. "How was your day?"

The bony shoulders shrugged under their oversize jacket. "Normal."

He started to leave the room.

"Sit down," Roz invited, hanging up the phone because the kids came first. "Let's chat."

"I gotta lot of homework to do."

"Please, Sam, just a few minutes."

He plonked himself down and stared at her.

Roz cleared her throat. "Okay, maybe *I* could start." Mentally, she scrolled through her morning. "Made breakfast, did dishes, housework, grocery shopping, read the kids stories…." Her voice trailed off as his eyes glazed over. Nothing that would interest a teenager. "It was a normal day," she finished, "like yours. But normal will do, right?"

His gaze flicked to hers in a brief moment of shared grief, then he shrugged.

Roz kept trying. "Oh, and laundry…I did lots and lots of laundry."

Sam frowned. "You didn't go into my room, did you?"

"Yes, to grab the washing." She didn't mention the mess.

He shoved back from the table and stood up. "I don't want you poking around in my room when I'm not here, Roz. That's *my* space."

"Okay, calm down."

He glared at her. "Can I go now?"

"After you've watched the kids for ten minutes while I call my senior manager."

Sam groaned and rolled his eyes.

"Thanks, Sam." Ignoring his long-suffering sigh, she picked up the phone and dialed her boss.

"I got an irate call from Quentin Gillespie a half hour ago." Chantel's normally warm voice was decidedly cool. "He said he got hung up on by a toddler." Gillespie headed a leading Internet provider, and Roz was implementing a best practices policy for his telephone help desk.

"Ouch." No point mentioning he wasn't supposed to be ringing the home line. A self-important jackass, Gillespie phoned whatever line—at any time—he wanted. "At least he wasn't redirected to the toilet."

Chantel laughed, but sobered almost immediately. "Roz, we're going to rethink your working from home."

Outside the kitchen window, Cassie trotted into view. She looked behind her for pursuers, then started picking daffodils in the front garden border. The road was mere meters away.

"Hang on!" Without waiting for a response, Roz dropped the phone and raced outside.

"You know you're not supposed to go near cars." She led Cass toward the house. "Where's Sam?"

The child thrust out the flowers. "I picked 'em for you."

Roz melted. Carefully, she took the too-short stems. "That's so sweet of—"

"Now I want noodles."

Sighing, Roz picked her up. "Let me finish my phone call and we'll talk."

Inside, she shifted Cassie to her other hip and picked up the receiver. For someone who didn't eat, the toddler was surprisingly heavy. "You're right, Chantel, this isn't working." She took a deep breath. "I have to resign."

For a moment there was absolute silence. "You sure know how to take the wind out of my sails, don't you? But let's not be too hasty here. Just tell me you'll get back to your usual efficiency."

Cassie squirmed and Roz put her down. "We both know that Gillespie's project needs someone available 24/7. But right now, so do these kids. He won't tolerate mistakes, and the contract means too much to the firm to jeopardize on my domestic learning curve."

There was a new scrawl of pencil near the skirting board, a squiggle disappearing into the worn carpet. Roz averted her gaze. "Promote Stephanie…she's been my right-hand woman on the job, and I think she's capable of rising to the challenge."

"I really don't want to lose you, Roz… How about Steph takes over the Gillespie contract, and we all pitch in with your other clients until you're back."

She was touched. Her associates already put in long hours. Still, maybe this could work.

"All I need," continued Chantel, "is your commitment to return after Christmas."

Or maybe it couldn't.

Roz slid down the wall until she was sitting next to the pencil mark. "I can't give you that guarantee," she admitted. "There are too many unknowns right now." If she succeeded in convincing Jack to keep the kids in New Zealand, she'd need to make herself available. "I think it's better for everybody if I resign."

"Be very sure, Roz. Between you and me," Chantel lowered her voice, "you're on target for a promotion."

Roz hesitated. For the last six years she'd invested a lot of energy into her career. Giving up the certainty of a great job for the long shot of convincing Jack to accept permanent custody was a huge gamble.

She took an eraser from the kids' activity table and absently rubbed at the pencil mark.

And even if he said yes to keeping the kids, then what? Was she willing to be a full-time homemaker? She stared at the smudged mess she'd made with the eraser.

So far, she was useless at it.

It was one thing letting Jack financially support his niece and nephews, another to expect him to indefinitely support his ex-wife. Not that Roz would let him… she'd never accepted a penny in alimony and she wasn't going to start now. She had some savings, but when they were gone, then what?

On the other hand, she'd survived the very worst that could happen to a person—nothing could be that bad again. Oddly, there was courage in that. Life was too uncertain not to put people first. The practicalities of how to share custody with her ex could come later.

"You want to sleep on it?" said Chantel hopefully.

"No, my resignation stands." Roz got to her feet, moving the activity table to cover the pencil mark. "Just promise to give me a good reference when I need one."

Sometimes you had to burn the bridge to find the courage to jump.

CHAPTER SIX

Roz opened the door, looking terrible. Jack knew his instinctive relief was unfeeling and quashed it—an attempt not wholly successful.

However bright—and fake—her smile, her hair was unkempt, she wore not a lick of makeup and there were water stains on the front of her sweatshirt.

He smiled back. If she was finding parenting tough, it would be easier for her to surrender the kids to Fiona. He handed her a shopping bag. "Presents for the kids… So how have you been managing?"

"A duck to water."

Jack looked at her sweatshirt, and his smile broadened. A waterlogged duck, maybe. Stepping inside, he scanned the living room. It was tidy, but there were suspicious bulges under the cushions. He picked one up and found Barbie in a compromising position with Teddy and Thomas the Tank Engine.

Roz dumped the bag and hastily replaced the cushion. "Obviously there are a few kinks to iron out." Unconsciously, she lifted a hand to pat her hair, and Jack's amusement faded because she wasn't wearing a bra. "But I'm coping…. What?"

"Nothing." He realized his hands had curved to the

exact shape of his ex-wife's breasts, and he shoved them in his pockets. "So how are the kids?"

"As expected—good days and bad." Poaching Barbie's pink scrunchie, Roz lifted her arms to tie back her hair, and Jack succumbed to temptation and looked. Why *wasn't* she wearing a bra?

"I'm most worried about Sam," she added.

"Talk to me, not about me," said a disgruntled voice above them, and Sam clomped down the stairs. "I'd be fine if she stopped treating me like I'm the same age as the kids," he complained to Jack.

"I don't think it's unreasonable to want to know where you are," Roz answered quietly.

"She even brought my lunch to the bus stop today."

"Okay, I admit that was a mistake, but I was running late and—"

"In a Thomas the Tank Engine lunch box."

Jack looked at Roz.

"It was all I could find!"

"*And* she's given me an eight o'clock curfew during the week."

"It's what your parents did—"

"Yeah, but now rugby training's kicked in for the reps team—"

"Which finishes at seven," Roz pointed out. "Not eight, like you told me."

"So I made a mistake." Again he appealed to Jack. "See what I mean about checking up on me?"

Jack tried to keep his tone neutral. "He is sixteen, Roz." At Sam's age, Jack had been working and living an adult's life.

Sam punched the air. "Yes!"

"*Nearly* sixteen," Roz corrected grimly.

"Oh, come on," said Sam. "Like three weeks makes a difference."

Jack looked from one stubborn face to the other. "Let's reassess on your birthday," he said to his nephew.

Roz folded her arms, throwing those distracting breasts into relief. "Fifteen or sixteen, Julia and Ants wouldn't want him out carousing on a school night."

"Carousing." Sam wrinkled his forehead. "What the hell kind of word is that?"

"Don't push it," Jack warned him. "She's in charge."

Sam opened his mouth to argue, thought better of it and shrugged. "My birthday then. I'm gonna take a shower before dinner." At the top of the stairs, he looked back with an impish grin. "Roz, got any warnings about touching the hot tap?"

"The curfew can always get earlier," Jack reminded him.

"Sheesh, can't anyone take a joke around here?"

With a glint in her eye, Roz called, "I'll be up to wash your hair in a minute."

The bathroom door slammed. Hearing the key turn firmly in the lock, Jack grinned. But the glint remained in Roz's eye. She waited until the shower was running, then said tightly, "Nice of you to remember I'm the boss—even if it was a bit late."

"Natural though it is, given the circumstances, you need to fight the tendency to wrap him in cotton wool."

"In front of the kids, you have to back me up, Jack. Besides, you haven't been here. You don't know what Sam's been like."

"I thought you said you were coping?" he challenged.

She bit her lip. "I am. Forget I said anything. Listen," she added awkwardly, "the younger ones ate early, but I waited to eat with Sam. I made enough for you."

He became aware of the scent of beef and wine wafting from the kitchen as she smiled at him, and for a split second Jack nearly smiled back before he remembered the situation. For the kids' sake she had to be pleasant. With bleak humor he wondered if she'd factored in that cost when she was bargaining with him for temporary custody.

But he had no intention of forcing his company on her or Liam. Nor of torturing himself with what he'd lost. "Thanks, but I ate on the plane. And I can't stay long. I still need to go to the office."

"But it's 7:30 p.m."

Jack shrugged. He'd begun working late the day Roz remarried, and never got out of the habit. If feeling nothing could be called balance, he'd regained his equilibrium in the years since their baby died. And he intended to keep it.

Frankly, his sanity depended on it.

"Let's talk about renovations. I want to get the place on the market immediately after Christmas, which means getting a crew in as soon as possible."

On paper it was a large, two-story brick house circa 1950 with a half-acre garden. In reality it was what estate agents always described as a handyman's dream.

It had certainly attracted a lot of dreamers, because every successive owner, including his brother, had started a renovation project and never finished it. Jack remembered Ants and Ju raving about the old fireplace, the high, molded-plaster ceilings and the wood-paneled study, and ignoring him when he'd pointed out the lack of insulation, the pokey bathrooms and the need for a new roof.

"Let's buy it if they don't," Jack's own dreamer had suggested.

"Roz, I'll build you one better than this, I promise. We have our own five-year plan." With their new baby in a pack on his chest, Jack had kissed her in this very hallway.

And just over a month later, their marriage was over.

"About the renovations…" Roz colored up in a way that immediately made Jack suspicious. "I don't want any work done while the kids are here. It's too unsettling to have strangers demolishing their home."

"But—"

"Come say hello to the children." She picked up his bag and shoved it at him with a bright smile. "They're in the family room."

"Roz!" But she was already leading the way down the hall.

Cassie and Liam were cuddled up on a beanbag chair in their pajamas, watching some cartoon. "Hey, look who's here," Roz called enthusiastically. "You guys chat while I make coffee."

Cassie took one look at him, clutched Blankie and shut her eyes, and Liam scrunched deeper into the beanbag. Jack felt like Captain Cook faced with a strange—and potentially hostile—tribe. But like Cook, he'd come prepared. "I brought presents."

Immediately he was surrounded, though both kids retreated after hooking the shopping bag out of his hands. Jack sat down and watched.

Picture books were a hit with Cassie. But he stiffened when the little girl clambered into his lap. "Read it to me."

She smelled of talcum powder and baby shampoo and dryer-warmed cotton. He read the story woodenly, every muscle tensed against memory. Thank God the book was short.

"'Nudder one."

"Maybe later." With relief, he lifted her from his lap and stood up. Liam was tugging on the stiff latch of a wooden box with shiny brass hinges. "What is it?"

"A kids' carpentry set." Jack crouched down, ignoring Liam's instinctive recoil, and opened it. "See, they're scaled-down working versions of real tools. A saw, claw hammer, mallet, plane, bradawl…"

He touched the tools as he described them. He hadn't meant to spend so much, but when he'd seen the craftsmanship Jack hadn't been able to resist them.

Across the toolbox, Liam was looking at him blankly. "I know it's a bit advanced," Jack admitted, "but you'll have them forever. One day you can pass them down to your own son. And look, there are some precut wooden pieces you can nail together to practice your hammer skills. Go ahead…."

Politely, Liam picked up the hammer and gave it a token swing. "Thank you, Uncle Jack," he said without enthusiasm.

Roz came into the lounge, holding two steaming cups of coffee. "Wow! Aren't *you* lucky."

Oh, God, thought Jack, *did I choose as badly as that?*

"Try it on some wood this time." Rather desperately, he started a nail for Liam.

The boy looked at Roz, who nodded encouragingly.

Sitting on his haunches, the wood between his knees, he raised the hammer and closing his eyes, brought it down hard. It missed the nail and cracked into his knee-cap.

Liam's eyes flew open and met Jack's in accusatory shock. Then his face crumbled and he started to howl.

Jack reached out to comfort him, and Liam stumbled backward to get away from him, tripping over the rug and landing on his bottom. Realizing he was only making things worse, Jack stepped back, watching help-lessly as Roz put down the coffee cups, then did the cuddles and consolation routine. "You'll be fine.... He's fine," she assured Jack when things calmed down. "A bruise maybe, but no major damage."

Liam glared at Jack. "I want him to go."

"Why, Silly Billy?" Roz tickled him into a smile. "It's not Uncle Jack's fault you need some practice."

But Jack agreed with Liam. He was out of place here. Loosening his tie, he stood up. "I'll leave."

THIS BONDING SESSION wasn't working out the way Roz had planned. "You haven't touched your coffee," she protested, sliding Liam off her lap. "Let me reheat it."

"No, you need dinner, anyway so…see you, kids."

"Bye, Uncle Jack," Liam said with obvious relief. Cassie ignored him.

Jack was halfway down the hall before Roz reached the family room door. Emergency action was needed. With a quick twist, she wrenched off the handle.

"Jack, wait!" Adopting a woeful expression, she waved the handle, trying to look helpless, and praying he'd forgotten how much he'd taught her. "I need some repairs done." If it was one thing her ex-husband couldn't resist, it was fixing things.

He frowned, then crossed his arms, and his biceps bulged under the fabric of his white business shirt. "You said you didn't want any renovations while the kids were in residence."

"I said I didn't want strangers here."

"Roz, I haven't got time to play handyman."

"Well, okay." Deliberately, she stood on the loose board in the hall so that it creaked ghoulishly. "I'll just keep the kids away from the danger zones." She waved the handle. "I can go through the window if the kids accidentally shut the door…and I'll use towels to stop the leak in the upstairs bathroom."

He said through gritted teeth, "What's wrong with the upstairs bathroom?"

Nothing. Yet. But surely she could loosen a nut or a washer. "Not sure," she said vaguely. "Lots of water under the sink."

His mouth tightened. "Okay, I'll do the urgent stuff now."

"Thanks, Jack."

"There are tools in my car. Go write me a list."

Oh yes, a list. A long, long list.

"And I guess whatever I do now will shorten the workload when the kids go to Fiona."

Her optimism dipped slightly, but she smiled and nodded.

"I'll start with the upstairs bathroom."

Oh, hell. "Great." Roz forced herself to hold his gaze, but folded her arms defensively. And realized she wasn't wearing a bra. Cass had called out when Roz was in the shower, and she hadn't had time to dress properly. Casually, she lifted her arms higher across her chest.

"And do something about that."

She blushed. "A gentleman wouldn't have mentioned it."

"I disagree." His smile reconnected her to everything they'd ever done together naked. "A gentleman would have told you earlier."

The front door clicked shut behind him. It took several seconds for Roz to realize she was leaning against the wall for support, having been turned on by a single look from her ex-husband. She straightened, then raced upstairs to sabotage the sink.

And find a bra.

GRIMLY, JACK HAULED his toolbox out of the trunk of the car, stripping off his dress shirt and replacing it with a T-shirt from his suitcase. A passing car honked and he muttered, "Yeah, yeah, haven't you seen a bare chest before?"

Upstairs a light snapped on, and he saw Roz haul open drawers and retrieve a pink bra. If she didn't close the curtains he doubted he'd have the moral strength to look away. Fortunately, she didn't test him. Things were complicated enough without his having to fight a sexual attraction to his ex-wife.

For another five minutes he stood by his car, battling the impulse to drive away. Finally, with an exasperated sigh, he reentered the warm house.

He hunted Roz down to the family room, where she sprawled on the carpet with Liam, photo albums open around them. Cassie sat opposite in an armchair.

"We're all looking at family pictures. You want to join us for a few minutes?"

"Hell, no!" His sharp tone drew Liam's wondering gaze, and Jack added lamely, "I remember what Ju and Ants looked like." He couldn't understand the urge to twist the knife. He hesitated, then said awkwardly, "Liam, you want to get your new hammer and come help me fix the bath?" He really wanted to repair his relationship with his brother's son.

But Liam didn't even look up. "No, thanks, I'm busy with Roz."

Cassie dropped her album and slid off the armchair, her feet landing on the carpet with a determined thud. "I'll help," she said generously.

"Umm…" Caught off-guard, Jack didn't know what to say.

"But don't you want to look at more photos, Cass?" asked Liam.

"Remember what I told you, hon," Roz murmured in a low voice. "Cassie is so little, she won't find them comforting like you. I'd be grateful," she said in a normal voice to Jack. "I'm running out of other things to give her."

"You know," he stated, searching for excuses, "some of my tools are dangerous."

Cassie eyed him. "Daddy lets me help."

"Fine, let's go."

In passing, Jack picked up the album she'd discarded on the floor, and saw it was one of Roz's. Which meant the baby pictures were… His heart started pounding in his chest and his grip tightened on the handle of the toolbox as dizziness clouded his vision.

In the distance, he heard Roz talking to Liam. "I

remember that house," she said. "It was the first one your parents bought after they got married. The wisteria was all that held it up."

Then Cassie's small hand grabbed Jack's, grounding him. "C'mon," she said, tugging impatiently. "Let's fix stuff."

In the upstairs bathroom, Jack shut the door and slid down it to the floor, then hid his face in his hands. Then silently, painfully, shoulders heaving, he cried, the pain of walled-off memories pouring out and merging with the still-raw grief for Ants and Julia.

Hadn't he and Roz suffered enough?

He could feel Cassie's curious gaze but as much as he tried, Jack couldn't stop his emotional hemorrhage, couldn't do anything but bury his head deeper into his arms.

"Are you havin' a rest?"

"Yes," he rasped.

There was a silence while she digested that. "Where's the hammer?"

Desperately pulling himself together, Jack retrieved it from the toolbox and handed it to her.

She looked curiously at his wet cheeks. "Did you hit your finger?"

Unable to speak, Jack nodded.

"Show me."

He stuck out his thumb and she kissed it. "All better?"

Her brisk sympathy moved him as much as the unexpected kiss. But then, she'd seen a lot of adults crying lately. "Yes." He smiled at her through his tears.

"Jack?" Roz tried to open the door he was leaning against. "You need some help?"

"Hang on, let me move the toolbox." After wiping his face on a towel, Jack stood up. When Roz opened the door he had his head in the cupboard under the basin.

"Uncle Jack had an owwie," announced Cassie.

"It's nothing," he said brusquely. "You're right, this is a bad leak. There's water everywhere."

"He cried."

In the semidarkness, Jack closed his eyes. There was a brief silence.

"Honey," said Roz, "go tell Liam I said you could have a cookie." The tattletale dropped the hammer on the tiles with a clunk and scampered away.

There was a tentative touch on his arm. "Jack, come out."

"No wonder this is leaking," he said. "Someone's loosened the connection on the S-bend."

"Forget the damn repairs. You're upset."

"I'm fine, and I don't want to talk about it." He rescrewed the loose fixture. "I'll tighten this to stop the kids doing this again. I just need—"

A wrench appeared beside him.

"Thanks."

He had no excuse to stay in the cupboard now. Reluctantly, he came out and returned the wrench to his toolbox. "What's next on the list?"

Her fingers brushed the tearstains on his face. "You still won't let anyone mourn with you," she said sadly.

Jack picked up his tools. "I'll fix the door handle next."

"Fine." She stood back to let him pass. "I'll stop trying to help."

Twenty minutes later, Jack had finished the most urgent repairs and was heading toward the front door.

"Why don't you stay and put the kids to bed?"

"Yeah, I can just see Liam's face."

"If he gets to know you, Jack…"

"Will you stop feeling sorry for me? It's driving me crazy."

"Will you stop pushing people away?"

With his free arm he caught her to him. "What's the alternative. This?" She'd always made him hard, and this time was no exception. She'd always softened against him and this time was no exception. "Do you really think we have any hope in hell of making this work, given our history?"

He should never have agreed to temporary custody.

She obviously hadn't thought about this complication; he could tell by the shock on her face. Releasing her, he stepped back. "Trust me," he said heavily, "It's better that I stay away. For everybody's sake." *Especially mine.*

"You're not leaving?" Sam came down the stairs, drying his wet hair with a towel. "But I thought you'd be moving in…you know, for the time we're here."

Jack looked at Roz. "Yours, I think."

She cleared her throat. "You do remember that Jack and I are divorced, don't you?"

"Oh, yeah…I guess that was a stupid thing to think." Through Sam's adolescent self-absorption, Jack could see memory start to surface. Sam had been almost ten when Thomas died.

"I really have to go."

Sam fell into step beside him. "Are you coming back tomorrow?"

"It might take me a couple of days to get a handle

on things at work. We've got big things happening at the moment."

"Oh, sure, I understand." The teenager affected nonchalance, but twisted the towel in his hands. And Jack realized Roz wasn't the only one who hadn't thought things through. What expectations had he raised in his oldest nephew?

Roz said nothing, but Jack could feel her tension as she opened the front door for him. Unable to help himself, he looked into her eyes, saw the unspoken plea, and began to drown. It wasn't a pleasant sensation. *Don't,* he wanted to say, *don't need me like this. We broke all the links, remember?*

"Good night." He could feel Sam's disappointment following him down the driveway, and tried to chase it away with rationalizations. A multimillion-dollar construction project didn't run itself. Over previous months he'd lined up designers, suppliers, construction crews and subcontractors in a finely balanced schedule that would topple like a row of dominoes if he made any mistakes.

Jack jabbed his remote in the direction of his Mercedes SUV. What Roz and Sam didn't realize was that delays on a project this size would cost hundreds of thousands of dollars—effectively, his profit margin. Opening the car door, he paused, then barked over his shoulder, "What time's your game on Saturday?"

"You wanna come watch? Really?" The teenager's face lit up before he remembered his habitual indifference. Shrugging he said, "Kickoff's at three o'clock."

"I'll *try,* okay?"

"No biggie…I mean, it would be great if you came. But whatever."

Jack waited for Roz's nod. But he wasn't expecting the smile that came with it, and its warmth hit him before he could put up a firewall. Reminding him what being loved by Rosalind Valentine had been like.

Before he'd lost the right to it.

CHAPTER SEVEN

ROZ WATCHED JACK DRIVE away, feeling a momentary wistfulness that had nothing to do with the kids' need for a father figure.

In his actions, she'd glimpsed a remnant of the soft-hearted tough guy she'd married, not the inaccessible stranger who'd divorced her. She realized suddenly that she was staking the children's future on the man he'd been, not the one he'd become.

She must need to have her head examined.

Particularly for assuming their sexual connection had been broken along with everything else.

Oh, God, I'm in trouble.

No, you're not.

Closing the door firmly, Roz checked on the kids, then went into the kitchen to dish up dinner. The casserole was perfect, the meat so tender it all but fell apart on the plate. Jack hadn't eaten on the plane; he hated airplane food.

I should have made him stay.

The serving spoon hit the kitchen bench with a clatter and she started to laugh. Like she'd made him stay six years ago? Hadn't she learned anything?

She remembered Jack in the bathroom earlier,

rugged, macho and terse—with tearstains on his cheeks. Roz sighed. The trouble was she understood him now, in a way she hadn't when he'd broken what had been left of her heart.

She understood that losing a child to crib death could make even the strong weak. They'd both been strong people before Thomas's death; and they'd both been broken by it, though she'd only fallen apart when he'd left her.

Reverting to type, her parents said, because Jack Galloway had been wild before settling down with their daughter. Thank God they lived in Australia now and couldn't disapprove of this situation.

"Gorgeous," Julia had said eight years ago of her prospective brother-in-law, "but dangerous. The kind of guy you crash and burn on."

He'd sounded like a jerk to Roz.

Recently graduated from university, she liked her men educated, and Jack Galloway had left high school before graduating. As a PR executive working for an ad agency where image was everything, what would she possibly have in common with a blue-collar construction worker?

When Jack missed his brother's wedding because of a long-standing estrangement from his aging father, a legend in New Zealand sport, her view hardened, though Julia was already expressing reservations about her new father-in-law.

Roz finally met Jack when she was twenty-four. "I don't approve of you," she'd told him, giddy on her best friend's housewarming champagne; more so on the lazy intensity in Jack's green eyes when he looked at her.

"I'm going to change your mind," he said.

She'd married him three months later, when Jack took out an overdraft to follow her to a convention in Las Vegas.

And they'd been happy. Even happier when their son was born. The first of a dynasty, Jack had toasted, and captivated by their perfect newborn, Roz had recklessly agreed to have five more.

Thomas. Through the sleeve of her sweatshirt, Roz fingered the thin silver chain around her wrist, finding the heavier link of Thomas's charm bracelet and tracing his name through the cotton.

Not that he wasn't etched in her heart. But she'd learned that embracing—not resisting—the pain was the only way to push through it. "It was worth it," she whispered.

If only his father could reach the same conclusion.

LIAM SAT ON THE COUCH with Cassie, watching a cartoon, his lower lip stuck out. Usually he liked to swing his legs, but he couldn't now because it hurt too much. He looked at the bruise, red turning purple, and it started hurting more.

It *was* big, though. Imagining how impressed his friends would be at school tomorrow, Liam cheered up. But then he thought of admitting that he'd hit himself with the hammer, and pushed his lip out again.

Cassie leaned on him and he squirmed away. "Don't sit so close!" Normally he liked how big and protective he felt when Cassie cuddled up to him; right now he felt mean.

She growled, but moved away, still looking at the picture book Uncle Jack had given her.

Liam glanced at his present, lying where he'd opened it. Dumb old tool stuff. Uncle Jack should have got him something fun, not something *he* wanted to play with.

Liam tried to think what he would have liked better. A baseball bat and mitt maybe…that's what Mum and Dad were gonna get him for Christmas.

Dad used to pitch to him in the backyard with his heavy old bat, and said Liam's swing was really coming along. Sometimes Liam even hit the ball. The urge to cry was very strong.

Cassie turned the page of her book and the heavy cardboard thwacked against his knee. "Oww," he cried, letting the tears fall, even though it didn't hurt much. "Say you're sorry."

But she was distracted. "Look." Cassie pointed. "A butterfly."

Liam glanced at the pink shimmering fabric sewn into the wings. "Dumb girls' book," he muttered, and she growled at him again.

"Dumb old Uncle Jack," he said. "He's a bum-bum," he added, and her eyes widened. She knew it was a naughty word. "We don't like Uncle Jack," said Liam.

She looked at him doubtfully, then scrambled off the sofa. "You the bum-bum."

"You are."

"No, you."

He pretended to get off the couch, and she ran out of the room. "Good riddance," he shouted after her, then sat back, feeling lonelier than ever.

He could write to Mum and Dad in heaven, and tell them about his accident, but today he resented having to. Today it didn't feel like anybody was listening.

The butterfly book lay open beside him; Liam kicked it onto the floor with his good leg, then had an idea and hid it under the couch. When Cassie was looking for it at bedtime, he whispered, "I bet that bum-bum Uncle Jack took it."

JACK ARRIVED AT Sam's rugby game at the start of the second half. He'd left an important site meeting to manage even that, and was in a foul mood.

As he strode along the perimeter of the playing field, Sam caught sight of him, and at the relief on the boy's face, some of Jack's ill humor evaporated. He gave his nephew a thumbs-up, then scanned the huddles of spectators for Roz and the other kids. He'd been up since five, yet only now did he notice the late spring sun, the smell of turf and grass churned up by rugby boots, and the light breeze, still brisk enough to make him dig his hands in the pockets of his jacket.

He passed through a group of teenage girls prematurely embracing summer in tight tees and cutoffs that revealed goose-bumpy blue flesh. Their voices rose and fell with intermittent shrieks of laughter as, flicking back hair, they glanced at the boys and practiced their flirting on each other.

Then Jack caught sight of Roz. And despite his irritation he had to smile.

She wore jeans, chunky socks, a thick jumper and a crimson beanie pulled low over her ears—and still she was shivering.

"It's about time," she hissed as soon as he was within earshot. "Sam's missed I don't know how many passes, scanning the crowd for you."

"Then leave your cell phone on so I can call you," he snapped back, taking off his jacket and placing it around her shoulders.

"What? So you could cancel?"

"Better than a no-show."

"I knew you wouldn't do that," she said. "You're too honorable." She seemed to realize she was wearing his jacket. "Jack, no, you'll freeze."

"I'm fine…. Hello, Cassandra." The little girl wore earmuffs that made her look like an Ewok, a sheepskin coat in the same pink, with fake fur trim that had turned into dreadlocks. On her feet she had a pink pair of Uggs. She sat on a picnic rug surrounded by books.

She didn't acknowledge him, but neither did she close her eyes. That was progress, he guessed.

"What's the score?" Jack asked Roz. She still looked exhausted. He reminded himself that taking the hard road had been her choice.

"No idea," she confessed, "but I think we're winning." Her eyes were very blue as she shot him a sideways glance. "Look, I'm sorry. Thanks for coming. I know it means a lot to Sam."

I also did it for you. He shoved the thought aside and turned to watch the game. "Where's Liam?"

"At a birthday party. I'm picking him up on the way home."

Jack tried to be ashamed of his relief. He couldn't seem to get it right with that kid, and Liam's continued fear of him cut him to the quick.

In Liam's world, dinosaurs, hobbits and Santa brushed shoulders with the tooth fairy, God and baby Jesus, while Ants and Julia checked the heavenly mailbox. Such blind faith made Jack uncomfortable. The sooner Liam dealt with the reality of his parents' death, the better the kid would recover from it.

Roz would disagree with him, but then she was an optimist. Which was one of the reasons he'd fallen in love with her. The wind picked up and Jack shivered.

"You *are* cold," said his ex-wife. "Look, take this back. Sam's got a jacket in his sports bag. I'll wear it until he needs it."

She retrieved the jacket and tugged it on, putting her hands in the pockets. A strange expression came over her face. Roz pulled out her hand and opened her palm, and the foil of a condom packet gleamed in the sun.

She and Jack looked at each other.

"It's probably wishful thinking," he assured her. "Most boys carry one around for years before they get a chance to use it."

"You didn't," Roz reminded him.

Jack had lost his virginity at fifteen. "Nothing about my teenage years was normal," he reminded her. "But Sam has fam…" His voice trailed off.

"You're going to have to talk to him, Jack."

"Roz, it's not my place." Damn it, he knew he shouldn't have come to the game.

"You're his guardian."

"So are you," he countered.

"Oh, yeah," she said tartly. "Teenage boys love discussing sex with mother figures. Maybe Fiona and I can set up a three-way conference call."

"What about one of the school counselors?" But Jack knew he was fighting a losing battle.

"He looks up to you, Jack," she argued.

"What am I going to say?"

"What you once said to me about it—however physically mature you are, emotionally you're still a baby."

"How about we just decide that this demonstrates a sense of responsibility?"

"I have one question for you. Did you regret having sex so young?"

"Absolutely not…at the time."

"And looking back?"

He hadn't been ready for the emotions that went with sexual intimacy, and they were messy, bewildering years. "Fine, I'll talk to him."

"Chocolate!" Cassie jumped up, practically vibrating with glee.

Hurriedly, Roz palmed the foil packet. "No, hon, it's not chocolate."

"I want chocolate." The toddler dumped the books and hauled on Roz's pocket. "I want some." Her voice rose in a wail, her face turned red and she threw herself onto the picnic rug in a full-blown tantrum.

Jack really, really wished he hadn't come. "Tell me why we're doing this again?" he asked Roz, who was crouching down, trying to pacify her goddaughter. He leaned over and picked Cassie up by her jacket, lifting her until she hung in the air like a bellowing fairy. Surprised, she stopped. "It's not chocolate," he said. "It's a preventative against accidents like you."

"I'm flying." Cassie flapped her arms. "Uncle Jack, you make me fly."

As he swung her gently around a couple of times, the final whistle blew.

Sweaty and muddy, Sam weaved his way through the

crowd, grinning from ear to ear. A few people turned to stare after him as though they could see the tragedy clinging to him; a couple whispered behind their hands. "Good God, are people always this insensitive?" Jack muttered to Roz.

"Yes," she murmured back, then overcompensated by giving Sam a hero's welcome, which the teenager shrugged off impatiently.

"We won," he told Jack.

"Great game." Jack lowered Cassie to the ground. "What was the final score?"

"Forty-thirty. But you missed the first half, right?" Sam launched into an enthusiastic account of the first forty minutes. Jack listened intently, seeing Julia in the excited gestures and passionate delivery.

Roz obviously saw the likeness, too. Her eyes widened; her hands grew clumsy as she folded the picnic blanket. His attention still on Sam, Jack took over the job. "I'll bring Sam home while you go pick up Liam," he told her. This was why he needed to stay away. She kept slipping past his defenses....

Surreptitiously, she swiped at her eyes with her sleeve. Face averted, she picked up Cassie. "Thank you."

"No problem." He watched her cross the field, carrying Cassie, who surprised him by waving. Jack waved back.

"Mind if I hang around with the guys a few minutes?" Sam gave a thumbs-up to his teammates, still milling excitedly on the pitch.

Jack thought of all the work he had to do, then looked at the longing on Sam's face. "Sure...I'll make a few calls in the car." His cell phone rang before he finished speaking. He looked at the caller ID and frowned.

"Roz?"

"Stay for dinner." Her voice was steady again.

So was his resolve. "Other plans," he said brusquely.

"Tomorrow night then?"

"My Japanese business partner is in the country for a few days. I'll be entertaining him."

Frustration mixed with the cheerfulness in her tone. "We'll expect you at six on Thursday."

"I'll check my diary and get back to you about dinner on Thursday, Roz." He had no intention of going.

"See you then," she stated firmly. Jack looked beyond the field to the car park and spotted the bright crimson of her beanie. She was trying to make him play happy family with the kids, but it wouldn't work.

After the trauma of the other night, any future encounters with the children would be on neutral ground—like sports fields and the movies. Places they didn't have to talk.

As he and Sam walked past the group of teenage girls, the greetings started.

"*Hi*, Sam!"

"Hey, Sammy, nice legs!"

"Whatever," replied his nephew. But Jack noticed his shoulders straighten, his neck flush, and hid a smile. The condom was definitely wishful thinking.

Behind them the girls giggled and whispered, then one voice rose self-importantly. "Yeah, his mum forgot she was supposed to be driving on the right-hand side and pulled into the path of a truck. It took five hours to cut the bod—"

Jack spun on his heel and cut the speaker off with a

look, but when he turned back Sam's shoulders were hunched again. Casually, he threw an arm around them. "So that drop-goal I missed. How many meters were you away from the posts again?"

"It's okay," Sam mumbled, "I'm used to it."

Jack tightened his hand on his shoulder. "They'll find something else to talk about soon." But it would be there for the rest of his life, the tragedy that marked him as different.

"Don't worry. I can handle it." Now it was Sam doing the reassuring.

"In the U.K. with Fiona, no one will know you. You can start again."

"Yeah." But the boy's enthusiasm was gone.

Brooding, Jack didn't notice his nephew had by-passed his teammates until they were almost to the car park. He stopped. "Wait a minute. Didn't you want to hang around?"

"Nah, it's getting cold. Let's just go home."

Wordlessly, Jack unlocked the car. On the drive home, he didn't raise the subject of the condoms. Didn't give his nephew the spiel that a childhood didn't last long, and when it was gone, it was gone forever. They both knew Sam's was already over.

"Next week I'll be there for the whole game."

"You don't have—"

"I want to."

He drew up to the curb in front of his brother's house; Sam got out of the car. For only the second time since his parents died, Jack saw Sam smile. "See you at dinner Thursday," said Sam.

"But—"

The car door slammed shut.

Jack waited until his nephew was inside, then punched the dashboard. "Shit!"

It looked like he was committed.

CHAPTER EIGHT

"OBVIOUSLY THE SCHOOL'S trying to make allowances for Sam's recent tragedy, but his deteriorating behavior isn't the only problem." The headmaster had left his formidable desk and sat next to Roz on low, comfortable chairs "because we're informal here at North Shore High."

Still reeling from the phone call this morning asking for an urgent meeting, she could only nod.

"In addition to being sullen and uncooperative, this week he's started skipping classes, and with final exams coming up…"

Mr. Coutts looked at her gravely. "Well, I thought the sooner I brought it to your attention, Ms. Valentine, the sooner we could up with a solution."

"Yes, of course… Shouldn't Sam be at this meeting?"

"Except he's not here, Ms. Valentine. Hence the reason for my call." There was a touch of impatience now in his kind tone.

"I'm sorry," said Roz, "I'm finding this difficult to assimilate. You see, every morning, including today, I make him lunch and give him money for the bus." Propelled by a growing anxiety, she stood up. "If he's not here, then where is he?"

"Probably hanging out at a mall or a park somewhere. If he's been coming home after school, you should see him at the usual time."

Roz bit her lip. "He's been telling me he's had sporting commitments after school…getting home around six, sometimes seven. Is that a lie, too?"

"I know he wouldn't miss rugby practice," said Mr. Coutts. "That's Mondays and Wednesdays."

"That doesn't explain the other two…"

"How's his behavior at home?"

"The same as at school. Except with Jack…his other guardian. Sam listens to him. But he's not living with us and we only see him occasionally."

Roz knew she was rambling, but could only think about where Sam might be. It was two-thirty now. She might not see him for another four hours…. Then the time registered. "Can I call you when I've had a chance to talk to Sam? I need to pick up his siblings at three."

"Of course. And if you feel a counselor would be helpful, we have a good person on staff."

For a moment Roz thought he meant for her. Because that's how clueless she felt right now. She'd had no idea that anything was amiss.

"There was bound to be some fallout after the tragedy," he said kindly, "so don't blame yourself. The important thing is getting Sam stabilized before his exams."

"Thanks for being so understanding, Mr. Coutts. I'll get back to you."

Outside, Roz pulled out her cellphone and paused. So much for her plan to show Jack how easy the children were. But she had no choice. Her relationship with Sam was too rocky to handle this alone.

"Jack Galloway here."

"Jack, it's—"

"I'm not available right now. Leave a message and I'll call you back."

"It's me…Roz." Stupid! Of course he'd recognize her voice. "Listen, call me when you can. It's urgent."

She closed her phone, curiously steadied by his cryptic tone, even on a message service. Jack had the ability to measure tough situations with a glance and do what needed to be done with a quiet competence. And he didn't mind being the bad guy when necessary. It was one of the things Roz had loved about him.

"*PLEASE* DON'T TELL JACK." Sam looked at Roz with desperate, pleading eyes. "I'll stop skipping classes, I promise."

Her heart sank. "I can't do that, Sam. This is too serious." The insolent teenager she'd been remonstrating with for twenty minutes had vanished the instant she mentioned she'd left a message for his uncle.

They were in the study, because unlike Coutts, Roz had gone for formality, sitting behind Anthony's desk and making Sam sit opposite. She'd wanted to impress her nephew with the gravity of the situation, but nothing had worked until she'd mentioned Jack.

Sam leaned forward, fingers gripping the desk. "Man, I skipped maybe four days over three weeks. Cootie's overreacting."

"He also said you have an attitude problem, disrupting the class, arguing with teachers." *Like you have with me.* She didn't say the words.

Sheepishly, Sam dropped his gaze. "I get angry when

they act like the only thing that matters is sitting up straight and studying and passing exams…like it's life or death or something."

And he knew about life and death. "I guess school feels pretty trivial right now," she conceded. And so would remembering to bring his dirty clothes down, or interacting with the family, or any of the things she'd been nagging him to do.

Sam sensed her weakening. "I'll be better," he said earnestly, "Nicer. Only don't tell Jack. I don't want him to stop lik—coming to my games or anything. Please, Roz, I'll even talk to *you*."

She laughed, but she felt more like crying. Was she really that bad? Didn't he realize that she was trying to provide a routine—a safety net—while he processed his grief? "I understand that it will take a while for meaning to come back into your life after all you've been through," she said. "Give it time, Sam, and if you need someone to talk to, I'm here for you. Maybe if we—"

Her cell phone rang and she checked the caller. "It's Jack."

The chair hit the floor as Sam sprang to his feet. "Don't tell him. Please."

"Hi, Jack, thanks for calling me back."

"What's wrong?" There was a rough anxiety in his voice.

Roz looked into Sam's pleading eyes and wavered. Jack had a right to know, but she also wanted to give the boy the benefit of the doubt. Could she trust him to live up to his end of the bargain?

"Roz?" Jack said again.

"Please, Roz," Sam whispered.

And she wanted to maximize the chances of keeping the kids in New Zealand. "Do you know where Ants keeps his toolbox?"

Sam clasped his hands together and mouthed, *"Thank you."*

"That's it?" Jack's voice took on an even rougher edge. "Yeah, okay, Glenn, I'll be there in a moment.... Your message said it was urgent."

"The door handle has come loose again and it's driving me crazy."

"For God's sake, Roz, I was imagining all sorts... Back of the garage, second shelf. It should be obvious."

"Thanks. Sorry to bother you at work. So, we'll see you tomorrow for dinner?"

She despised the neediness in her voice. But right now she longed to have another grown-up in the house.

Reluctance was rife in his tone. "Yeah, I'll be there.... Are you sure everything's okay?"

Let me see...I'm lying to you, I need you, I'm exhausted and I don't know if I've just made the right decision. I'm trying to get you to love the kids so you'll keep them, which is the right thing for them, but fraught with peril for my peace of mind.

"Absolutely," said Roz. And because Jack couldn't see her, she rubbed the back of her neck.

LIAM WOKE AT A NOISE from Sam's room. It came again, a muffled bump, and he slid out of bed to investigate. The hall light was on, because although he was too big for a night-light, he'd told Roz leaving it on would put off burglars.

Quietly, he crept along the passage and opened his

brother's door. Light spilled into the bedroom, illuminating Sam, who was half in, half out of the window.

He heard a swift intake of breath, then Sam recognized his shape and gave a muffled curse. "Sheesh, give me a heart attack, why don't you!" he hissed. "Get in here and shut the door."

Liam did as instructed and was enveloped in darkness. Panicking, he fumbled for the light switch, but Sam grabbed the neck of his pajama top and hauled him away. "Leave that off."

His eyes adjusted, helped by the streetlight shining through the open curtains. "Where are you going?"

"To a friend's house."

"But it's late…everyone's in bed."

"I forgot something…something I need for school."

"Why aren't you going out through the door?"

But Sam didn't answer. He cocked his head, listening, and Liam listened, too. A car with one of those big exhausts was coming down the street, its loud roar softening as it stopped outside the house.

Sam ducked his head out the window and gave a thumbs-up. Liam wriggled in beside him to see. "Who's that?" The person in the car was old…maybe twenty or something. If Sam was going out with a grown-up, maybe this was really okay.

"My uncle…my real dad's brother. He was at the funeral."

Liam found it confusing that Sam had the same mother as him and Cassie, but a different dad. So he focused on the immediate situation. "If you're allowed to go out with him, why aren't you going out the door?"

"Okay, I'm sneaking…so don't tell Roz. Or Jack."

Liam was going to ask if he could come, but decided he didn't like the look of the man in the car. He had big arms with tattoos and a sort of frown on his face that made Liam think he could be mean. And he was smoking, which meant he probably wasn't very smart, because everyone knew smoking was bad for your health.

The man was tapping the fingers of his free hand on the dashboard, and he jerked his head to Sam, who started scrambling out the window again.

"Go back to bed and remember what I said. You don't tell anybody 'bout this." There was a wild look in his brother's eyes that scared Liam.

"You are coming back, aren't you?" he whispered.

"Of course I am, doofus."

The familiar insult comforted Liam, and he went back to bed. But it took him a long time to go back to sleep.

"Pivoting deck, kick tail, inclined caster trucks…this is such a cool present, Jack." With natural grace, Sam pivoted on the Ripstik caster board, leaving black rubber marks on the lounge's hardwood floor.

"I'm glad you like it, but test it outside," Jack said drily.

"After your homework," Roz added.

"C'mon, Roz, have a heart."

"Okay," she said, "half an hour…but no more, Sam."

Bang. The front door slammed and he was gone.

Jack turned to Liam, who was looking at his matching board rather doubtfully. "What does it do again?"

"It's a cross between a skateboard and a snowboard."

"Oh," said Liam. He sat astride it and scooted across the floor.

Jack suppressed his impatience. "You stand up on it, mate."

"No thanks," said his nephew politely. "I don't want to fall."

"How about I hold your arm?" Roz suggested.

"I'm okay like this." Sedately, he rolled into the hall.

Roz looked at Jack and started to laugh. "Your face!"

"I can't seem to win with that kid," he muttered.

"Give it time," she answered softly. "Let me go finish dinner."

"Want some help?"

"No, drink your beer and relax."

Instead he sat and brooded over his continuing failure to impress his brother's son. Liam was so like Ants in looks and disposition. By rights, he and Jack should have no problem getting along. Jack noticed the family albums stacked at the bottom of the bookcase, and reluctantly picked one up. Maybe he'd find clues to a relationship with his nephew.

The album started with childhood photos of Ants, glossy small prints from predigital days. Vision blurry, Jack paused at a snapshot of two skinny kids. He and Ants were standing at the edge of an Olympic-size pool, shivering in Speedos and goggles, mimicking a dive-ready stance. Only five and six years old and already in a 6:00 a.m. training schedule.

Ants had on his "try hard" expression and a slightly anxious smile. *Shit.* Jack took another swallow of his beer. Liam had just looked at him with that same expression.

Jack's face in the photo was sullen. Ants might have the right attitude to please their father, but it was Jack who'd had the athletic potential. He also had a stubborn resistance to conditional love, as evidenced by the scowl.

As always, Mum was a blurred figure in the background. His father had treated her as a service provider, and during their childhood the boys had largely followed his example.

She'd left her husband the day Anthony started university. "He would never have let me take you boys," she'd once confided to Jack after a large sherry, "and someone had to be a buffer."

And they'd needed a buffer.

All Jack's life, his father had called him a loser because he wouldn't bend to Frank's will. In retaliation, he'd done everything he could to prove his father right—skipping school, getting into trouble. But Mum had never let Frank hit them—though he did when she wasn't around.

Only months before her death, Jack had been able to buy her a cottage in the country where she'd taken up golf and bridge and reveled in "never having to look at bloody water again."

He missed her.

On impulse, he punched Luke's number. His foster brother had left several messages since the funeral, and Roz had mentioned that Liz rang the kids regularly from their home further down the country. It went to voice mail. "Luke…it's Jack." He hesitated, feeling awkward. "I'm just keeping in touch." He hung up. It wasn't much, but it was a start.

Cassie came into the room, hefting an aged tabby that weighed almost as much as she did. It hung passively in her arms with what was obviously a long-standing resignation.

"You wanna pat James Zombie Maisy?"

Jack and the cat looked at each other warily. Liam was right; the animal did have Jack's green eyes. "How about putting him down first?"

Instead, Cassie hoisted it halfway onto Jack's lap. The cat unsheathed claws to haul itself the rest of the way up.

Jack swore, grabbed the animal and lifted it clear. "Son of a—"

"She wants to be your friend," Cassie climbed onto Jack's lap, not careful about where she put her feet. He ditched the cat to resettle her.

Liam coasted past on his caster board and said in a tormented voice, "It's a boy, Cassie. How many times do I have to tell you!"

"It's a girl!" From her position on Jack's lap, Cassie grabbed the cat, which was about to make its escape. "Pat her!" she commanded.

"Him!" yelled Liam from the hall.

This was an old warhorse of a cat. Under the soft fur, Jack felt lumps of scar tissue, and one ear had been torn in a long-ago fight. The animal closed its eyes and started to purr. "Isn't she pretty?" cooed Cassie.

Jack started to laugh. Even the animal's purr had a freighter's growl. "Very pretty," he agreed.

"She's your friend," the tot reiterated, and Jack got it.

"I'm *her* friend, too," he confirmed. Satisfied they understood each other, Cass got off the couch and, with the cat still in her arms, staggered out of the room.

Sipping his beer, Jack picked up another album, looking for more recent pictures. As he opened the cover, Roz poked her head around the door. "Dinner's ready." She glanced at the album, then at Jack, shock on her face.

"I guess I've succumbed to memories," he conceded sheepishly.

She stared at him. "What am I supposed to say to that?"

"What do you mean?"

But she'd already turned away. "Dinner's getting cold."

Puzzled, he looked down at the album. It was open at a portrait from their wedding day.

His breath caught as he looked at his radiant, beautiful bride. In addition to loving her, he'd liked so much about Rosalind Valentine.

He liked how she pretended to be a hard-boiled sophisticate, yet had the natural exuberance of a child. He liked her laugh, her quick, precise movements when she was in a hurry, and the tiny frown that drew her brows together when she was engrossed in a book.

He liked the way she'd shivered and got goose bumps whenever he came up behind her and twisted her silky black hair aside to nuzzle her neck. He liked the texture of her skin, her smell, her taste and the way they fit together—in bed and out of it.

He liked her independence, and her willingness to be emotionally vulnerable. He liked her fairness and how she'd always tried to see the other person's point of view.

He liked the way she'd seen clear through to his soul—and still loved him.

Jack shut the album. That chapter of their lives was dead and buried with their son. And just as with Thomas, regrets couldn't change a damn thing.

CHAPTER NINE

"LIAM GALLOWAY SPEAKING…. Oh, hi, Uncle Wade."

In the middle of putting a forkful of steak into his mouth, Jack froze. No, it couldn't be Roz's ex. He looked across the table, where she was trying to "choo-choo" a spoonful of peas into Cassie's obstinately closed mouth. Roz's cheeks were turning a telltale pink.

Apparently it could.

"*Uncle* Wade?" he inquired.

"Come on, hon," Roz coaxed Cassie, "the train needs a tunnel, so open up."

Liam bounced back into the dining room in high excitement. "Uncle Wade's on the phone."

"*Uncle* Wade?" Jack repeated to Roz's back as she went into the hall.

"Wade," she said in a low voice, walking as far away as the phone cord allowed, "this is a surprise."

Jack tried to read "unwelcome surprise" in her tone, and failed.

"He's ringing from China," burbled Liam, "and he's gonna send me back a dragon kite."

His nephew preferred a mass-produced dragon kite from Roz's two-minute ex to a US$100 Ripstick caster board from his *real* uncle?

Cassie squirmed to get out of her chair. "I wanna talk to Uncle Wade."

"He's not your uncle," Jack snapped.

Through a mouthful of steak, Sam said, "Technically, Roz isn't our aunt, either, since you divorced, but we—" His eyes met Jack's, and he choked and started coughing. "Can you pass the water, please?"

"Yes." Roz lowered her voice so Jack had to strain to hear. "Of course I'm glad you called."

Water splashed onto the table as Jack thumped the jug down beside his nephew.

"Oh, dear," Cassie said in her Auntie Fiona voice. "What a mess."

Jack grabbed some paper napkins and mopped up. "So," he said casually to Sam, "you know him well…? Wade?"

Sam shrugged. "I guess. He and Dad played football together on Tuesdays."

His baby brother had been like that, inclusive, generous, warmhearted…even though Wade and Roz had only been together for eighteen months. *Ants, you bloody traitor.*

"That's very generous of you, Wade," said Roz, "considering—"

"I've finished my dinner," stated Liam. "Can I have ice cream now?"

"Yes," Jack said, but he'd missed the rest of Roz's sentence. Damn.

"I want some ice cream!" Cassie yelled. .

"You have to eat your dinner first," Liam reminded her.

"It's yucky." The little girl picked up the piece of

meat in front of her, licked it and put it back on the plate. "See, I don't like it."

"I wish things had worked out differently," Roz was saying, her voice rising to cut out the background noise.

Differently? Did she mean that she wished she and Wade were still together?

"But Auntie Roz said—"

"Just give your sister some ice cream," Jack barked at Liam. Because what Roz *said* wasn't half as interesting as what she was saying now.

"But that's not fair! I had to eat *my* dinner."

"So dish yourself twice as much…now just shush a minute, will you?"

"Jack wants to listen to Roz's conversation," Sam said helpfully.

"Of course I don't!"

Cassie looked at the ice cream Liam was heaping on his plate, then the meager portion he had dished her, and squawked in angry protest.

Jack grabbed the two-liter container and dumped it in front of her with the spoon still in it. "Here."

"But—"

"Quit being a baby," Sam said to Liam.

"Am not."

"Are too."

"Enough!" roared Jack.

Silence fell, except for the careful chink of spoons in bowls. "Sorry, guys. I…" His voice trailed off. What could he say? *I hate the fact that—however briefly—Roz was another man's wife?* Even though he'd left her in the hope she'd make a new life with someone else.

Liam kept spooning up his ice cream with a sullen

expression, but Sam shot Jack a look of sympathy. "Women," he said.

Roz came back into the dining room. "I had to cut the call short with all that racket," she began, then gasped.

Following the direction of her gaze, Jack saw Cassie was plastered in chocolate ice cream from hand to elbow, her lips stretched over a dessert spoon like a widemouthed frog. It was in her hair, smeared across her face, dripping down her bib into a puddle on the floor. Most of the two liters was gone.

Jack had to hand it to Cass; she knew how to take advantage of an opportunity.

"*Who* gave you that?"

"I did," he admitted.

"I told him not to," Liam said piously.

"Squealer," said Sam.

Roz tried to take the ice cream container away from Cass; the little girl growled and clutched the rim.

"Might as well let her finish," Jack commented. "It's nearly gone, anyway."

"I'll get a cloth." There was almost enough frost in Roz's voice to refreeze the melted ice cream. "Jack, can I have a word with you in the kitchen?"

She closed the door behind him. "Stop undermining my authority."

He folded his arms, leaned back against the countertop. "How does being divorced from my ex-wife entitle the professor to keep playing *Uncle* Wade to my family?"

"Oh, for God's sake. That doesn't mean anything—"

"Damn right," he said.

"I won't fight with you in front of the kids," she said

quietly, and Jack had a perverse desire to push harder, to provoke some emotion.

Instead he passed a hand over his face. "You're right, I'm overreacting."

"Wade was calling to offer his condolences from China…he's working there now. He and Ants—"

Jack's temper flared again. "Yeah, I know. They played football together. Whoopty-do." It killed him to know the man had stepped in for him on so many fronts. Judging from Liam and Cassie's enthusiasm, he'd been a much better uncle.

"You were the one who walked away," she reminded him coldly.

He barked a laugh. "And boy, was I easily replaced. The ink was hardly dry on the divorce papers."

Her eyes flashed. "A divorce instigated by you, Jack, so don't play the injured party with me. How many women had you bedded by the time I walked down the aisle with Wade?"

Far fewer than Jack had encouraged her to think. "They didn't mean anything…. He obviously did."

"Oh, so that exonerates you, does it? The fact that you didn't make any promises to anyone? Well, what about the vow to me you broke?" She stabbed at his chest. "Till death us do part?"

Death *had* parted them. "I'm not the only one who has trouble keeping vows." He caught her accusing finger. "How long did marriage number two last? Oh, that's right…excluding courtship, less than a year."

Roz yanked her finger free and slapped him. The crack resounded through the kitchen, but Jack barely flinched.

"Feel better?"

"Yes, damn you!" Her gaze shifted to something behind him, then her eyes widened.

Jack spun around to see Liam and Sam standing openmouthed in the doorway, and his anger evaporated amid overwhelming shame.

The kids gawked at his cheek. "Does it hurt?" whispered Liam.

It stung like hell. "No."

Sam pulled his shocked younger brother against him and glared at Roz. "That's so lame…hitting a guy when he's not allowed to hit you back."

"I deserved it," said Jack, "so don't blame—"

"There's a social worker's here," Sam said abruptly.

Behind Jack, Roz moaned. He turned around, and she moaned again when she caught sight of his cheek.

"We can fix this," he said, and began hauling open kitchen drawers. "Where's a cloth?"

She sprang into action and found one. "They said they'd drop by one evening when you were here to see how we were doing." She tossed the cloth to Jack, who ran it under the cold tap, then pressed it against his burning cheek.

"Keep the social worker talking at the door," he instructed Sam.

"I'll go clean up Cassie." Grabbing a dishcloth, Roz rushed toward the boys, but Sam didn't move aside.

He threw Jack an apologetic look. "You guys were yell…talking too loud to hear the doorbell so—" he stepped aside, pulling Liam with him, and a woman came into view "—I invited her in."

Somewhere in her late forties, she had a mass of

unruly dark hair over a round, kind face, a wide, warm smile and razor-sharp brown eyes. "Hello." She eyed the cloth pressed to Jack's face. "I'm Ellie Walters. I hope I haven't come at a bad time?"

CASSIE HAD HER FACE buried in the white plastic ice cream container, her sticky hands clutching the sides as she licked out the last of the contents, when Roz ushered Ellie into the dining room.

Jack stepped in front of Cassie, obscuring the woman's view. "Are you sure you wouldn't rather wait in the lounge?" He still had the towel pressed against his face. A toothache, he told Ellie.

Roz couldn't look at him directly; she was too ashamed.

She'd never hit him—or anyone—before, but he'd tapped into a rage she'd never really dealt with. Her palm was still stinging, and even now, anger simmered under her contrition. No, she hadn't forgiven him.

"I'm fine here." Ellie pulled out the spare chair at the dining table, her mild gaze settling on Cassie. "My, you have been a busy girl, haven't you?"

At the sound of an unfamiliar voice, Cassie lifted her head from the container. A line of melted ice cream from the rim bisected her hair. Seeing a stranger, she closed sticky, clumped lashes.

"She's shy," Roz explained, taking the opportunity to swipe a napkin across Cassie's face. Being cleaned up was the little girl's least favorite thing, and she emitted a warning growl.

Jack snorted—whether at Cassie's appearance or Roz's explanation, Roz didn't know or care. The other two males grinned before Liam noticed her frown and matched it with one of his own.

"Don't let us keep you, Jack," she said tartly, "if you have to go home." She concentrated on wiping Cass's face and hands, ignoring the growls, which were growing in ferocity.

"And be accused of desertion?" he countered with an answering glint. "I wouldn't dream of it. Sam, how about I reheat your dinner while Roz cleans up Cass?"

Roz registered the half-eaten food on the teenager's plate, and bit her lip. How much had the kids actually heard?

"No, thanks." Sam stared at her with accusing eyes. "I'm not hungry anymore. Hey, Liam, let's go watch *Smackdown*." He drew out the last word and, flustered, Roz dropped the cloth, then bumped her head on the table while retrieving it.

For a moment she stayed below the tabletop, wondering if she should bother coming up.

"Wrestling," Jack explained to Ellie. "How about I make us all a coffee? Where will I find it, Roz?"

"I'm sorry, but I'm confused." Ellie drew a notepad out of her pack and jotted a few notes. "Am I to understand you're not living here, Mr. Galloway?"

"No." Jack sat down next to Ellie and Roz took a chair opposite.

"He visits," she said nervously, "whenever he can." *Oh, God!* Jack had forgotten about the cold cloth, and the red mark on his left cheek was now a perfect handprint.

Roz coughed, but he was concentrating on Ellie, who, fortunately, sat to his right.

"Uncle Jack! Owwie!" Cassie sucked her breath through small white teeth.

Casually, Jack replaced the cloth. "Is that a problem?" he said to Ellie.

"The temporary parenting order that you and Ms. Valentine applied for was for day-to-day care. That means you're both required to live with the children." She hesitated, glancing from one to the other. "I couldn't help but overhear some of your…discussion. If living under the same roof is a problem…"

Roz lifted Cassie out of her chair and sat the little girl on her lap, heedless of the ice cream. *This is Jack's out*, she thought numbly. Whatever hold she still had over him had been destroyed by that slap. *It's over.*

"If those are the conditions, then I'll move in tomorrow." Across the table, Jack's bland gaze met Roz's. "I'd hate anyone to think I wasn't honoring my commitment."

"Well," said Ellie, making more notes, "that's fine, then." She smiled at Cassie, who shut her eyes again. "Let me give you a pamphlet on dealing with shyness." She riffled through her overflowing folder. "That's odd, I can't find it."

Cassie opened her eyes. "I bet bum-bum Uncle Jack took it."

There was a moment's stunned silence. "My goodness," said Ellie, "where did you pick up that lang—agggh!" She screamed as Liam's frog jumped onto the table in front of her, and she clutched at her heart. "Oh, dear Lord."

Jack flung the cloth over the frog, then scooped it up. "Liam, come get the bloo—your frog out of here."

Liam scooted back into the dining room and took

Froggie, his eyes like saucers as he looked at the hand-print. Jack jammed the wet cloth back against his face.

"Remember," Roz said, distracting Liam, "you're only supposed to let Froggie out in your room." She reached out to ruffle his hair and he stepped back.

"It's only Uncle Jack you hit, right?"

This couldn't—just couldn't!—get any worse, Roz thought.

On her lap, Cassie said, "Uh-oh," and threw up all over the table.

CHAPTER TEN

CASSIE HAD PROBABLY SAVED the day, Roz reflected later, coming downstairs after putting the kids to bed. Because in the ensuing chaos and cleanup, she and Jack had managed to concoct a story about some computer game they all played, where Jack was the target....

Whether Ellie believed them or simply gave them the benefit of the doubt, Roz didn't know, and was too mortified to care. Right now, she had an apology to make.

Despite the chill outside, she found Jack on the deck, waiting to leave. Always waiting to leave. The porch lights were too dim to reveal much of his face, and Roz was glad. Because if you knew where to look you could still see the faint mark of her handprint.

"I shouldn't have hit you," she said without preamble. "I'm sorry."

"I provoked you.... *I'm* sorry." He stood with feet slightly apart, arms folded, the masculine stance of a reluctant apology. Roz almost smiled.

"I was jealous," Jack conceded.

"Because the kids call him Uncle Wade?"

He was silent and, realizing why, she felt her anger rise again. "Because it hurts your male pride that I found someone else." Her laugh was bitter. "Given the brutal way you ended our marriage, Jack, why would I pine for you?"

"No reason at all," he agreed, as though he really thought she could get over him that quickly. And she wanted to hurt him as much as his ignorance hurt her.

"What bothers you the most," she challenged, "that he touched me or that I touched him?"

"How much you must have loved him to marry him," Jack answered quietly.

She turned away. Wade had been a tourniquet to stop the bleeding, not that she'd acknowledged that at the time. He'd loved her when she'd needed love. Only when she'd healed, had Roz realized he deserved better than gratitude. "He's the nicest man I ever met."

"And yet you divorced him."

There was an implied question that Roz wasn't prepared to answer. Turning back, she changed the subject. "Why did you support me with Ellie? You could have got rid of the lot of us, yet you committed to moving in here."

"For the same reason I agreed to temporary custody. I owe you for Thomas."

"Thom—" Her stomach swooped and she felt nauseous. This was a discussion they should have had sooner. "The debt you owe me is for how you ended our marriage, Jack. I don't hold you responsible in any way for our son's death."

This time *he* turned away, looking out at the quiet residential street. "So you always said."

She came closer. "And nearly six years later I'm still saying it."

"Six years on, be honest with me," he challenged.

Keeping his back to her, he jammed his hands in his jacket pockets, though it was a warm night. "You never once thought, if *you'd* been there, Thomas wouldn't have died?"

"Yes, at the time I thought that," she admitted, and he turned his head. "But I never—"

"And it tortured you, didn't it?" His jaw in profile was clenched, his voice fierce in the dark. "You replayed the scenario over and over again. Staying home that morning…not going shopping or to the hairdresser."

"Yes." Her throat closed, and she had to force the words out. "I replayed it thousands of times…but it doesn't make it true, Jack. It was a fantasy that comforted me. I knew that then and I know it now."

In some terrible way, she was lucky not to have been at home with them. Because it would have happened anyway, and she'd be in Jack's situation now, unable to move past the guilt. She took another step toward him. "How could I blame you? You were his father. I knew you would have died to protect him. We should have comforted each other, Jack." He didn't answer and her bitterness returned. "Instead, you left me."

He faced her fully, leaning against the porch railing. "I couldn't spend the rest of my life watching you pretend to forgive me, Roz."

Even after all these years he wouldn't hear what she was saying. That no one held Jack accountable but himself.

"Go away," she ordered. "Go away before I hit you again."

There was a flash of white teeth, more grimace than smile. "I'll be back tomorrow night with my bags."

Halfway down the steps, he paused. "Whatever you want to call this payment for, Roz, consider the debt discharged. And if it makes you feel any better? The day you married Wade crucified me. So you got even."

And he disappeared into the dark.

LIAM WAS ON A SECRET mission.

Yesterday, he'd discovered where Roz had hidden some Christmas presents—at the top of her wardrobe—and the temptation to look had been gnawing at him ever since.

And now he had the perfect opportunity.

Roz was cooking dinner; Cassie was watching a DVD with her blankie after her bath. Cautiously, he opened the door to Roz's bedroom, and froze at the faint scent of her perfume, a sort of lemony, flowery smell. Nope, he was alone.

Ignoring his guilty reflection in the mirrored door, he slid the wardrobe open. The presents were on the top shelf, in an innocent white plastic bag, but a curl of gold ribbon hung over the edge like a fishing lure.

He'd spotted it last night while he and Cassie were playing hide-and-seek. Liam was tortured by Christmas presents—hidden around the house like pirate's treasure, waiting for an intrepid discoverer.

Last year Mum and Dad had removed his presents from under the tree because he couldn't resist poking a tiny hole in the festive paper.

Not that he'd do so now that he was six.

No, all he wanted to do was check out the size, feel the weight and maybe give the big ones a tiny shake just to hear anything there was to hear.

Quietly, he hauled the chair in front of the dressing table over to the wardrobe.

"What you doing?"

Liam jumped. Cassie stood in the doorway with Blankie, hair tufted up from lying on the couch, brown eyes sleepy—and interested.

"Go away. I'm doing big kids' stuff." He grabbed her shoulders to turn her; she screeched. Liam dropped his hands. "Shush!"

"I wanna climb the chair, too."

"You can't, you're too little." She started that rising wail that would bring adult backup, and Liam knew he'd have to do something fast. Digging into the pocket of his jeans, he felt for the last jelly bean, the black one he'd been saving. "Here!"

There was white lint on the sticky licorice coating, but Cassie popped it into her mouth.

"You can watch," he said. "But you have'ta be quiet."

Sucking noisily, she nodded.

He climbed on the chair and, on tiptoe, reached as high as he could, but his fingertips only brushed the plastic handle. Frustrated, he glanced around the wardrobe for something else to stand on.

There was a heavy cardboard box on one of the lower shelves, half-hidden by a stack of woolens. Dragging it onto the chair, he clambered on top. The cardboard sagged, but held. Again Liam stretched for the presents, fingers straining…touching. Got it!

The box collapsed, he lost his balance and fell forward into the row of clothes, landing in a tangle of fabric and presents and coat hangers.

"Uh-oh," said Cassie. A drool of black licorice trickled from her wet mouth.

Liam scrambled to his feet. "Quick, go guard the door!" He had to clean up before Roz came.

Obediently, Cassie went to stand there, but her fascinated gaze stayed on Liam.

Frantically, he shoved the fallen clothes to the back of the wardrobe and squashed the presents back in the plastic bag. "I'm gonna be in so much trouble," he muttered, grabbing papers and jamming them back into the cardboard box. He suddenly recognized what he was holding and stopped in bewilderment.

"What on earth was that crash?" Roz's voice carried up the hall, then her head appeared around the door.

"Auntie Roz is here," said his lookout.

But Liam didn't care about being caught anymore.

"Liam Galloway, are you trying to find Christmas pre…" Then Roz saw what was in his hand and stopped short, her expression stricken. Guilty.

And his whole world collapsed.

A SENSE OF GLOOM pervaded the house when Jack carried his bags and laptop through the back door from the garage that evening. He put them down in the hall and listened.

Cartoons on the TV in the family room sounded normal. Something spicy was emanating from the kitchen, and he sniffed…. Lasagna, faintly overlaid by strawberry bubble bath from the downstairs bathroom.

Cassie, her small face solemn, appeared from the living room, dressed in pink flannelette pajamas and mouse slippers, and carrying Blankie. Silently, she came down the hall and wrapped her arms around Jack's legs, laying her head against his shins. Something was definitely wrong.

"Hey, Cass." He picked her up and she cuddled against him with a sigh, her soft palms curled around his neck. Her implicit trust startled him. "Where is everybody?" With her head still on his shoulder, she pointed.

In the living room, he found Sam, Liam and Roz standing in a loose triangle around the coffee table, which was covered with letters, colorfully drawn, with childish writing.

All of them had their arms folded—Roz and Sam defensively; Liam like a judge. Fleetingly, Jack was reminded of a crime scene on one of the television cop shows. The little boy's lower lip jutted out and his brows were drawn in a ferocious frown. None of them acknowledged Jack's arrival.

"Honey, I didn't post them because I knew your parents can still read them from heaven," Roz said desperately. Against Jack's advice, she'd taken over the task from Fiona.

"Why is it such a big deal, anyway?" said Sam. "I mean, you know Mum and Dad are dead."

"But you said you'd post them—both of you—which means you lied. And anyway, how can they see through the cardboard box?"

Roz brightened. "Superman can see through lead."

Momentarily, the scowl lifted. "No, he can't!" Liam's voice grew in volume until he was shouting. "He can see through everything *but* lead." Angry tears started coursing down his cheeks. "See, you don't know anything."

"What's going on?" Jack asked quietly.

Roz turned to him, her expression pinched with anxiety. "Liam found his letters to Ants and Julia in a box in my wardrobe."

"She said she'd posted 'em, and she didn't. Mum and Dad didn't even get them." The small boy lay down on the floor and started crying sobs of despair and anger that reached into Jack's chest and clutched painfully. He knew exactly what that moment of abandoning all hope felt like.

From Jack's arms, Cassie looked at her big brother, and her mouth trembled. "I want my mummy."

Clumsily patting the toddler's back, Jack fought the urge to cut and run. Roz fell to her knees beside Liam, tears in her eyes. "Darling, no. With all my heart I believe they're watching over you and know what's in those letters."

She tried to pick him up, but he pushed her away. "You'd say anything to make me feel better," Liam sobbed. "And now I can't believe you anymore."

Despairing, she looked up. "Jack, please." But he had nothing to contribute.

Liam pushed up to a sitting position and stopped sobbing. "You'll tell me the truth, won't you, Uncle Jack? You'll tell me the truth because you don't like me." There was no judgment in the child's voice; it was said simply, as a statement of fact, and Jack squirmed like a worm on a hook.

"Of course I like you, mate," he croaked.

"You tell me, Uncle Jack! Tell me the truth!"

Hugging himself, Sam started edging toward the door, and Jack knew he had to say something.

"Actually, it's a good thing Roz didn't post them, because it wouldn't have worked."

A muffled sob escaped Roz; Jack ignored it. With his gaze still locked to Liam's, he gestured toward the empty fire grate. "You have to burn them."

Out of the corner of his eye he saw Sam turn his head.

"You burn them," Jack repeated, "and the smoke carries them up to heaven." *God forgive me,* he thought, *for this lie,* then nearly smiled at the irony of an atheist praying. He must be more screwed up than he thought.

But Ants and Julia had believed, and this was their son. Jack had no right to destroy a child's faith because life had destroyed his. Liam was still eyeballing him, so he kept his expression transparent, let the child see what Jack did believe. That if heaven existed, Ants and Julia would be there, watching over their children.

The slight shoulders relaxed in a shuddering sigh.

Shakily, Roz got to her feet and collapsed into a chair. Jack remained standing, patting Cassie's back. She was heavy in his arms and he realized she'd fallen asleep, lashes curled over her cheek.

For a long time no one said anything. They simply sat or stood numbly, like people in the aftermath of a hurricane that had razed everything to the ground, but left them miraculously untouched.

Sam was the first to move, dipping his hand into the pocket of his jeans. "I have matches," he said gruffly.

Jack made a mental note to talk to him again about smoking. "You can light them, then," he said. "That is, if Liam wants to burn them now."

In answer, Liam wiped at his eyes with the sleeve of his sweatshirt and gathered up his letters. Kneeling before the fireplace, he laid them reverently in the grate. Sam lit them.

Jack watched the edges of the paper blacken and curl, the brightly colored drawings become distorted as the crayon melted. The large words disappeared as flames consumed and then exhaled them as smoke.

Tiny fragments of charred paper rose on the updraft while Liam and Sam watched solemnly, firelight in their eyes. And strong feelings—painful from being held back for so long—came to life in Jack.

The flames ran out of fuel and died. Liam grabbed the poker and stirred until the ash crumbled and fell through the grate, and there was nothing left. Then he went to Roz and buried his face in her lap.

She leaned forward and laid her cheek over the curve of his back, her long, dark hair spread across his green sweatshirt like a protective blanket. And Jack had to close his eyes because the beauty of that image was more than he could bear.

But he still heard her softly voiced "Amen."

CHAPTER ELEVEN

ROZ STOOD OUTSIDE Anthony's study, staring at the heavy, dark oak, then knocked and went in. The younger children were in bed, Sam was holed up in his room, and Jack was in here, unpacking.

"I just wanted to say thank-you…for what you said to Liam."

Looking up from the desk, where he was setting up his laptop, Jack shrugged. "Yes, well…I did what I had to do. But I don't believe any of it, Roz."

The weariness she'd been holding at bay overwhelmed her. "Most of the time I'm faking it, too, Jack." She started to leave, but he was at the door before her, leaning on it to close it.

"What's that supposed to mean?"

Throat tight, she lifted her chin. "You don't have copyright on a bleak world view."

Shock flickered in his eyes. "Don't *you* give up," he said. "Not you, Roz."

"I'm not giving up…at least, not permanently." A sob ripped from her chest. "I'm letting them down, Ju and Anthony…. Sam hates me, and now I've traumatized Liam." She'd flung herself into taking custody, so sure she was doing the right thing. So sure Fee was the wrong person for the job. With her efficiency, at least the other woman would have posted the letters.

Knuckling her eyes, Roz reached past Jack, fumbling for the door handle. His scent, crisp and clean, enveloped her, then his strong arms. She laid her head against his shoulder and wept.

"It was never going to be easy," he soothed. "And for what it's worth, I think you're doing a hell of a job, given the circumstances."

She couldn't allow herself to rely on him like this, couldn't handle the pain of the inevitable withdrawal. Safer, far safer to fight. She pulled away to glare at him. "Say I told you so and you're on diaper detail."

"I wouldn't dare." He drew her head back against his shoulder; she felt his smile against her hair. Ah, God, she remembered that smile, so rare these days. Could feel it in her heart. Under her cheek, the beat of his was solid and familiar.

How had they fallen into this dangerous intimacy so quickly? Roz freed herself. "I'm okay."

But Jack didn't move away from the door. "Liam will get over it," he said softly, "and Sam doesn't hate you."

"He never talks to me. Every time I try to chat—"

"Guys don't chat. In fact, even the suggestion of chatting makes us run for the hills."

"Liam talks."

"Not to me."

Roz said delicately, "You want to cha…talk about it?"

"I'm handling it."

"Huh." She imbued the grunt with skepticism.

He grinned at her. "Now you're getting the hang of guy talk…. No, don't ruin it with a girlie follow-up."

She laughed and felt better. Long ago, they'd bantered like this all the time, enjoying the male-female polarity until the teasing became intimate and they took the battle to bed. A similar awareness flashed in Jack's eyes, charged the air between them.

They started talking at the same time.

"I've got a cup of tea waiting," she blurted.

"I'm going to take a shower," said Jack, "get an early night."

Neither of them could leave the study fast enough.

In the kitchen, Roz turned on the tap and splashed her face with water. "You're not the only one who needs a cold shower," she muttered, reaching for the paper towels.

Instead, her fingers touched Jack. Roz yelped and looked up, water dripping from her face.

"You…you startled me." She refused to think about whether he'd heard her or not because then she'd blush, she'd gibber, she'd sink through the floor.

"I wanted to ask where you keep the towels." His jaw was clenched as he handed her the roll. Roz ripped off a sheet and buried her burning face in it.

"Linen cupboard at the top of the stairs, opposite my…bedroom."

"Thanks." His voice had dropped so low it was almost a rumble. Instinctively, she lifted her gaze to his—and found his pupils took up half the irises. Lust jolted through her and her fingers clutched the paper towel.

"You're welcome," she whispered.

His chest expanded. "Okay if I use the shampoo in the shower? I left mine behind."

"If you like bubble-gum-scented baby shampoo." She imagined lathering it on his wet head, imagined pink bubbles running down all that strong, naked muscle…. Roz shook away the vision. "If you like I can get you something more grown-up to use."

In his eyes, she saw the something more grown-up he wanted, and she gripped the sink rim for support. Yes, she wanted to be used. There was a throb between her legs, a need she hadn't felt for a long, long time. She knew exactly how he felt gliding inside her, filling her beautifully, tortuously.

The muscle in his neck corded as though under a terrible strain. "I don't think that's a good idea."

Her brain came back to earth, landed with a bump.

Where was her pride? This man had left her in her darkest hour, then added insult to grievous injury by immediately dating other women. Yet part of her still wanted him, despite everything. "You're right," she said, full of self-disgust, "Cassie's shampoo should do fine."

Roz knew today was going to be a bad day when at 7:30 a.m. one week later she opened the fridge to get milk for the kids' cereal, and remembered she'd left a bag of groceries in the car overnight.

Turned out she'd left the trunk open, too.

As she approached she saw James Zombie Maisy eating the minced beef destined for nachos tonight. The frozen peas were a flabby wet packet on the suit Jack had asked her to pick up from the dry cleaners.

So it wasn't all bad.

Since the kitchen incident they'd both used the kids as human shields to avoid being alone together—on the rare occasions Jack was home. Roz suspected he worked longer hours to avoid her. It seemed a bitter irony that while her goal was getting Jack to bond with the kids, her presence had become an impediment to him doing so.

And time was running out. Fiona and Roger's weekly calls were a reminder of how fast. The temporary custody arrangement was already a month old, and Roz was lying awake at night worrying about the kids' future and trying not to worry about the fact that she wasn't over Jack.

She popped the top of the milk and sniffed, then reeled back at the sour smell. Liam's sleeping bag from a birthday overnight lay in the backseat, and as she moved it away from the soggy peas, duck down fluttered through the car. Great, there was a hole in it.

Sighing, Roz went back inside for her purse. Sam was pouring cereal into a bowl and Cassie was playing at his feet. "We're out of milk," Roz said. "Can you make sure Liam gets up and dressed while I go get some?"

"I come," said Cassie.

"No, hon, stay with Sam."

"Why?" he complained.

"Because Jack's in the shower."

"I already have to sort Liam out."

She didn't have time for this. Roz picked Cassie up— oh Lord, she needed her diaper changed—marched to the car and buckled the toddler in her car seat, still in her pajamas.

"Feathers!" Cassie cupped some in her hand and blew.

The old man behind the counter wrinkled his nose when Roz dumped the milk on the counter and counted out coins from her purse. "Kid smells worse than wartime trenches."

"Sorry," she said, "it was an emergency. Here you go."

"What about the candy she's eating?"

Looking down, Roz saw Cass stealthily chewing her way through a chocolate fish from the display at the front of the counter.

"Cassie, no!" She took the headless fish away from her, and Cass promptly threw a tantrum.

The old man yawned. "That'll be an extra dollar fifty," he said over the wailing.

Roz emptied her purse and found herself short. "Can I pay you later?"

He pointed to the sign next to the counter: Do Not Ask for Credit for Fear a Refusal Will Offend.

"It's only fifty cents."

"No exceptions," he said. "It's a slippery slope. An' you got feathers in your hair."

Anxiously, Roz glanced at her watch. She could leave and come back, but that would make Sam and Liam late for school. It was already touch and go.

"Leave your watch as security," he suggested.

"You expect me to leave my two hundred dollar watch for half a chocolate fish?" She looked down at Cassie, who was still writhing on the floor. "How about I leave the kid?"

"You think I didn't learn things in 'Nam?"

On the way home, Roz opened the windows because the stench had got so bad, and her temper was ready to blow.

Cassie stopped howling and tried to catch the flying feathers.

Jack was in the kitchen when they walked in, looking in the fridge. His hair curled damply over his collar from a shower, and a spicy aftershave cut through the smell of last night's leftovers. His broad shoulders were covered in a fine wool suit jacket that suggested he was heading for one of his corporate meetings.

No doubt, thought Roz meanly, with an interior designer in a Karen Walker suit and Manolo Blahnik heels, who'd just spent an hour buffing up at the gym and was currently enjoying a skim latte and a low-fat muffin and—

She realized she was jealous of a woman that existed only in her imagination, and not just because of her latte, but because she might flirt with Jack.

Putting the milk on the counter, Roz took a deep, deep breath and was reminded that Cassie's diaper needed changing.

Head still in the fridge, Jack said mildly, "There's no milk."

"It's here."

He turned around and blinked. "You have feathers in your hair."

Feathers in my brain, as well. "Fashion accessory," she said, shepherding Cassie toward the bathroom.

"And all over your back," said Jack, "and what the hell is that smell?"

"*Real* life."

Cassie ducked under her arm and ran to Jack.

"You mean you two went out like that?" His tone had the incredulity of a man in charge of his world.

Roz's temper rose, hot and hard. He was only in charge of his world because he refused to step outside its boundaries and get messy like everyone else.

"Yes, we went out like this! Because Sam— Wait,

where is Sam?" She checked the clock. "Oh, hell, he's left for the bus and he hasn't had breakfast."

"Relax, I gave him some money." Jack picked up the milk and poured some into his coffee. "You know, Roz, you could save yourself a lot of stress with more forward planning."

Her anger chilled to an icy rage. "What would you suggest?" Mentally, she slipped a big fat noose around her ex-husband's neck.

"A daily planner, getting things ready the night before, making sure you're always well stocked with the basic foodstuffs…"

"Gee, I never thought of that." Something in her voice—or maybe it was survival instinct—made Jack look up as he buttered his toast.

Roz smiled sweetly and fed her ex-husband more rope. "Any other tips?"

"Liam." Jack scraped the last of the jam out of the jar. "You know he's a dawdler. Maybe you should try getting him up earlier. And Cassie, well, I've been flicking through a few of Julia's books…shouldn't she be potty trained by now?"

He handed Cassie a piece of toast; she licked off the butter and stretched up, her little belly pale over the top of her pajama pants, to dump the rest on the table.

"And her eating habits are atrocious."

Roz kicked open the trapdoor and let the bastard swing. "Okay, hotshot, you've obviously got all the answers." She was tired of acting as a buffer between Jack bloody Galloway and the realities of child care. "Here!" She thrust the wet wipes and the clean diaper at him, and automatically, he took them.

"What are you talking about?"

"You know, this is my fault." With jerky movements Roz put on her coat, picked up her bag. "In trying to get you to bond with the kids I've kept all the bad, sad things from you—Cassie's toileting regression, Liam's obsession with his health, Sam's tru— All the ways they've been grieving. But I've been deluding myself, haven't I?" She picked up her car keys. "You're never going to let yourself feel anything for anyone again. If these kids were the von Trapp family from *The Sound of Music,* you still wouldn't let yourself love them, would you?"

He didn't answer; he didn't have to. The look on his face said it all.

"Well, I've had it up to my laundry-soaked elbows doing this alone. As they say on *Wrestling World* or whatever the hell that bloody show's called—" Roz tapped his arm "—tag, partner. I…give…up!"

"You can't," Jack said reasonably. "I've got a heap on today…meetings, a site visit. I can't take a pre-schooler to a construction site." He was obviously under the misconception that she'd respond to logic.

"Why not? Cass would be great at demolition."

"Roz…" Uneasiness drew his brows together. "I'll never say another word of criticism, I promise." He put his hand to his heart.

"You're in charge of the walking bus this morning, so I suggest you get a move on."

"For God's sake, you can't leave me alone with these kids. I'm not qualified." Now there was panic in his voice, a deeper thread of disquiet.

"Don't worry, you won't be in charge…they will."

She felt great—light-headed with power and vented anger. "Today you're spending time with them— whether you like it or not. Oh, and that daily planner you're so keen on is stuck to the fridge."

On her way out, she bent to kiss Cass on the top of her silky head, whispered, "Give him hell, sweetheart."

"Roz, this is crazy. Come back."

She kept right on walking. Outside, she hauled Cassie's car seat out of the back of the station wagon and dumped it in the garage.

She was backing down the driveway when she heard a small, panicked voice. "Roz!" Liam hung out of an upstairs window, alarm on his face, and she braked. "Where are you going?"

"Uncle Jack's looking after you today."

"I don't want him to."

She nearly lost her nerve. "He's…he's a good guy, Liam. You'll be fine."

"But when will you be back?"

"I'll be home in time to tuck you into bed, I promise. Now finish getting ready for school. Jack's going to need your help."

She drove two blocks and pulled over, knuckles white on the steering wheel and guilt making her stomach churn. What if Cassie didn't eat? What if Jack and Liam had a fight? What if Sam didn't come home after school? For twenty minutes Roz sat there, fighting one of the hardest battles of her life. If she went back, nothing would change. Jack was their family, and she needed a break—she'd used up all her reserves. She wasn't Superwoman; in that area Fee was way ahead of her.

Roz couldn't protect the kids—or Jack—any longer. If they were ever going to forge a relationship, they'd have to find their way together, without her interference or intervention.

She drove home to her tiny designer apartment in a tower block in the central city. The first thing she did was open all the windows to release the mustiness and let in the warm spring day.

Then she opened her mail, pulling a wry face at the half-dozen "Sorry you're leaving" cards sent from her former colleagues. Right now, quitting her job seemed like an act of sheer lunacy.

Disconsolately, she turned on the shower, then remembered she'd switched the hot water off, and swore. It was good to use rude words aloud again.

What was she going to do for the two hours the water took to heat? She pulled back the sheets on her bed and crawled in. Jet lag was like this—gritty lids, heavy limbs and a feeling of dizziness when she shut her eyes.

The apartment was very quiet. The water heater clicked and gurgled. She closed her eyes and slept.

CHAPTER TWELVE

JACK STOOD IN THE KITCHEN amid the debris of break-fast. *She'll come back. No way would she leave me alone with young children.* The thought steadied him. Ten minutes tops, and she'd walk through that door.

He sat on a stool at the kitchen counter and watched the minutes tick around the clock while Cassie pushed James Zombie Maisy around on Liam's Ripstik board.

Then realized he was being pathetic. The least he could do was get the kids ready.

"You got everything you need for school, mate?" he asked Liam, who was lurking in the hall.

"Yeah, but I can't find Froggie to put him in his tank."

Jack hid his impatience. "Okay, let's look." That bloody amphibian went walkabout so often it should have a swag on its back.

They checked the obvious places first—the sink, the bath and the toilets; anywhere there was water. Nothing. Next were the dark places—wardrobes, cup-boards and under beds. On his hands and knees, Jack lifted Liam's bedspread and peered into the gloom, while Cassie jumped on the mattress. A spring hit Jack's head.

"Sh—"

"Is he there?" The cover lifted on the other side, and Liam's hopeful face appeared, upside down.

"No!" Dropping the cover, Jack stood up, rubbing his scalp. "Listen, Liam, if you're given responsibility for something, you have to look after it properly." He knew he should stop there, but he was pissed.

Ten minutes had come and gone, he was late for work and Roz should have been back by now. "This halfhearted, got-something-else-better-to-do mentality isn't bloody good enough. Froggie depends on you to keep him safe."

Jack caught sight of himself in the mirrored wardrobe—a big, angry man standing over a small boy with bowed head—and shock sent him stumbling back a step. He'd become his father. In the frozen moment that followed came another painful realization: *And a damn hypocrite.* "Halfhearted" was exactly the way he'd tackled this guardianship.

Liam shot him a scared glance that made him want to crawl into a dark hole with Froggie. "You know what?" Jack said quietly. "Most of the time you do a good job looking after that animal. He's just the Houdini of frogs. Let's keep looking." Eventually the three of them found him in a plant pot in the lounge.

Liam's watch beeped, and he glanced at it anxiously. "We need to go soon. That's my ten-minute warning for Auntie Roz."

"Maybe we'll call in sick today."

"No, we can't! You're in charge of the walking bus and I'm doing the morning talk."

"What the hell is a walking bus?"

"Parents take turns walking kids to school. Kids get collected outside their houses."

"Okay then." Jack accepted the inevitable. "What's left to get ready?"

"Make my lunch, change Cassie, sign my homework book—"

Jack raked a hand through his hair. "How about I give you money to change Cassie's diaper?"

Liam looked doubtful. "I don't think I'll be very good at it."

"Ten bucks. Fifteen if you can do it in five minutes."

Liam grabbed Cassie's hand and she growled. "If you let me change you," he wheedled, because he really, really wanted all that money, "I'll buy you a lollipop."

Obediently, she came with him to the bathroom and lay down on the changing mat.

It wasn't easy and Liam used a lot of baby wipes, but he managed. Cassie balked at the clothes he dragged out of the drawer, so he let her pick what she wanted to wear.

They were back in the kitchen in twelve minutes. "I did it!"

But Uncle Jack only nodded distractedly. He had the phone jammed between his shoulder and jaw, and was slathering peanut butter on bread. *And* using the same knife in the butter, which Mum would've told him off for. "I'll try and get on-site by ten. Find a kid's hard hat for me, will you…? Hell, I don't know. How tall are you, Cassie?"

"Free," she said proudly, giving Uncle Jack her age.

"Three…no, that's not right. About knee height."

He hung up. "What on earth is your sister wearing?"

Liam eyed Cassie. She looked all right to him, in orange jeans and a pink sweatshirt, with her sparkle shoes and yellow sun hat. "Clothes," he said helpfully, watching Uncle Jack parcel up his sandwiches, hoping he'd be able to unwrap the cling film when the time came, 'cause his uncle used so much. "I need a cookie, a drink and an apple, too."

Uncle Jack opened every cupboard, searching for what he needed, and Liam had to help him. For an adult, he really wasn't very good at this. Liam started to panic. "We're going to be very late."

"I'm hungry," whined Cassie.

"Uncle Jack, we need to go!" Liam started to feel tearful.

Uncle Jack scanned the pantry shelves. "Here." He gave a surprised Cassie an open box of cornflakes, then plonked her in the stroller in the hall.

"You have to strap her in."

Uncle Jack got mixed up with the straps and buckles, so Liam had to do it.

The doorbell rang. Uncle Jack stopped fiddling with the straps and sat back on his heels. "Of course she'd come back," he said, and gave a strange laugh. "Why was I worried?"

Excited, Liam wrenched open the door. "Auntie Ro—"

His five-year-old neighbor stood on the other side. "I brought flies," said Marcus.

Liam forgot about Auntie Roz. He took the jar and held it up, trying to count the buzzing contents. "How many?"

"Eight," Marcus stated, turning red with pride, "and one blowie. I got 'em from the compost heap. I wuz gonna bring 'em after school, but Mum wanted them out of the house…. Is that your uncle?"

Liam was still trying to count the flies. He glanced

over his shoulder. Uncle Jack was standing behind him, staring at the jar. "Yeah."

"Marcus Cunningham," said Marcus, and held out his hand. His mum was big on manners and looking adults in the eye and stuff.

Uncle Jack seemed to wake up. "Jack Galloway." He shook Marcus's hand. "The, ah…flies are for?"

"Froggie," Liam answered authoritatively. "He has one a day. If you don't catch 'em, you have to buy 'em."

"I better go to school," said Marcus.

Through the glass jar, Liam caught sight of his digital watch. "We should'a left five minutes and twenty-three seconds ago, Uncle Jack!"

Cassie said, "I want to hold the flies."

"No! She'll break it."

His baby sister started to howl. Uncle Jack gave her the jar of flies and she shut up. It was Liam's turn to protest.

"If it breaks I'll catch more," Uncle Jack promised. "Let's just get you to school…. You know where we go?" Liam nodded. "Okay, let's roll."

Outside the front gate they picked up speed, half jogging, half walking. Cassie's stroller bounced over the curbs and she laughed. "Go faster."

Liam noticed she was making a mess with the cornflakes, which bounced out of the box and cascaded down her pink sweatshirt, but she kept a tight grip on the flies. Actually, it was kind of fun, running like this, his rucksack bouncing on his back.

"This is Molly's house," Liam panted, waving to Molly, who was swinging on the gate ahead. Her mum caught sight of Uncle Jack and stopped frowning, standing up straighter, pushing her shoulders back like Mrs. White told them in assembly. It must be hard with such big bosoms.

"Hi, Liam." Molly picked up her rucksack and grabbed his hand, and he pulled free, scowling.

"You have to," she said in her bossy voice, "it's the rules."

It tortured him to hold a girl's hand; still, Liam was a great respecter of rules. Reluctantly, he let her take it again. Her hand was warm and slightly damp, and he jiggled from foot to foot. "Can we go now, Uncle Jack?"

But his uncle was smiling at Molly's mum in the way grown-ups did when they wanted the other person to do something. Liam hadn't known Uncle Jack had dimples like Dad. "So, now you can understand my predicament, Karen," he was saying. "I don't suppose you can take over the walking bus today?"

"Well, I would, but I need to get to work." Molly's mum did look sorry. "But honestly, Jack, it's so easy. They walk in front, holding hands, while you take up the rear. And there's only six kids—"

"Six?" Uncle Jack looked shocked.

"Don't worry, you'll be fine, a big strong guy like you." She laughed, tossing her head and reminding Liam of the horse in the field next to his school. Molly's hand was getting wetter and wetter; he let it go to wipe his palm on his sweatshirt.

"Can we please go now, Uncle Jack?" The next place was his friend Findley's house. He'd much rather hold hands with Findley.

Uncle Jack had lost the dimples. "Yeah, mate," he said glumly.

"So anyway, I finish work at two," Molly's mum called after them. Come to think of it, she kinda had teeth like the horse, too. "So I'll give you a call in case you still need help…with Cassie or housework."

That was weird. Liam had been into Molly's house once and it didn't look like her mum did housework.

"Will you be my boyfriend?" Molly whispered.

"No," said Liam, jerking his hand away.

"Just till you go to England?" wheedled Molly.

"I don't like girls!" And thinking about living with Auntie Fee made his tummy go funny. She wasn't like Mum or Auntie Roz. She expected kids to act like grown-ups.

"You have to hold my hand." Molly tried to grab it again, and Liam pushed her away.

"Go away, bum-bum."

"Liam, you don't push girls," Uncle Jack said.

And suddenly he'd had enough. "I can't be good anymore," he yelled. "I've used up all my goodness."

He expected his uncle to yell back, but he just said quietly, "Okay, mate," and let him and Molly hold the stroller instead.

"'THE RAIN WAS SO NOISY on Pinky's biscuit tin roof that he'd run outside with his fruit bowl, thinking plums were falling off the tree above his home.'" Jack stifled a yawn, and from her perch on his lap, Cassie elbowed him in the ribs.

"Keep reading."

"'Then the big raindrops would splash on his up-turned face, soaking Pinky to the skin. This was the only time he ever washed, so it was lucky he lived in a country where it rained a lot.'"

Across the Italian restaurant's white linen tablecloth, Liam stopped sucking up the last of his Coke through a straw. "Uncle Jack, I'm starving." The whine in his voice was getting more pronounced.

"It's been forty minutes since we ordered," Sam agreed. "I wish they'd hurry up."

"So do I. Then I can stop reading." Jack had never noticed how slow service was in his favorite restaurant. But then, he'd never been here with hungry kids. Or eaten dinner at six-thirty before. Cassie growled and jabbed him in the ribs again.

Dear God, Jack hated this mouse, but unless he read, Cassie would be getting off his lap and creating havoc. She'd already startled the wine waiter into dropping their first round of drinks by growling at him from under the table.

"'Once there'd been a drought and it hadn't rained for three weeks. Pinky had got so smelly no animal would stand downwind of him.'" All Jack's sympathy was with the other animals; he'd changed four diapers today. And Cassie smelled as if she needed another.

Surreptitiously, he turned five pages together and resumed reading. "'And so they went in and had plum jam on hot buttered crumpets and…lived happily ever after.'" Jack slammed the book shut. "Finished."

"Nooo!" Cassie took the book and, frowning at him, reopened it at the right page.

"You can't read!" Jack declared.

"She knows it off by heart," said Sam. "We all do."

"Fifteen bucks to change her diaper," he offered.

Sam leaned back in his seat, scrawny arm slung across the back of the chair's tubular frame. "Thirty."

"You did it for twenty dollars two hours ago."

Sam inspected his nails. "Yeah, but we're in a restaurant, under difficult conditions…."

"Okay, twenty-five." They both knew he had Jack over a barrel.

"I'll do it for twenty." A round-eyed Liam piped up.

Jack thought of the mountain of used baby wipes and the dirty diaper he'd found discarded in the bathroom on his return home this morning and blanched. They hadn't needed Marcus's imported flies.

"You can be Sam's assistant," he said.

"I'm not giving him any of my money."

Jack handed over another ten. Today was costing him a fortune. His conscience had prevented him looking for a babysitter, but he'd had no compunction about calling a housecleaning service—not that he was going to tell Roz that.

Getting a cleaner had been one of Luke's many pieces of advice. Jack had rung his foster brother in desperation when Cassie had thrown a tantrum in the middle of the supermarket because he wouldn't let her push the cart. After laughing at Jack, Luke had talked her down. The incident had evaporated any lingering constraint between the two men. Jack had brought the kids to Antonio's for dinner because his cooking skills didn't extend past barbecuing meat.

"C'mon, Cass." Sam picked up his sister. The three trooped off to the bathroom, and Jack found himself alone for the first time that day. Well, not quite. Cassie had left Winnie the Pooh sitting opposite, wearing a diamanté headband with pink feathery things sticking out of it.

"So, you're a girl now, too, huh?" Jack said, thinking of the cat.

He heard a cough behind him. The owner was standing there. "Apologies for the delay, Jack. The chef had trouble locating cheese slices." There was a culinary artist's disdain in his voice. "Let me buy you a drink...a glass of Chianti."

"Thanks, Dario, but if I start drinking, I'll never stop."

The old man inclined his head and gestured to Pooh. "Something for the lady, then?"

Jack leaned back in his chair and considered his old acquaintance through narrowed eyes. "It's been a long—*very* long—day."

Dario backed away, palms raised, but his liquid black eyes glistened. "Ahh, your food arrives and also your *famiglia* approaches." In an undertone he added, "And the little bella mafiosa."

Jack grinned. "Please, let me pay for those water glasses."

"No, no...I only ask you to bring her again—when she's twenty."

The kids returned to the table. Sam took a long draft from his Coke. "I undercharged you," he muttered, but brightened as the veal parmigiana was laid in front of him.

Liam looked doubtfully at his bolognese. "I thought it would be spaghetti hoops out of the can," he said.

Jack leaned over and tucked a large napkin into the kid's T-shirt. "Welcome to real food," he said.

He tried to show Liam how to twirl the spaghetti around his fork, but the boy ended up looking as if he'd been on the receiving end of a gangster drive-by shooting, splattered in red sauce.

In the end, Jack cut it up. Beside Jack, Cassie licked all the garlic butter off the dinner rolls, ate three olives and pronounced herself finished. Until Jack's crème caramel arrived and she ate the lot.

The younger kids fell asleep on the drive home. He carried them in and laid them in their beds, fully clothed, then made himself a tall bourbon on the rocks and collapsed on the couch. "Is it always like this?" he asked Sam.

"Pretty much."

Jack noticed that the school bags still needed unpacking, and remembered the other jobs on Roz's daily planner he hadn't done—the washing, the ironing, making something for a bake sale at school, buying a present for a birthday party Liam was attending tomorrow.

Over the last week he'd seen his ex-wife do so much more. The ice chinked in his glass as he took a long swallow. Kissing owwies, helping with homework, listening to troubles in addition to cooking, cleaning and coaxing Cass to eat. Being the good mother she was.

The sweet pain of watching her had driven him to take refuge in work, but today he'd realized that he owed these kids more than lip service as a guardian. No matter how hard it was being around his ex-wife.

And he had to admit, in some odd way, today had been fun.

Cassie hadn't let Jack out of her sight, but she'd been in her element, playing in a heap of sawdust on-site, and growling at any construction crew who made friendly overtures, much to everyone's amusement.

As long as Jack let her do whatever she wanted, they'd got along fine, and for the sake of his schedule he pretty much had. The stop at the toy shop, DVDs on demand, fries for lunch…he didn't fool himself that these things were anything but a stopgap. If he'd thought for a moment that he was making progress with his brother's children, Liam's disapproving face would have set him straight.

Despite Jack's best efforts, he couldn't please that boy, and it prickled him like a hair shirt. He wanted Liam to look up to him like his daddy had when they were kids. But the child—this clone of Ants—persisted in disliking him.

At least he and Sam were cool. Jack glanced over to the teenager, who was text messaging on his cell phone, and tried to think like a parent. "You got any homework you should be doing?"

"What? Yeah…it's a group project, so is it okay if I go to my friend David's house to study?" Sam waved his cell. "He just invited me and he only lives a couple of blocks away."

"Sure, just be home at nine-thirty."

When the teenager left, Jack glanced at his watch. Roz had promised to be home at Liam's normal bedtime, in twenty minutes. He picked up another album—this one of Ants, Julia and their kids. Some of the events depicted were familiar, but then the photographs became more recent.

Sipping his bourbon, Jack lingered over every one, hungry to know more about the years he'd avoided Ants and his family because they were too painful a reminder of what he'd lost. Yet his brother had never reproached him, and the invitations had never stopped coming, though Jack turned most of them down. How that hurt now.

But Roz was always in the background at the big occasions…clapping as the birthday candles were blown out, raising her glass in a toast. She had kept faith with them, even when Jack couldn't.

In some of the pictures, Wade was with her, but he didn't look as if he belonged, and even with his arm around her shoulders, Roz seemed just as alone. For the first time, Jack was able to look past his jealousy and see that.

Look past his jealousy and regret her failed second marriage. Because he didn't want to think she'd suffered as much as he had. He'd deserved it; she hadn't.

That big blond brainiac was meant to heal her. Otherwise what had been the point of Jack giving her up?

CHAPTER THIRTEEN

THE FIRST THING ROZ noticed about the house when she arrived at 7:25 p.m. was the silence.

Normally, Liam and Cassie were racing around in pajamas in a final play frenzy, while Sam had the sound on *The Simpsons* cranked up, trying to drown out their noise, and Roz called for everybody to please use their inside voices.

Surely Jack hadn't got them to bed early?

She dropped her car keys on the telephone table, and they skittered off the polished surface to the floor. He'd found time to clean? As Roz bent down to pick them up, she noticed the pencil marks on the skirting board had disappeared, and her astonishment grew.

Not just cleaned, but spring-cleaned?

She sniffed. The whole place had the unmistakable tang of solvents and chemicals. Climbing the stairs to the kids' bedrooms she found both sound asleep, tucked neatly under the covers. Sam's room was empty, not just of Sam, but of clutter. She'd been trying to get him to clean his room for a month.

Fighting a growing sense of failure, Roz started for the stairs. Halfway down, she caught sight of Jack sprawled asleep on the couch in the living room, and immediately cheered up—he looked as disheveled as she usually did at this time of night. On the other hand, he'd achieved a hell of lot more, so he'd earned it. Still, his success wasn't unqualified, if Sam had gone out.

Roz crouched down beside Jack and reached out to shake him awake. Then paused. How many times had she watched him sleep? His hair had fallen forward over his brow and she had to fight the urge to smooth it back, slide her fingers through that silky springiness.

But she couldn't resist a slow visual journey over his face. This close, she could see his eyelashes and brows were tipped with the same honey-gold as his hair. Once the only lines he'd had were when he smiled, that slow-burning, lip-curving grin that crinkled those green eyes and never failed to ignite a melting, come-to-me-baby response.

Fortunately, he didn't smile at her anymore.

Now new lines added harshness to the Hollywood good looks that had once bowled her over. Before Jack, she'd been dating the kind of guys who invariably gravitated to nurturers—boyish charmers with mommy complexes. There was nothing little-boy about Jack. Comfortable in his masculinity, he admired smart women and relished being challenged intellectually. During their marriage, he'd been a huge supporter of Roz's professional goals, and not the least threatened when she started earning more than his fledgling business.

Playing hard to get was the sensible course to follow with a man used to women falling all over him, and Roz had a reputation in that area to uphold herself.

But faced with the raw vitality of a man she'd instinctively recognized as her soul mate, she'd folded on the second date and all but dragged him into bed. Ironically, it was Jack—the player—who wanted to take things slowly, but Roz figured he'd had it his own way for far too long. At which point she did discover that Jack played games….

Her gaze drifted down his body with a guilty pleasure. He'd changed into jeans since this morning, the denim faded in all the right places, and the black T-shirt molded to the curves of muscle and bone. He had one arm under his head, and the pale skin of his inner biceps was as smooth and tempting as an apple.

Her throat tightened. Dear God, how she'd loved him. But a woman needed a man who'd stand by her in the bad times, one who'd let her stand by him.

Heaven knows she'd tried. After he'd left her, she'd been convinced they would get back together. She wasn't going to give up on her perfect marriage; Roz had lost enough.

Within weeks she'd heard rumors of other women, and hadn't believed them. No, he wouldn't do that to her. Couldn't. Until she'd arrived unannounced at his rental apartment after receiving notification that he'd filed for divorce.

He'd opened the door bare-chested, a thumb tucked casually in low-slung jeans, his eyes flat. Beyond him, some barely dressed skank poured bourbon into shot glasses.

"Now," he said, "do you believe it's over?"

And she'd hated him then…. Roz shut her eyes briefly, and when she opened them, Jack was awake, staring back. So close, she could see the small flecks of rust and gold suspended in the green irises. So close she could read every emotion.

He still loved her. She reeled in shock, and Jack shot out a hand to steady her.

But when she looked up, he had the customary blinds down. Nobody home…

"Don't you ever pull a stunt like that again," he said.

"I won't." Roz stood up. She'd only been imagining things. "Look, I'm sorry."

He wasn't expecting an apology; she could tell by his blink. But she was weary of conflict. And anxious for information. *Did Cassie eat? Did Sam play up? How did you get on with Liam?* She perched in the armchair opposite and asked casually, "How was your day?"

Stretching his arms above his head, Jack yawned and sat up. "Fine."

Roz waited for more; he only yawned again. She resisted the urge to shake him. "I wasn't expecting them to be in bed so early. Was Liam worried that I wasn't back?"

"No, they…it was fine."

"Where's Sam?"

"Studying at some guy called David's house."

Odd. David wasn't in the same class. She gestured to the room. "You even cleaned."

His gaze shied away from hers. "The place needed it."

The phone rang and, frustrated, she went to answer it. It was Molly's mother, Karen. At last she'd get some information.

But Karen only wanted to talk about Jack. "My God, Roz, what a hottie Anthony's brother is. You could have warned me he was doing the school run. I looked a mess. Tell me he's free."

Honesty fought with possessiveness and won. "Yes."

"Give me the guy's number."

Possessiveness made a counterattack. "He's gay."

"Really?" Karen sounded doubtful. "He's so rugged and macho."

"So were the Village People." There was a business card on the telephone table; Roz picked it up. *Al Cleaning Services—Thanks for your custom.* She smiled. "Listen, Karen, I've got to go. I'll see you tomorrow…yes, sorry, it'll be me again."

Jack was in the kitchen making tea. She flipped the card onto the counter in front of him and he looked at it ruefully. "I meant to hide that." He put a steaming mug in front of her. "Have you noticed that the kids are sleeping in their clothes yet?"

She breathed a long sigh of relief. "I thought it was just me."

"Honest to God, I don't know how you do it."

"It has its rewards. A laugh from Liam, a cuddle from Cass—"

"A chat with Sam," Jack finished drily, and Roz laughed.

"Why aren't you madder?" she asked. "I expected a lecture at best, a flogging at worst."

Sipping his tea, Jack took a moment to answer. "Well, I did want to kill you around 8:45 a.m. But you were right. I should be pulling my weight in this arrangement."

Hope blossomed, but before Roz could ask questions, the phone rang again.

She picked up the kitchen extension. "Oh, hi, David, does Sam need a lift home? He's not there…? But isn't he studying with you tonight?" She looked across the kitchen at Jack and sighed. "I must have heard wrong. Sure, I'll tell him to call you. Bye."

"Sam definitely said David." Jack eyed her closely. "You don't seem surprised."

She busied herself with dialing. "Let me try his cell…. It's going to message."

"He doesn't know my number. Maybe I'll have better luck." Jack dialed in turn. "Sam? You're busted. I'm giving you twenty minutes to get back here. Every minute you're late after that, you'll be grounded a week." He rang off. "This has happened before, hasn't it?"

"Not since we had the talk after—" Roz stopped, suddenly in deep water.

"After?" He picked up his tea again.

She wouldn't lie to him. "Sam was skipping classes. He's not now."

"And you were going to tell me this when?"

"I wasn't," she admitted. "Because you'd see it as another reason they should go, not another reason they should stay. But now that you're considering permanent custody—"

In the middle of sipping his drink, Jack choked. "Whoa, right there. I do need to foster a relationship with the kids, but I'm not keeping them."

"Let me just tell you how I see it working." Roz almost tripped over the words in her eagerness to divulge her plan. "I'll sell my apartment and use the money to contribute to running this household—that will ease your financial burden and let me stay home until Cassie turns five. Then I'll go back to working school hours. The kids and I will stay in this house—obviously it's not feasible for you and me to live here together—but you'll be involved as much as you can. At some stage we'll need to buy this house from them, but…" Her voice petered out because he was staring at her with an odd expression on his face.

"My God, you're really serious about this, aren't you?" Jack turned and tipped the dregs of his tea down the sink. "In terms of your scenario, I wouldn't let you sell your apartment—I can easily support the kids. But that's a moot point. Fiona and Roger are having them."

"Fee might have changed her mind," Roz argued. "Or maybe she'll settle for a guarantee of contact. We could pay for the kids to go visit a few weeks every—"

"I promised her she could have them," he interrupted. "So there's no use talking about it."

"What?" Anger constricted Roz's chest, making it difficult to breathe. "You had no right to make that arrangement without me."

"*We* had an arrangement, too, remember? That they go to England after Christmas."

"Our arrangement was to discuss it again!"

"Stop splitting hairs. You always knew where I stood."

Roz tried to calm down, press her case. "She's not the right person to raise them, Jack."

"Why?" he challenged. "And remember, I've already disagreed with your home and community argument."

"I'm not convinced she'll raise the kids the way Julia and Ants would have wanted. Did you know her children go to boarding school? No, I didn't think so. I have no idea whether she intends sending our guys…but you need to find out. And remember her behavior at the funeral? Sam's well-being came a poor second when she was under pressure. Is she capable of putting the kids' interests first? And speaking of Sam—he's made it plain he doesn't want to go to the U.K."

"Okay, let me tackle your points one by one." Jack leaned against the counter and started ticking items off on his fingers. "One. I admit Fiona can be a little uptight, but her heart's in the right place and Roger balances her out. Let's not forget he's involved in this." Jack waited for Roz's reluctant nod. "The boarding school thing we can make a condition of custody. Two. You saw how Sam was treated at the rugby game, like some kind of sideshow. England will be a new start for him. Finally, Fiona's performance at the funeral…well, we all make mistakes when we're grieving."

"But—"

"Accept that they're going to England, Roz." He turned and stacked his cup in the dishwasher. "You hit the nail on the head this morning when you said I can't love them."

"No, I said you *won't,* Jack. There's a difference."

"Then I won't," he said brutally, his back still to her. "I don't want children in my life. That desire died with our son."

There was such anguish in his voice that she reached out to touch his shoulder. Then saw a shadow hovering at the door. "Liam, what are you doing up?"

Jack turned around, consternation in his eyes.

The small boy stretched and yawned. Hopefully, he hadn't registered Jack's comment. "I meant to stay awake until you got home."

His T-shirt was covered in some kind of sauce; his pants were rumpled. Roz picked him up and his thin arms wound around her neck. "Let's get you back to bed." Passing Jack, she said quietly, "You know, you used to be the bravest man I knew."

Upstairs, she helped a sleepy Liam change into pajamas, then tucked him in. "Did you have a good day?"

"It was okay." He was nearly asleep again. "*You* love me though, right?"

Fervently, she pressed her lips to his forehead. "Always. And Uncle Jack just needs practice again, that's all."

He snuggled down. "Me and Cassie don't want to live in England. We want you." As though that settled the matter, his breathing deepened into sleep, while Roz sat rigid on the side on his bed.

Now what?

She tried to look at the progress made today. Whatever he said, her ex-husband was obviously softening. Look how far he'd come already. She could still change his mind. But if he wouldn't love them… No, that was defeatist thinking. She could still change his heart.

She had an idea of how to break through his emotional roadblock, if she could get him to her apartment. For a moment she balked at causing him such pain, then reminded herself he'd had no such qualms when he'd cut her out of his life.

This time around it's not over until I say it is.

Downstairs, she found Jack reading Sam the riot act. The teenager threw her a hostile look. "You promised not to tell."

"Hey, you're the one who can't be trusted here," said Jack curtly. "Treat your aunt with more respect."

"She's not my aunt anymore," the boy mumbled, then added with a flare of defiance, "And you're not even my real uncle."

"Fake uncle or wicked guardian, the boundaries your parents set still apply," Jack said shortly. "Roz might have the patience of a saint, but I don't. Now go to bed before I lose the last of what little I have. We'll talk again in the morning."

As Sam stomped out of the room, Roz called after him, "I know you're grieving, but we're still your family, Sam. Let's stick together."

His scornful gaze flicked from her to Jack. "What?" he jeered. "You mean, like you guys did?"

CHAPTER FOURTEEN

SAM WAS HOME FROM SCHOOL, sitting at the kitchen table eating cookies, when Roz came back from the supermarket with the kids the next afternoon.

He'd appeared contrite in front of Jack this morning, but he barely gave Roz a glance now. Did she have too much patience with his behavior, as Jack had suggested? Roz knew some of his acting out was a grief response, but at some point he had to accept her authority.

She poured everyone a glass of cold milk and they joined him at the table. "Learn anything interesting at school today?"

He upended the packet, caught the last cookie crumbs in his mouth. "No."

Liam chipped in. "I learned that Venus is the second hottest planet after the sun."

"Wow—" Sam faked a yawn "—that's *so* fascinating." Liam's face fell.

"Please," said Roz, "make an effort."

Sam rolled his eyes. "And what did *you* do at preschool today, Cassie?"

"Pooped my pants," she announced, and won an involuntary laugh from her biggest brother. Liam started to giggle.

"You're a little stinker." Affectionately, Sam grabbed a napkin and wiped a trail of milk off her chin. For once, Cassie didn't demur.

The gesture, and Cassie's response to it, suggested a history of care, and Roz wondered if she'd done Sam a disservice in doing so much for the younger ones. She'd wanted to lighten his load, but maybe he needed a sense of being necessary to his little brother and sister.

On impulse she stood up. "I need to get to the post office before it closes. Sam, you're in charge."

Immediately, he scowled. "Can't you take the kids with you?"

Roz picked up her bag and kept on going. "I'll only be half an hour. See you soon."

She shut the door on his protests, then realized she'd left her car keys inside. Going back in would be fatal. The mall was only a brisk ten-minute walk away and it was a nice afternoon. She headed down the drive and set off, trying to remember the last time she'd traveled this lightly.

Normally, there was a stroller, diapers, snacks and drinks…. It had only been a month, and already she felt incomplete without them.

What was it going to be like when the kids went to England? She stopped at the thought and, because she was alone, leaned against an oak, its mottled trunk silky smooth against her palm. *Not so brave now,* she mocked herself silently. *Not nearly so brave now.*

In the wake of Sam's home truth last night, she and Jack had said an awkward good-night. But this morning Roz had organized a babysitter, then rung her ex-husband and asked him to meet at her apartment, saying there was something she needed to bring back to the house that was too heavy for her to carry alone.

If this didn't work, then nothing would.

SAM GOT UP when Roz left, went into the lounge and turned on the TV.

"It's rude to leave the table without asking to be excused," Liam yelled after him, but his big brother didn't answer.

"I'm finished." Cassie set her glass on the edge of the table. It fell to the floor, splintering into sharp, milk-filmed shards. She and Liam looked at each other. "Uh-oh," she said, and made a move to get down.

"Stay there," Liam yelled, "you've got bare feet. *Sam!*"

His brother came and looked at the mess on the floor. "Aww, shit."

"You're not s'posed to swear. Roz says."

"Who's gonna stop me, you? Look at this bloody mess." Sam grabbed a broom and started sweeping. Cassie made another attempt to get down, and he grabbed her arm. "Stay there, dippy, till I've picked up the glass."

"Down!" she ordered.

Sam picked her up and set her in the hall. "Liam, keep an eye on her until I've cleaned up."

"I've got bare feet, too."

"Do I have to do everything around here?" But Sam swung him down from the table. "Now bug off, you two."

"Bug off," agreed Cassie, and didn't move.

"I can help if I get my shoes…." Liam offered tentatively. Maybe then Sam wouldn't be so mad. "Roz says I'm a good helper."

"Roz says, Roz says!" Viciously, Sam swept the

broken glass into a dustpan. "I'm sick of hearing about Roz. What about quoting what Mum and Dad say? Or do you want Cassie to forget them?"

"No!"

"Because she will, you know. She'll end up thinking Roz or Fee is her bloody mother…. It's not right." Sam looked at him wildly. "It's not right, Liam."

"I d-d-don't forget, Sam. I write to them every day."

"Do they ever write back? Well, do they?" He flung the broom across the room and Cassie started to cry. "Jeez, am I the only one in this bloody house who gets that they're dead and never coming back?"

Liam started to cry, too. He didn't want to, but he couldn't help it. Then Sam was kneeling on the floor and hugging him and Cassie. "I'm sorry, I'm really sorry, you guys."

"Were you tricking, Sam?" Liam pulled away. "I mean, Mum and Dad are watching over us, right?"

"Yeah, I was tricking. Is that one of your letters on the table? Can I write something on the bottom?"

With Liam and Cassie watching, he found a pen and scrawled, "P.S. Love, Sam." For a moment he stared at the words he'd written, then started to cry, big shuddering sobs that sounded like they hurt coming up, like he was going to be sick or something.

Liam got the bucket out of the laundry that Mum used to put by their bed when they had tummy bugs, but Sam only cried harder when he saw it, so Liam took Cassie out and closed the door. They weren't s'posed to watch TV during the day, but since Sam had turned it on, they huddled on the couch, watching it. The phone rang beside him and he answered it.

Ten minutes later, Sam came quietly into the room. His lids were all puffy and red, but at least he wasn't crying.

"What'cha watching?" he asked gruffly.

"SpongeBob SquarePants."

Sam picked up his little sister and sat her on his lap, taking her place on the couch. "Liam?" he began tentatively.

"I know." He didn't shift his gaze away from the TV. "Don't tell Auntie Roz and Uncle Jack."

He didn't mention that he'd just told Auntie Fee on the phone, figuring it would only get him into trouble. Just telling her Sam was looking after them had made her mad at Auntie Roz, though she'd gone quiet when he'd mentioned Sam was crying. Then she'd said it had been a mistake letting them stay on in the house.

"Who was on the phone?"

"Um…Marcus." Uh-oh. Lying was tricky. He was supposed to get Auntie Roz to ring Auntie Fee back, but now he couldn't. Besides, then she'd find out about Sam crying, and he'd get into trouble with Sam and—

Liam chuckled as SpongeBob tried to teach his pet snail, Gary, to fetch, and leaned into his brother's arm before he realized. He caught his breath, but Sam didn't shift away.

"Do you think they have SpongeBob SquarePants in England, Sam?"

"Dunno."

"I don't want to go live there. I'm gonna stay here. I told Auntie Roz."

"She can't do anything. It's all settled."

His brother's tone was brusque, so Liam didn't tell

him that he trusted Auntie Roz to change things so they could stay.

"Liam?" Sam cleared his throat. "I'm staying in New Zealand."

"But you just said we can't."

"I said you and Cassie can't…you're too young. But it's my birthday next week, which means I'm sixteen, and my uncle—my real one—says when you're sixteen you can do what you want. I'm gonna move out and get a flat."

"If Auntie Roz can't keep us, we could live with you."

"No, they won't let us, but when this house sells I'll have enough money to visit you in England, and you'll visit New Zealand."

"They're gonna sell this house?" Liam got a scared feeling in his stomach.

"It's okay, we'll get the money."

Liam didn't want money; he wanted Auntie Roz. He started to panic, then remembered she knew that, and relaxed back against his brother's arm. Sam liked to pretend he was big and knew stuff, but Liam was backing Auntie Roz. She was the boss, not Sam.

"So how long have you lived here?"

While Roz unlocked the door of her ground floor apartment, Jack studied the building. Judging from the design and materials, it had been built in the 1980s.

"Since I left Wade…" There was a loaded silence as she swung the door open.

Though tastefully furnished, the place was a shoebox compared to Jack's spacious apartment. "Why didn't you accept the alimony I offered?" Mention of Wade always made him irritable. "Then you could have bought something larger."

"This meets my needs," she said stiffly. "Besides, it's still bigger than the apartment you and I lived in."

Mentally calculating, Jack realized she was right. Yet that place had never felt cramped…maybe because they'd spent so much of their leisure time in bed. "You didn't answer my question about the alimony."

She gave him a considering look. "I wanted to hurt your pride. You'd hurt mine and I was damned if I was going to let you have everything your own way."

"It worked," he admitted, taken aback by her honesty.

"Good," said Roz, and slipped off her coat. Her high heels clicked against the hardwood floor as she walked down the hall, and Jack took note of her outfit, a soft, swinging dress in navy. His mouth went dry because she was so lovely. In their roller-coaster world of child care, he could—almost—remain unaware of the silky fall of her long hair, the curve of lashes on a smooth cheek… other curves. "You're dressed up."

"I had an early dinner with the elderly neighbor who's looking after my cat. Listen, I still have a few things to pack, but it won't take long." She paused at what must be her bedroom door. "Make yourself comfortable, and I'll call you when I need a hand."

Make himself comfortable in a place imbued with her? He even recognized the scent of the furniture polish. "I'd rather be doing something."

"You could water the plants for me." She gestured. "There's a jug under the kitchen sink."

Red geraniums wilted in their pot on the white granite countertop. Jack attended to them first, then prowled the house looking for others. He noticed she'd kept the furniture he'd made for her—an ornately carved mirror frame, a bookshelf and even a kauri dining table, squeezed into the tiny alcove posturing as a dining room.

Jack ran his hand across the table's golden, butter-smooth surface, breathing in the lemony beeswax. The smell of a world lost to him. However big his apartment, it lacked the homey touches. Who the hell was he kidding? It lacked—

"Roz," he called harshly, "are you nearly ready?"

"Five minutes."

He waited by the front door next to the hall table he'd restored for her twenty-fourth birthday. Scattered across the kauri slab top were half a dozen greeting cards, all embossed with the same message—"Sorry you're leaving." Jack swept them up and stalked into Roz's bedroom, where he tossed them on the open suitcase she was packing.

"Tell me that you didn't have to quit your job to do this."

"It's no big deal." Roz picked up the cards and threw them in the bin, then glanced at his face. "It *isn't*, Jack."

"I don't get it. Surely with your seniority, they could have managed a couple of months leave."

"They did." Roz closed the lid of the suitcase and started to lift it. Instinctively, he took it from her. "But I wanted to keep my return date open in case you saw sense and accepted full custody."

Jack dropped the suitcase. "What?"

She shrugged. "Win some, lose some."

He wanted to shake her. "Damn it, I should never have agreed to this temporary custody thing. It's got completely out of hand. And you…you're just plain crazy. You're like a moth hurtling against a hot bulb, determined to get burned. For God's sake, Roz, protect yourself."

"From what? Loving anybody again?" she challenged. "How's that tactic *really* working for you?"

It wasn't, and the sudden empathy in her eyes told him she knew it. He couldn't bear it. Jack said brusquely, "What do you want help moving, Roz?"

Oddly, her compassionate expression didn't change. "It's behind you."

He turned around and his vision telescoped to the large picture on the wall next to the door—three black-and-white photographs taken in action sequence and set in a rectangular silver frame.

In the first shot, he and Roz smiled down at their solemn baby, who was frowning at the photographer. In the second, they laughed as a bored Thomas chewed at his hands, while a blurred squeaky toy waved frantically in the foreground. Their son had been cranky that day, unwilling to cooperate. Though hilarious, the session had been a disaster.

Jack's stunned gaze shifted to the third shot. Having given up, he and Roz kissed, unaware that Thomas was laughing up at them, with a beatific gummy smile.

Jack had never seen these photographs, taken only a few days before their son died. They were funny and real and poignant, and they had the same impact as a crack on the head with a two-by-four. For a moment, the room swam and Jack couldn't breathe.

Roz came to stand beside him. "I got it out when I

came back here yesterday. It seemed like time to put it up again."

He didn't answer, because he felt as if his whole body was braced against a dam about to burst, and he needed to concentrate. He closed his eyes against Thomas's laughing face, but the image still burned on his retinas.

"Maybe I am crazy," said Roz, "but I'm tired of being scared all the time, Jack." Gently, she cupped his clenched fist. "Aren't you tired of being numb?"

He wanted to respond then, because there was a break in her voice, but if he moved a muscle, the dam would burst. And that way lay chaos.

After a few moments, she withdrew her hand and he knew this torture was nearly over. Then Roz sighed, the softest, saddest sound of defeat, and Jack could no longer stop the flood of emotion.

CHAPTER FIFTEEN

ROZ WATCHED TEARS stream from under Jack's closed lids, and a wave of love swept away everything else. She tugged his bowed head down to hers and kissed them away with an aching tenderness, her lips tracing the warm saltiness across his face to his mouth, firm, full and heartbreakingly familiar.

Though he stood stiff and unyielding, he didn't pull away, and his biceps tightened under her fingers when she gripped his arms. "Come back to me, Jack," she murmured fiercely against his lips. Cupping his face in her hands, she kissed him harder, demanding a response.

She felt the moment his control broke; a ragged sigh shuddered through his body, and then his tongue met hers with a desperate, uncontrolled yearning that rose to passion in one frantic heartbeat. They clung to each other, body to body, mouth to mouth in a savage, possessive embrace. And all the emotions Roz had struggled to suppress for six long years—love, grief, fury, compassion, revenge—rose in her like bloodlust.

Her teeth grazed his lips as she fought the urge to bite; her fingernails dug into his shoulders.

"Roz, I'm so sorr—"

"Shut up!" She yanked at his shirt until the buttons

flew open, then shoved him backward onto the bed and straddled him, her fingers tangling in his honey-blond hair to pull his head back, her mouth seeking his surrender. And he gave it to her, trusting her even in her anger until the violence seeped away and her caresses grew tender again. Roz looked at his bleeding lower lip, the ugly marks she'd nipped across his neck, and passed a shaky hand across her brow. "I'm sorr—"

"Your turn to shut up," whispered Jack. With a hand around her nape, he held her close and kissed her again, his tongue moving against hers with a devastating gentleness that made her tremble harder. For long hypnotic minutes he kissed her, and she drank in the sweetness of his taste mixed with the metallic tang of his blood, his scent, his touch on her body as he unzipped her dress, his fingers as unsteady as her own.

Her lover, her husband, the man whose child she'd borne, the man she was supposed to grow old with. She must have moaned because he stopped peeling down her dress. "I can stop if you've changed your mind."

But Roz wasn't that strong, not with his half-naked body, warm and heavy, on hers. Not with the heavy-lidded intensity in his eyes and the wet aching need between her legs.

She touched a finger to his mouth, rasped, "Your turn again. Shut up."

His lips curved under her finger; then he took it into his mouth and sucked gently. A jolt of pure lust shot to her groin. He dropped his head to her left breast and did the same to her nipple, with much more heat, and she gasped and gripped his hair. Every touch evoked a sensory memory—the slow assured slide of his hands on her body, the way he moved teasingly against her, and the intent purposefulness that made her hum with a sizzling anticipation.

With the same urgency, Roz explored him, finding and tracing old haunts—the scar on his shoulder from a childhood injury; the swell of pectorals and indentation of ribs; the hard, tight stomach scattered with fine hair. Absorbing the beauty of him, and the magical sensual connection they'd once taken for granted.

Any woman would have loved his body—those massive shoulders, the corded forearms dusted with gold, his broad chest, muscular legs and tight male butt, pale cream in contrast to the rest of his tanned physique. But for Roz the sexiest part of Jack was his eyes, and the way he looked at her as though she was everything he'd ever wanted.

The way he was looking at her now.

Their hunger grew; their caresses became more intimate; senses sharpened and merged. They stripped each other naked and threw their clothes on the floor. She could hear his heightened breathing—and hers. "Jack."

With his hand between her legs, Roz verged on coming, but she couldn't lose control before he did. She pushed his clever fingers away, pressed him back against the pillows and took him slowly into her body. Reality was so much better than memory.

"Roz." He started moving under her, and instinct and need took over.

Her orgasm roared through her, hard and scorching and fast. Dimly, she heard Jack groan, felt him shudder underneath her. With a gasp, she collapsed on his chest, lips pressed against the salty dampness right over his heart. Gradually their breathing eased. With one arm cradling her, Jack stroked her hair, then massaged her nape in the way she loved. Time slowed until she was suspended, half-asleep, in the quiet spaces between his heartbeats. Completely and utterly spent.

And everything they needed to say to each other could wait.

IMPATIENTLY, Fee stopped stirring her tea and started walking with the phone. "I thought you said you were expecting them home around seven? Well, has either of them even rung to say why they've been delayed…? No? And it doesn't bother you?"

It was eight in the morning in Surrey, England, 9:00 p.m. in New Zealand, and this was Fee's third call since getting up at 5:00 a.m. to see Roger off on his drive to London.

"I said I was happy to stay until ten," said the baby-sitter. "Maybe they went out to dinner."

Her girlish voice made Fee wonder how old she was. At least they'd hired a babysitter this time, rather than relying on Sam. Roz seemed to be taking her responsibilities very lightly, completely blasé about the fact that Sam had been terribly upset earlier.

Fee wanted to talk to him and confirm that he was all right, but apparently he'd been shipped off to a friend's house so Roz and Jack could go out.

"Do you want to leave another message?" asked the babysitter.

"I've already left one and she hasn't returned my call. I'll try again tomorrow." Given the thirteen-hour time difference between New Zealand and England, there were narrow windows of opportunity to phone, and she'd just missed another of them.

Irritated, she hung up, gulped her tea and went to dress. She was due at the thrift shop in twenty minutes for her volunteer shift. Opening her wardrobe, Fee chose a simple ensemble—she didn't want to make anyone in the thrift shop uncomfortable—then applied light makeup for the same reason. Was it so hard for Roz to ring her back?

Initially, Fee had used Jack as her point of contact, but he'd proved hopeless, completely vague about details, and more often than not at work, with no time to chat. So she'd been forced to start phoning Roz, who was always pleasant, but slightly defensive when Fee delved into the nuances of domestic life.

And talking to the children directly didn't furnish much information. They were clearly reluctant to be on the phone, and Roz's whispered encouragement in the background only exacerbated Fee's annoyance that her niece and nephews had to be instructed to be nice to her.

Fee realized she was dabbing on the blush with a heavy hand, and reached for a tissue to rub away the excess.

Leaving Jack and Roz with temporary custody had been a mistake; it had disrupted the tentative relationship she'd begun to forge with the children, and given her husband time to question whether Fee wasn't taking on more than she could chew. Roger meant well, but his inference—echoing Roz's—about her ability to cope, stung.

Recalling her mortifying behavior during the funeral brought a sudden and entirely natural blush to Fiona's cheeks. Thank God Roger hadn't been there to see her shameful display. Fortunately, she'd had time since to regain perspective on the accident.

Of course she hadn't killed Julia and Anthony; the truck driver and Julia's lapse of attention had. Fee started to apply mascara, but her fingers shook and she put the wand down.

Christmas would be a very sad time for the children, and it occurred to her that they might find it easier to cope with festivities here, where winter and snow and roasted chestnuts were nothing like New Zealand's summer celebrations. Her two sons would be home from boarding school and it would be a warm, welcoming introduction to their new family.

Fee phoned the babysitter back and canceled all her messages for Roz. Jack was the person more likely to say yes to allowing the children to come over earlier.

She would talk him into it tomorrow.

ROZ DREAMED.

She and Jack were skimming in a fairy tale sailboat across a moonlit sea. Traveling alongside the craft, just under the glassy water, Thomas was a dolphin baby, a pale white blur of joyous speed, as he dipped and reappeared.

Ahead was an island, black jagged cliffs rising to a plateau of lush green, where a white cottage nestled amid trees. She knew the other children were inside, waiting for them.

They sailed around the island, looking for anchorage, but the rocks were as sharp as fangs and the water sucked and spat around the cliffs' base like a malevolent mouth.

Thomas beckoned and Roz dived into the water to follow him through a safe gap in the rocks, but black seaweed tightened around her legs like cold fingers, pulling her under.

Gasping for air, she struggled free and broke the surface, but Thomas had gone and Jack was sailing on, oblivious to her plight. She screamed, "Jack, I'm over here!" But he didn't hear her. Panic consumed her. "Jack, come back!"

Roz woke up, her body rigid and heavy with dread, and cold sweat prickling her forehead. The bedside clock showed 9:00 p.m. and it took her dazed brain a moment to process why that was.

She became aware of a familiar warmth and scent beside her, of slow regular breathing fanning her right shoulder, and turned her head.

Jack.

They needed to get up, go home and relieve the babysitter. But Roz made no move to wake him because the dream had seemed so real—a premonition and a reminder. *Don't trust him.*

His face in the moonlight was smooth and untroubled; it tugged at her heart like an anchor. Could she risk loving him again?

She got up and dressed quietly, then stole to the door. No. She couldn't.

A gruff voice said behind her, "You're not even going to leave a note?" About to turn the door handle, Roz froze.

JACK STARED AT his ex-wife's guilty face and had his answer. He'd woken with a sense of well-being, a feeling of hope he hadn't experienced in years, to see Roz sneaking to the door.

"I told the babysitter I'd be home by ten."

He'd forgotten all about the kids. Jack shoved back the sheets. "Give me five minutes."

"I don't mind going alone if you want to take a shower…or something."

The awkwardness in her voice stopped him. He flicked on the bedside lamp, the better to see her face. "You regret what we did."

"No!" The immediacy of her response reassured him, but his relief didn't last long. "Only, it probably shouldn't happen again." She hugged herself. "We have too many other things going on." It was a lame excuse, and by the way her cheeks colored, he could tell she knew it.

It occurred to Jack that she might have slept with him to sway his decision about custody. She wanted those kids, and she must know he still had feelings for her. A little softening up might change his mind…. Then he looked into her eyes and saw the same vulnerability that was making him scramble for reasons to push her away.

But he couldn't. He couldn't do it anymore.

"I never thought I could love anyone as much as I loved you," he said. "And then Thomas was born and somehow my heart grew bigger."

Roz crept to a chair and sat down.

"When he died I blamed myself. You knew that. It didn't matter what the autopsy said, what you said, what anyone said, because rationality doesn't come into it. I had to suffer."

"So you left me," she said bitterly, "and we both suffered."

That had been his real punishment, when he'd regained sanity enough to regret it—the pain he'd caused her. "I salved my conscience by telling myself that you'd heal faster without having me around as a constant reminder."

Jack looked at the pictures on the wall. Thomas had her clear, all-seeing eyes. "In hindsight it was probably the other way around."

He owed her this unflinching honesty. His gaze traveled over her pale, still face. It was impossible to guess what she was thinking. Jack took a deep breath. "I knew you wouldn't give up on our marriage easily, so I deliberately took myself beyond your forgiveness."

Her lips barely moved. "Other women."

"When you came to my apartment, I knew I'd succeeded."

He'd thought he'd known the final dimensions of hell then, every crevice and crack of it.

Until Roz married Wade and Jack realized the very marrow of his bones could be ground down with pain until there was nothing left of hope. And in that void, he'd finally found some sense of atonement.

"Roz, I'm so sorry. I had reasons, but I offer no excuses. I know no apology can make up for what I did, but I'm going to ask anyway. Is there any way forward for us?"

"I don't know!" She buried her face in her hands and was silent for a long time.

Eventually she gave a laugh that was half sob, and sat up. "I took Cassie to see Santa this morning."

It wasn't what Jack had expected, but he nodded encouragement.

"We've been reading books about him and she was hyped. Even insisted on getting dressed up."

They exchanged an involuntary smile.

"Exactly. She teamed some of my best jewelry with a pair of antlers and a clown nose she found in Liam's toy box that reminded her of Rudolph."

Abruptly, Roz stood. "So we got there and lined up, and she watched him ho, ho, hoing and lifting kids onto his lap. And the closer we got, the tighter she held my hand. When it came to our turn, she froze."

Roz walked to the dresser, picked up some jewelry and put it down again. Her eyes met Jack's in the mirror. "Santa was so kind," she continued in a shaky voice. "Beckoning and smiling and encouraging her. So Cassie would take another tiny step, and then panic again. And she started to cry in frustration because she wanted to visit him so badly but she just…couldn't… do it."

Jack's hands clenched on the sheet as he realized what was coming.

"Right now, that's how I feel about you." She turned around and looked at him directly. "I'm a one-man nurturer who ended up a two-time divorcee. Because when my baby died, my soul mate left me."

He flinched but said nothing. Another apology would be an insult.

"And I thought…" She swallowed hard. "I thought I was going to break into tiny pieces unless I found someone to hold me. You hurt me so much, Jack—and then I hurt Wade."

Roz went to the suitcase, picked it up. "I'm sorry, but I can't do this again."

There was only one thing an honorable man could say, so Jack said it. "I understand."

And the worst thing was, he did.

CHAPTER SIXTEEN

"LIAM, YOU WANT TO COME with me and Cass to the hardware store?" Jack asked the next morning.

His nephew didn't even look up from his Lego. "No, thank you."

Jack persisted. "You know Roz is too busy to play?" She was helping Sam with his exam revisions and avoiding Jack, and he was equally intent on doing the same.

Neither of them had any idea how to take this from here.

It was Sunday, which wouldn't normally have stopped Jack going to the office, but he'd already agreed to look after the younger ones today. Which meant pretending everything was fine.

But he was a man used to going after what he wanted, so passively respecting—not challenging—Roz's decision was making him crazy. He had to get out of this damn house and think, and the hardware store was the place to do it.

Liam glowered. "I wanna stay *here!*"

Oh, great, he was in his nephew's bad books again. You'd think he'd be used to it.

"Fine." Still, Jack brooded as he bought a packet of tacks and a tube of silicon, while Cassie played with chunky reels of gold and silver chain links. He felt bad about Liam overhearing him the other night; the next present would make it up to him. He could afford to buy him a big one because the project was ahead of construction by several weeks and Hiro was talking more joint initiatives.

By rights I should be walking on sunshine, not wallowing in an emotional quagmire.

Damn it, why had Roz brought him back to life, if she was only going to stab him in the heart? Okay, she had a right to second thoughts, but couldn't she have had them *before* she made him feel again?

He rubbed the back of his neck, trying to ease the tension. "C'mon, honey," he said to Cassie. "Let's go get some timber."

Enthralled with the shiny metal, she ignored him. Jack glanced unseeing at his list. Four more weeks, he told himself, and he'd be free to crawl back into his cave and roll the rock across the door. The kids would go to England…and Roz would have her heart broken again.

Hating his thoughts, he barked, "Cass, let's go."

"I'll watch her if you like," offered the store's owner, who was standing on a ladder in the same aisle, refilling the nail boxes.

"Thanks, Phil." Jack headed for the timber supplies.

The wail started when he was at the far end of the warehouse, and rose to a scream so shrill, so petrified that he dropped the plank he held and ran.

Skidding around the end of the aisle, he saw Phil crouched down on rheumatic knees, trying to placate Cassie, who stood rigid, cheeks scarlet, screaming her head off.

She caught sight of Jack and flung herself on him, clawing at his shins until he hunkered down to her level, and then her arms closed in a choke hold around his neck. Bewildered, he tightened his grip and stood up, while she sobbed in his arms.

"I don't understand it." Phil was white-faced. "One second she was fine, then she looked around and saw you were gone, and started to scream. She bit me when I tried to pick her up." He showed Jack the neat indentation in his wrinkled palm. "I tried to tell her you were coming back."

The older man was obviously shaken. Jack felt a trifle unsteady himself. The terror in that scream had been palpable.

Cassie raised a tearstained face. "You went away," she sobbed accusingly. "You went away, Uncle Jack." Enraged now that her fear had worn off, she whacked his chest with a tiny fist. "Bad Uncle Jack."

Her parents had left her in an unfamiliar place and not returned. Horrified, he patted her back. "Shush, baby, it's all right. I won't disappear again."

Except he would, Jack realized with a sinking feeling. In four weeks, when she went to Fiona and Roger.

Grimly, he drove home and went through the motions of domestic harmony, but his anger had a focus now. After lunch, when all the kids were occupied, he dragged Roz into the study and told her about Cassie's meltdown.

"I should never have agreed to temporary custody. It's not good for them to bond with us like this."

"The kids and I had already bonded," she reminded him calmly. "And didn't you want a better relationship with them?"

"Yes, but…" It hadn't included being needed. Jack hung on to his righteous anger. "Obviously Cassie was going to become attached to the people who cared for her immediately after the accident…. It should have been Fiona and Roger."

"They had the kids in New Caledonia for three days immediately after the accident, and Fiona stayed here with Cassie for a week before she flew home."

"So Cassie hasn't spent as much quality time with them as she has with me?" Jack had glimpsed the buzz-word in one of Roz's child care books. "Is that what you're saying?"

"Actually, if you add the twelve-day holiday they had together before the accident, then they're way ahead of you in terms of quality time." She was watching him closely. "Cassie loves them, Jack, but she was Daddy's girl and it's you she associates with Anthony. You should be flattered…not scared."

He ignored the last part. "This isn't right."

Roz's voice was very gentle. "Is it really such a big deal that a little girl loves you?"

Yes. "It is when we're not going to keep her. Even if I changed my mind, how can we possibly make this work after what happened last night?"

"I don't know," Roz said honestly. "I've been asking myself the same question all morning."

"Now you regret it, don't you?"

"If it's stopped you reconsidering permanent custody? Yes."

It hurt so much more than he expected. "I should never have let you put them through this," he said savagely.

Roz gasped, then went pale with anger. "I'm not

doing this for me. I'm doing it because it's what the *kids* want. And it's what Ants and Julia wanted. The reason you're so pissed is because you've realized that."

He couldn't deal with the truth, so he headed for the door. Roz was up from the desk in a flash and barring his way. "Sam worships the ground you walk on. Liam and I have always had a special bond, and Cassie considers both of us as her property." Her blue eyes flashed. "Sure, you and Liam have problems. Sam and I do, too—but you know…you *know,* Jack," she repeated in a low, passionate voice, "that we're their best option. Ants and Ju didn't just choose me, Jack, they chose you."

"They chose the person I was at the time, not the person I am now." He couldn't stop the bitter laugh. "If there wasn't a difference you wouldn't have said no to me last night."

"Don't you know how desperately I want you to prove you're still that man?"

He looked in her eyes and saw hope. The phone rang loudly beside them, and they both jumped. Roz picked it up. "What?" Immediately her tone softened. "Oh, hi, Fee. Yes, Jack's here."

He waved in dismissal. Right now there were more important things to discuss. Like what Roz meant.

"While you talk to him, I'll get the kids to come say hello," she was saying.

Reluctantly, Jack took the phone. "Hi, Fiona."

He listened to what she had to say with mixed feelings. "Let me think about the kids coming early for Christmas, and get back to you…. No, I won't tell Roz before I've made up my own mind." He hung up and turned around to see Liam in the doorway. "Sorry, buddy, I forgot you were going to talk to her."

"Does she want us to go over early?"

"Yeah." Jack hesitated. "How would you feel about that?" He'd never asked them what they wanted before, fearing the wrong answer. Now he had to know if Roz's assertion was true.

"I don't want to live with Auntie Fee," Liam declared passionately. "I want Auntie Roz."

You and me both.

"And Auntie Roz wants us, I know she does."

There was the difference. Roz didn't want him. Or had she implied Jack still had a chance? He needed to think.

Liam was eyeing him anxiously. "Sam said we get the money when you sell our house. Is that right?"

"Yes. It will go into a trust for your education." *Along with money from me.*

"Well, you know how you paid us to change Cassie's diapers?" Liam's next words came in a rush. "I'll give you our share if you don't make us go to Auntie Fee. It's okay, I asked Cassie…she said it's all right to give you the money."

Appalled, Jack stared at his earnest nephew. "Liam, I can't—"

"Don't answer now," the child interrupted. "You think about it and let me know."

And Jack didn't have the heart to tell him the answer was already no.

ROZ WAS IN CASSIE'S ROOM pulling back the curtains after the little girl's nap when Liam bounded in. "Uncle Jack's gone out."

"Go 'way." Cassie growled at her brother from her bed, where she sat with pillow hair, rubbing her eyes. With a quivering bottom lip, she held up her arms to Roz. "Cuddle."

"But he was going to look after you while I went to the market." Roz picked her up and Cass burrowed into her—a soft, warm bundle of lovable grumpiness, fragrant with soap, perspiration and damp diaper. "Was he called into work?"

"Dunno." Liam wrinkled his nose in Cassie's direction. "He said not to save dinner 'cause he doesn't know when he'll be back."

"Oh!" Roz tightened her hold on Cassie, suddenly needing the hug as much as the baby did. *I challenge him to be old Jack and new Jack runs away.* She'd thought she was getting through to him.

Last night she hadn't been thinking about the children, only about him. It had taken daylight for all the implications of sleeping with him to sink in. Along with the truth. She'd turned him down not because she was scared to love him again, but because she'd never stopped loving him, and that vulnerability terrified her.

And judging by his withdrawal now, she'd been right to protect herself. "Who wants afternoon tea?" she croaked.

Cassie perked up. "Me!"

"Okay, then." Roz made an effort to be cheerful. "Let's go. How's Auntie Fee?"

Liam scowled. "She wants us to go early for Christmas."

"What?" Roz stumbled and had to grab the upper hall balustrade. "What did Jack say?"

Liam shot her a furtive look. "Um, he's thinking about it," he mumbled. "Can I have carrot cake?"

"He's *thinking*—!" She bit her lip. "Carrot cake it is." She never said anything to raise Liam's hopes, and always talked enthusiastically about England, taking pains to foster the kids' relationship with Fee and Roger through regular phone calls.

She figured that wherever these children ended up living, they needed all the extended family they could get.

As soon as she could, Roz found a private corner and rang Jack's mobile phone. It went straight to message. She tried Fiona…no one home. For the next few hours she alternated between calm rationality—Jack wouldn't dare make that decision without her—to blind panic. He'd already made one deal with Fee behind Roz's back and was probably out buying air tickets now. And still neither Jack nor Fee answered their damn phones.

By the time she put the kids to bed, Roz was a nervous wreck, and predictably, both youngsters played up. Liam was relatively easy to settle, but at nine o'clock, Cassie was still awake.

"I'm going to bed," said Sam in disgust when Cassie came down for the fourth time, and Roz didn't blame him. She carted Cassie back to bed and lay down beside her to coax her to sleep, taking the file of custody documents with her. She hadn't read the guardianship clause in the will, but maybe it held something she could use. What she found made her drop the file and curl up closer to Cassie.

"Auntie Roz." The little girl took her thumb out of her mouth and patted Roz's cheek.

Roz closed her eyes in sudden anguish. "Go to sleep,"

she said gruffly. Her deepest belief—that her best friend hadn't wanted Fee to raise her kids—was wrong.

Cassie gave her cheek an imperative tap, and obediently, Roz reopened her eyes, but heard nothing of the little girl's chatter. Jack had said he'd relied on Grimble to give him the salient details of the will. Obviously, he'd never read the subclause appointing Fee and Roger guardians should Jack and Roz be unable—or unwilling—to fulfil the obligation in the event of Joyce Galloway, Jack and Anthony's mother, being unable to do so.

The shadows lengthened and the night-light brightened. Gradually, Cassie's lids drifted shut, and her breathing deepened to childish snores. Hearing a door close downstairs, Roz edged inch by careful inch to the side of the toddler's bed. Jack must be home.

Cassie opened sleep-drugged eyes, and she froze. When the little girl closed her eyes again, Roz resumed her incremental escape. *Quietly,* she reminded herself. *Don't hurry.* But she was impatient to hear what Jack had decided. Rolling off the bed, she began tiptoeing toward the door. A floorboard squeaked; instinctively, Roz dropped to the carpet, but Cassie only sighed and turned over.

Taking no chances, Roz stayed on her hands and knees until she was in the hall, coming to a halt in front of a pair of size eleven shoes.

"Having fun?" asked Jack.

"Shh!" Roz bolted to a sitting position and listened.

"Roz…Auntie Roz…" Cassie's wail spoke of an unspeakable betrayal.

"I'm com—"

Jack leaned down and put his hand over her mouth. "It's Uncle Jack," he called. "Go to sleep."

"Story," said Cassie.

"Tomorrow."

"Auntie Roz."

"Tomorrow."

There was silence while Cassie digested that. "Water." But it was a halfhearted request.

"Cassie," Jack said again, in a warm rumble that sent a shiver up Roz's spine, already shivery from having his equally warm hand over her mouth. "Go to sleep."

He removed his hand and pulled her, half-resisting, downstairs. Roz opened her mouth to fire accusations, reproaches and counterarguments.

"You win," said Jack. "I'll tell Fiona we want to keep the kids in New Zealand."

She sat down before her legs gave way. "But...but what changed your mind?"

"You wore me down with home truths, but I guess if there was a definitive moment, it was Liam offering his inheritance to sweeten the deal.... Oh, and Cassie's prepared to buy me off, too, apparently." His mouth twisted in a wry smile. "He was so earnest I'm pretending to think about it."

Roz was finding her victory difficult to assimilate. "Where on earth would Liam get the idea to offer you a bribe?"

"Me, of course." Jack caught her hands and pulled her up, his green eyes suddenly very serious. "I need you and they need you—at least, Liam and Cassie do. I'm sure Sam will realize he does, too, once he knows he can stay in New Zealand." Jack raised her fingers and kissed them. "I love you, Roz, and if this is what it takes to get you to give me another chance…"

Uneasiness flashed through her joy. "But you do want them, too, don't you, Jack?"

"I want the best for them and you're it," he answered, pulling her closer. "I can't fight that anymore."

He lowered his head and, as always, her breath caught in anticipation. But there was one more question she had to ask him. "You will love them, won't you?"

He paused, his mouth inches from hers. "I'm fond of them."

If he wasn't doing this for the right reasons it would never work. For any of them.

Roz turned her head so his lips brushed her cheek. "Bully for you," she said.

Jack drew back. "Why is that so important? You keep telling me this is what the kids want."

"And I do care what they want. But I care about what they need more." How could she make him understand what she only dimly understood herself? Roz could do single parenthood if she had to—but she didn't have to. The guardianship clause in the will had made that clear. "These children had two great parents, Jack. And however much I want them—and you—I'm not going to shortchange them with a father figure who's halfhearted about his commitment."

"I'm not halfhearted," Jack said impatiently. "For God's sake, Roz, they're my brother's children. Of course I'll do everything Ants would have done with them."

"But will you *be* everything to them, Jack?"

He didn't even think about it. "No. Not to the level you're asking. Not like a father."

If Jack couldn't love these kids, then morally she had no right to keep them, not when Jo and Ants had listed Fee and Roger as alternatives. Whatever Fee's faults, she and her husband loved the children and had never wavered in their willingness to raise them. They had the alternative of a loving family. The very thought of losing the children made Roz want to grab a shotgun and barricade everyone in the house. Her impartiality was long gone. Which meant she had to ask herself what she'd once asked Jack of Fiona.

When it really mattered, was she capable of putting the children's interests before her own?

Roz swallowed and stepped back. "Then let Fee and Roger have them," she said, "because that's not good enough."

CHAPTER SEVENTEEN

SHE ASKED TOO MUCH.

Jack put on his shades against the glare as he skirted the prefab classrooms on Liam's sports day. The sky was the joyous blue of early summer; the sun heated his face and bare arms. Birds chirruped with the orgiastic fervor of nest-builders and chick-raisers. Caught in an internal argument that looped and relooped through his brain, Jack noticed none of it.

He couldn't commit to loving these kids the way he'd loved Thomas, with that hurl-over-the-cliff leap of faith. With Roz there was no question of holding back, but with the kids...

Avuncular would have to be enough, and it drove him nuts that Roz insisted on more. It wasn't as if the kids noticed any difference. In the sea of colorful picnic blankets, and seething, excitable children, his gaze met Liam's.

Licking a popsicle, the boy stood on a tartan picnic blanket, dressed in his house colors—red. They clashed fiercely with his hair, which flamed copper in the sun, and his freckled face shone with sunblock.

As always, Jack felt himself measured and found wanting. Forcing a smile, he waved. Liam's expression didn't change; he said something to Roz, who knelt beside him, slathering sun lotion on Cassie's scrunched-up nose. Her own nose was pink, but she looked as fresh as a mint julep in white capris and a green-and-white-striped tee, her hair gleaming like a blackbird's wing.

She raised her head and her expression was as guarded as Liam's, but at least she waved. Couldn't she see that even being fond of these kids was a huge step for him?

He hadn't had a chance to talk to either Liam or Sam about permanent custody yet, but Jack figured once he'd marshaled his troops, they could take her. Because this time he wasn't bowing out quietly.

He hadn't wanted to be dragged back into the land of the living, but now that he was there, Roz was going to have to accept the consequences. And that was the two of them living happily ever after with Judgmental, Angry and Bossy.

"Uncle Jack!" Cassie spotted him and stood up, waving her lemon popsicle imperiously. She looked the picture of innocence in her pink overalls and white T-shirt, with her fine, light brown baby hair fluffed up in the breeze.

He was about to wave back when a female hand caught his arm. "Why, Jack, how nice to see you again." He turned politely to Karen, wishing Liam hadn't told him that Molly's mother looked like a horse. "Roz said you probably wouldn't make it," she added.

Did she now? "I had an hour free." Jack made an effort. "So how are you?"

"Oh, you know, keeping out of trouble…unfortunately." She still had her hand on his arm. Gently he freed it, only to have it grabbed by her daughter.

"Can you make Liam do the three-legged race with me?"

"Why don't you just ask him?"

Molly pouted. "I have, and he says he's not doing it with a dumb girl, but we get extra house points the more people who go in the race, and there's no one else left to go."

Jack glanced toward the picnic blanket and caught a glimpse of Liam's back as he disappeared around the side of a classroom. Roz had the innocent expression of an accomplice. "Looks like he's disappeared. Sorry, kid."

"I'll find him," Molly said with grim determination, and trotted off on the hunt.

"So, following my daughter's example…" said Karen, falling in beside him "…there's a parents' three-legged race next. How about partnering up with me, Jack?"

"Gee, I'm sorry, I'm already promised to Roz." He reached the picnic rug, leaned down and kissed his astonished ex-wife full on the mouth.

"Oh, is that how the land lies?" said Karen placidly. "I should have guessed when she joked that you were gay. But if you like, I'll look after Cassie while you two race."

With a blush spreading across her face, Roz spluttered, "I…we're not—"

Jack swung Cassie into Karen's arms. "Thanks," he said, "we appreciate it." He grabbed Roz's hand and hauled her off the blanket. "Let's go cream the competition."

"What the hell are you playing at?" she muttered as soon as they were out of earshot.

"You wanted the old Jack back…well, I'm back." He caught and kissed her again, making it thorough.

And for a second she responded with all the yearning he felt for her, before turning her head. "Please let me go."

Instead, he grabbed her hand and headed for Liam, who was hiding behind one of the silver birches shading the sports field. "Liam, come watch Auntie Roz and me in the parents' three-legged race."

A delighted grin spread across the boy's face. "You're gonna race, really?" He scampered out from behind the tree.

"You don't play fair," Roz muttered.

"I know you think you're doing the right thing, but in this case you're wrong."

"Yep, that's the way to change my mind," she began, but then Liam tugged on their joined hands.

"Hurry up, they're gonna start soon."

They jogged down to the starting line and were issued a stocking. Jack tied Roz's left ankle to his right, then looped his arm around her slim waist, scanning the competition. There were at least two couples with the smiling, relaxed smugness of regular exercisers.

"Doesn't this tell you something?" he asked as they did a quick run to warm up.

She sighed. "What's that?"

"We're in perfect step without any practice. We used to be a good team, Roz, and we can be again. You take care of the kids' emotional needs, I'll take care of the material ones."

"You mean the way you were brought up?"

Jack mistimed his step and had to catch her as they

stumbled. "Now who's not playing fair? My father didn't give a damn about us, and I do care about those kids."

One of the teachers blew a whistle. "Line up, parents."

Obediently, they toed the line. "The Jack I fell in love with gave one hundred and ten percent to everything he did," she said. "Do you really think I'm going to settle for less?"

"Love me, love the kids. Is that the deal?"

"You got it."

"I'll get back to you."

"You do that."

"Ready, parents," called the teacher. "Steady...*go!*"

Fueled by frustration, they flew down the field, passing one couple after another. Jack suddenly saw the comedy in their situation and started to laugh. Roz's arm tightened around his waist. "Concentrate!" she panted.

He'd forgotten how competitive his ex-wife was, and it only made him laugh harder. Under his arm, her ribs shook as she tried to hold back a chuckle, but by the time they crossed the finish line they were both in stitches.

Liam was almost beside himself, punching the air. "Second!" he screeched. "You came second!"

"See what I mean about teamwork?" Jack said hopefully, but she only shook her head at him as she untied the stocking from their ankles.

Karen approached, carrying Cassie, and Jack let the subject drop. For now. As the pair drew closer he noticed Cassie's face was tearstained, and he forgot his levity. "What happened?"

"We had a bit of drama with a bee sting, but she's okay now."

From her position on Karen's hip, Cassie reached out her arms to Roz. "Owwie," she said plaintively.

"I rubbed lavender on it," said Karen, handing her over. "It helps with the stinging, but I notice it's swelling a bit, so put some ice on it when you get home."

Roz looked at the puffy area and frowned. "I'll go now and drop in to a chemist for some antihistamines. Jack, will you hold her while I find my car keys?"

"I'll walk with you to the car." Gently, he took Cassie, and they headed for the exit. "Hey, baby girl," he said. "Bet you're mad at the mean old bee.... Roz, how long has she had this rash?"

Pausing from rummaging in her bag, Roz frowned at the blotches on Cassie's forearms. "The hives weren't there this morning. Could she be having an allergic reaction to the bee sting?"

"Maybe. Let's be on the safe side and head to E.R."

His tone was calm, but Roz fumbled, trying to fit the key into the lock. *Don't overreact.* This was what Thomas's death had done to her—made her expect the worst from every tiny incident.

Jack's hand closed over hers, squeezed briefly, then he took the keys. "I'll drive. Liam, jump in front with me, and we'll let Roz sit with Cass."

Roz got in and took Cassie, fastening her in her child's car seat. The little girl started to whimper. "Owwie, Roz."

"It's okay, honey, I'm here.... It's probably my imagination, Jack, but her lips look puffy."

Wordlessly, he started the engine and pulled into traffic. "I'm still putting on my seat belt," Liam complained. "And I'm not supposed to sit in the front until I'm thirteen 'cause of the airbag."

"I'll drive carefully," Jack promised. "How's our girl?"

Roz stroked Cassie's hair back from her pale forehead, unsure if the clamminess she felt was the child's or her own palms. Panic was a rolling fog around her brain, making it difficult to concentrate. Cassie had stopped whimpering, but her breathing seemed strained. "Liam," she asked, "has Cass ever had a bee sting before?"

"I don't *think* so."

"Anyone in your family, Jack, ever had a reaction?"

"No." He pulled his cell out of his pocket, keyed in an auto-dial. "Fiona, it's Jack. Anyone in your family allergic to bees…? Uh-huh. Yeah, can't talk now. I'll call you back."

He dropped his cell and stepped on the accelerator, his face grim. The car picked up speed. His eyes met Roz's in the rearview mirror, and she kept stroking Cassie's hair, murmuring foolish endearments all the while.

But even as she prayed, the small face swelled before her eyes, the gasps become a wheeze and Cassie's lids fluttered shut. "Jack! She's lost consciousness."

Roz's shoulder hit the window as Jack slammed on the brakes and swerved to the curb. He jumped out and hauled open her door. "Change places," he said. "Drive, Roz, as fast as you can."

Terrified, she scrambled into the driver's seat, flicked on the hazards and pulled into traffic, treating every set of traffic lights as a free intersection. Beside her, Liam started to cry. "Be brave for me," she croaked.

"Liam?" Jack's tone was low and urgent. "Give me your drink bottle—quickly now, son."

The road, Roz reminded herself, *concentrate on the road.*

Liam unbuckled his seat belt and hung over the back of the seat to hand him the bottle. "What are you doing to her?"

"I'm sticking the plastic tube down her throat to help her breathe."

Oh, God. With a massive effort Roz shoved the panic back, staring so hard at the black tarmac flying underneath the car that her eyes ached. Her knuckles tightened to white on the steering wheel as she fought the urge to glance in the rearview mirror, because she knew one glimpse of Cassie's face and she'd lose it. *It's going to be okay. She's going to be okay.* In her mind she chanted it, prayed it, demanded it…pleaded it.

"Why are you breathing down the tube, Uncle Jack?"

Roz's concentration faltered and the car slid into a skid; she corrected it. "Sit down, Liam," she rasped. "And put your seat belt on again."

She started to weep, lips pulled back in a silent grimace. The traffic lights ahead turned amber; Roz put her foot down and shot through them, ignoring the blare of horns. Left at McQuarrie, right into Drover Street, brakes squealing at every corner, while Liam cowered beside her…

And somewhere behind, Jack was breathing air into Cassie's lungs. Tears, hot and salty, trickled into Roz's mouth. She swallowed them and kept driving, though her hands shook so hard on the steering wheel she had to keep adjusting their position.

At last, the neon medical cross of St. Bart's, blue against white, shone through her tears and she swerved into the sweeping hospital bay, nearly sideswiping an ambulance. After slamming on the brakes, Roz shoved open her door and ran toward the paramedics milling around it.

"Bee sting allergy. Three years old. She…she's stopped breathing. Please!" A sob escaped in a strangled heave that shook her whole body. "Help us."

There was a whir of activity around her, a whir that got faster and faster. Roz put out a hand to steady herself against the ambulance, and then everything went black.

ROZ WOKE UP on a gurney in a corridor, and for a moment, she didn't know where she was. There was a crack like an earthquake fault zigzagging through one of the ceiling tiles, and she stared at it while her brain resurfaced.

Cassie.

She jerked to a sitting position, then almost fell over her knees as she bent forward to counter the wave of dizziness. A nurse approached and put a cool hand on the back of her neck to steady her. "You fainted, so take a minute."

"Cassie!"

"Your baby's been given adrenaline and taken to intensive care. Your husband went with her, so she's not alone. We're looking after your son at the nurses' station, so don't worry about him."

Roz slid off the bed. "Where are they?"

"Through the double doors, turn right and follow the signs." She smiled reassuringly. "He probably saved her life…your husband. Lucky he'd had first-aid training."

But Roz didn't hear her; she was already halfway down the corridor. She didn't need to look at the signs. She knew exactly where she was going, because she'd been here before.

Six years ago.

She recognized the sharp stench of disinfectant, the antiquated hum of the air-conditioning and the fluorescent glare reflecting off the easy-wipe walls of an interminable corridor. Her rubber-soled shoes squeaked on the pale green linoleum, while her heartbeat gathered speed like a mouse on a treadmill, racing faster and faster.

If anyone passed her, she didn't know it. Trapped in a terrible sense of déjà vu, Roz only knew one fact. Cassie was dead.

Roz stopped.

The last time she'd made this journey she'd had hope. When she'd received the brief, shocked call from Jack saying that paramedics were resuscitating Thomas, she'd abandoned a cart of groceries and sped to the hospital. Terrified, frantic, but with a heartfelt conviction that her baby would be okay. No logic held sway; she'd simply believed that if he'd died she would know. This tiny person, bone of her bone, flesh of her flesh, connected by that mysterious, symbiotic intimacy of mother and newborn.

Then she'd seen Jack. Sitting in one of the bucket chairs, elbows on knees, callused hands covering his face and his broad shoulders shaking with uncontrollable sobs. *Reaction*, she'd told herself. *He's relieved that it's over.* Until he'd lifted his head and looked at her, his eyes transmitting an agony that hit her like a thousand volts.

Roz realized she was hyperventilating now, and tried to regulate her breathing. Two seconds on the in breath, four out…the way she'd been taught to counter the panic attacks that had plagued her after Thomas's death.

Cassie was dead…but she had to make this journey.

Hugging herself, Roz took one step, then another—a condemned woman taking her last walk. She watched her feet, willing them to move, the grass-stained trainers of her fun afternoon a rebuke and an obscenity now.

There was the sound of running footsteps. "Roz," Jack called. "She's fine. Cassie's going to be okay."

"No," she whispered to her trainers. "She's dead."

Jack reached her and grabbed her shoulders. "Listen to me!" Dazed, she lifted her head and his gaze pinned hers. "The doctors have given her epinephrine. She's breathing on her own. She'll make a full recovery."

Roz moaned; immediately, his arms closed around her. "I thought…"

"I know."

She broke down. "I can't do this again, it's too hard." She buried her face in his shoulder, feeling hot tears soak and spread through the cotton of his shirt. "You're right not to take this on," she sobbed. "We'll give custody to Fee."

His hands gently circled her back. "You don't mean that."

"I d-d-do."

"No," he repeated. "You don't."

There was a utility room next to them. Jack guided her inside and shut the door. They stood in the dark, surrounded by the smell of musty wet sponge mops and cleaning products.

He gently peeled strands of hair back from her face. "I was the one deluding myself, thinking I didn't love these kids…." His voice got stuck in his throat, and Roz realized the hot tears on her face weren't all hers.

She wrapped her arms around his neck and lifted her face blindly in the dark. Their first kiss was clumsy. On the second, their mouths melded, hard, hot and honest, all about seizing life and second chances.

The nurse's words came into her mind again. *Luckily, your husband had training.* "How did you know what to do?"

He hesitated. "I took some courses in emergency first aid a few years ago."

She didn't have to ask why. Her heart broke for him. "I'm sorry," she whispered, "so sorry you were alone with Thomas when he died."

"Until it happened, I thought I was a strong man," he said. "And when I shattered, I didn't care who I hurt— you, Ants and Julia. I'm sorry, Roz, for all the pain I—"

She put a finger on his lips. "How about we just forgive each other?" Under the pad of her index finger, she felt his mouth lift in his special smile.

"I can do that."

"You're going to have to give me that smile sometime when I can actually see it," she said, starting to tremble from delayed shock. "Now I need to get to Cassie."

"I'll fetch Liam. Then I'll ring Fiona."

They stepped out of the utility room, blinking against the light. Jack's eyes were red, there were traces of tears on his cheeks and his hair stood up. Roz figured she looked as bad when he used the tail of his shirt to wipe her face. She thumbed his cheeks free of tears, finger-combed his hair. He caught her hand, held the palm against his face, and for a long moment, they simply looked at each other.

Jack brought her hand to his lips, kissed her knuckles passionately, and they parted.

LIAM SNEAKED AWAY from the nurses' station and the babyish toys they'd given him to play with, and tried to find Cassie. He had to tell her it was all right that a boy cat was called by a girl's name.

The nurses had told him again and again that she'd be okay, but he didn't believe them because his baby sister was never still, and she'd been so floppy in the car when Uncle Jack had been breathing air down the novelty straw. Liam shut the picture out of his mind because it made him want to cry again.

Uncle Jack had been very calm while he'd done it, and at the time Liam had found that reassuring, because if Uncle Jack wasn't panicking then maybe things weren't so bad. Now he thought maybe Uncle Jack hadn't been trying hard enough.

He told himself that if Cassie died she'd be with Mum and Dad in heaven, but he was so tired of everybody leaving him.

First Mum and Dad, then Sam getting all funny and not caring if they stayed together. Auntie Roz loved him, but she couldn't stop Uncle Jack from sending them to England. Liam knew Uncle Jack wouldn't say yes to taking the money. It probably wasn't enough.

Liam wandered down the hall and pressed his nose against the glass of a room, hoping Cassie would be there, but all he saw was an old man dressed in a green sheet, skinny legs hanging over the edge of a hospital bed. The old man frowned and made a shooing gesture, and Liam ducked.

"Liam, where are you?" called Uncle Jack.

For a split second he considered not answering, because he'd wandered off when he wasn't supposed to. But Uncle Jack would know about Cassie.

"I'm here."

Uncle Jack came around the corner and gave him the smile Liam had once seen him give Cassie when she was asleep. Liam's tummy went all funny, like there was a milk shake sloshing around or something, and all the worry whooshed out of him like air from a party balloon.

He smiled back.

CHAPTER EIGHTEEN

JACK KNEW IMMEDIATELY that he shouldn't have raised the issue of custody with Fiona. He should have left it a happy call, all about Cassie making a full recovery.

But euphoria and fatigue had skewed his judgment, made him utter the fatal words. "How would you feel about Roz and I having permanent custody?"

Turned out she felt a lot of things, betrayal and anger chief among them.

Now her niece had experienced a life-threatening allergic reaction. It didn't matter that this was Cassie's first sting or that her brothers had escaped the disorder. Roz and Jack should have asked the doctor about genetic predispositions at the beginning of their guardianship.

"I promised myself that I'd look after her children, and I've been negligent, Jack, as negligent as you. Well, no longer."

"Fiona, I—"

She hung up on him. Jack listened to the dial tone and thought, *Serves me right. Hitting her with a bombshell when she's been frantic with worry for the last...* he glanced at his watch *...hour and a half.* Of course she'd overreact.

It occurred to him that it was three-thirty in the

morning over there. He'd call her back at a civilized hour, apologize for being an insensitive jerk, and start again.

FEE HUNG UP and burst into tears. Roger was in London, the boys at boarding school. She was alone in her Georgian mansion in Hampshire. Outside, the first snow dusted the hawthorn hedge with white, and the driveway was a dirty, icy sludge under the security lights.

She fumbled in the drawer of her antique rosewood bureau for a box of tissues and blew her nose, wanting to call Roger at their flat, but terrified of a woman answering. He'd had an affair last year with a workmate, a midlife foolishness he bitterly regretted, and though Fee knew he'd never do it again…well, some fears never really went away.

His lover hadn't been young, or even pretty, but Fee knew her as kind. That was when she'd realized some of the blame lay at her own door—though Roger accepted all of it. An early menopause had made Fee shrewish and carping; sex only happened when she thought it was time, and the act inevitably began with her resigned sigh.

So she'd forgiven him and they'd made a new start. Roger had been so loving since…. Odd that an affair had repaired their marriage.

Her husband had always been forbearing, letting Fee direct their lives, organize the boys' education; putting up with the pokey London flat during the week and making the long commute home on the weekends, where she'd put him to work in a too-big garden.

The country house she'd insisted on had been a mistake. She missed her London life and she missed her sons. By the time she realized that giving them the best education couldn't compensate for their absence, they loved the place and wouldn't leave.

She would do things differently if she had another chance. And now she did—with Julia's children. Fee picked up the photograph of Julia and Anthony and their family, and grief washed over her. Warmhearted, easygoing Julia, effortless to love.

Fee, on the other hand, was hard to love; she knew that. An overachiever, she was smart enough to rue it, and compulsive enough to be unable to change it.

The holiday in New Caledonia had not been a success. Fee hadn't been able to relax; she'd organized tours when everyone would have been happy by the pool. It was she who'd insisted on rental cars because she had a distaste for public transport. She who'd sent Julia and Anthony on their last journey.

And the better sister had died. If only Fee had let go of the reins, it would never have happened. She felt that deeply, keenly. She would give her sister's children everything she had, because she desperately needed the chance to atone.

To hell with it. She called Roger—who answered on the third ring, obviously dragged from sleep—and told him what she wanted to do. As always, he gave her his full support. Then Fee dressed, drank tea and scribbled on a notepad in the kitchen, waiting for dawn. At exactly 8:30 a.m. she rang her lawyer.

JACK PULLED HIS SUITCASE out of the taxi. It was a fine day in early December, three days after the bee sting, and he was returning from a two-night business trip to Tokyo.

It was meant to be longer, but he'd cut it short, citing Cassie's accident—though his niece had needed to spend only one night in hospital for observation. Roz had stayed with her, and Jack had barely had time to kiss them a hasty goodbye when he dropped them home before heading to the airport.

In truth, it was Sam's sixteenth birthday, and Jack didn't want to miss it.

And he really needed to see Roz.

Stupid to worry she'd change her mind, but Jack wasn't used to happiness anymore, and he didn't trust it. Their phone calls had been frustratingly brief. And they hadn't told the kids they were keeping them, because the custody issue hadn't been finalized with Fiona. She must be away, because she wasn't returning messages.

They could set the custody wheels in motion, anyway, but they both felt strongly that they needed Fiona's approval first. It had to work for all of them.

Walking down the driveway, Jack noticed that summer had come in his absence. The lime-green leaves of the spindly Robinia tree fluttered in the breeze like pennants of welcome, while bougainvillea exploded into bursts of scarlet across the trellis to one side of the patio. On either side of the driveway, tight white buds on the standard roses gave the effect of a row of giant bridal bouquets.

And the strangest feeling unfurled in him. He no longer looked at the house as something that needed work—though God knows that hadn't changed.

For the first time, Jack saw the good bones underneath the worn exterior, the comfort and warmth. It was like noticing the twinkle in the eye of an old lady who'd lived a satisfying life and was still game for a jig, given the right partner.

"Uncle Jack! Uncle Jack!" Cassie sat in the window seat, banging on the pane. She was wearing a smart red dress, purple earmuffs and a pair of bright green satin evening gloves, the long loose fingers of which flapped as she waved, making her look like Edward Scissorhands.

He laughed. Liam came to the window, his smile more tentative, but Jack figured he had the present to turn the tide. In fact, he was damn sure he'd finally got it right.

Inside, he scooped Cassie up and kissed one round, silky cheek, breathing her in, and realized how much he'd missed her. She squirmed to be put down, intent on only one thing. "Where's my present?"

"It's Sam's birthday today, not yours," Jack teased, winking at Liam, who still stood beside the window seat. "Hey, mate." He thought about crossing the room to hug him, but as he hesitated the moment passed.

Impatiently, Cassie smacked Jack's thigh. "You been in a plane. I get a present."

"Okay, maybe I got you a small one." He dumped his suitcase on the table and opened it, handing her a parcel. "Liam, I have one for you, too."

Gloved fingers flying, Cassie ripped into the wrapping like a lioness on its kill.

"So where is the birthday boy, anyway?" said Jack. "And Roz?" Saying her name made his heart skip beats like a teenager's.

"Some urgent appointment came up," Sam said from

the doorway. "Umm, how come you're home today? We weren't expecting you until tomorrow." For some reason, he sounded nervous.

"Because today's too important to miss. Happy birthday, Sam." He gave him a hug as he handed over the present. The moment was awkward, it was uncomfortable, but hey—they'd live. His own face hot, Jack grinned at his blushing nephew. Holding his present, Liam stood watching them with a wistful expression, and Jack thought, *I should've hugged him.*

Cassie started to jump in sheer joy. "Look what *I* got." He'd bought her a hammering toy—a stand, inset with brightly colored wooden dowels that could be hammered flat with a mallet, then turned over. The perfect present.

And he had another one. "Go ahead, open it," Jack encouraged Liam.

"Sam first," the boy said manfully, "since it's his birthday."

The teenager's face lit up he unwrapped the latest cell phone. "Choice! Thanks, Jack…man, this is rad."

"It's got some weird and wonderful features," said Jack. "Read the brochure."

The home phone rang and Sam jumped. "I'll get it." Ignoring the handset in the lounge, he disappeared into the hall.

Jack turned back to Liam, who was laboriously peeling the last of the tape back from the wrapping paper. "It's a baseball training set," he said eagerly. "The ball pops up from the base, so you can practice hitting it out of the air. Then when you've mastered that, this pitching machine lobs the ball to you." He switched it on and nothing happened. "Damn, it needs batteries. I'll pick some up next time I'm out."

Liam looked at the pitching machine, then at his sneakers. "Thank you," he said in a very quiet voice.

And Jack finally accepted that he was never going to win over this kid. "Guess you should go wash your hands for dinner." Something in his tone made Liam shoot him a nervous glance. "Will you stop being so bloody scared of me?" Jack snapped. "I'm not going to hurt you!"

The kid scarpered.

Angry with himself, Jack sat down on the couch and stared moodily into space, only half aware of Cassie happily banging away on her new toy.

"I told you she's not here right now," Sam muttered from the hall. "I can take a message…okay, call back later if you don't trust me…."

Jack experienced a twenty-year-old sense of déjà vu. Himself fielding just such a call. He strode into the hall and confiscated the receiver. "This is Jack Galloway, Sam's other guardian. Is there a problem?"

He wasn't surprised by what he heard. As he listened, he looked gravely at his nephew, who fidgeted from one foot to the other, crossing and uncrossing his arms, striving to appear unconcerned and failing miserably.

"Yes, Roz and I can come and discuss the situation on Monday. Ten o'clock?" Mentally, Jack reshuffled his appointment schedule. "See you then."

Sam started babbling before he'd replaced the receiver. "They're making a big deal about nothing…a few cigarettes…anyone would think we were smoking dope. And okay, maybe we were stupid to bring beer onto the school grounds, but…man, it's not like it's hard liquor."

The torrent of words ran out, and there was silence except for the bang, bang, bang of Cassie's mallet. So this was what parenting a teenager felt like. A cocktail of frustration, worry, fury and helplessness when they repeated your mistakes. Not trusting himself to speak, Jack counted to ten.

"It's only a few days," Sam said in another rush. "I'll use them as study leave…I mean, Roz has been hounding me to put in more hours, anyway."

The front door opened; Roz came in, and Jack felt sick for having to do this to her. But she was already pale. He took three steps, shielding her from Sam's view. "Roz?"

"I've been with Grimble," she said in a low voice so that Sam wouldn't hear. "Fee's in town and she's suing for custody." As he stood, stunned, she pasted on a smile and looked past him to Sam. "Hey, *that's* not a birthday face."

"I've been suspended," said Sam.

THIS WAS THE SUCKIEST birthday dinner ever, Liam decided, washing down his dry roast chicken with a big sip of water and glowering at his big brother.

Dumb old Sam. Why did he have to go get 'spended on his birthday, anyway?

Now no one except Liam and Cassie wanted to wear party hats or play with the balloons or pull the Christmas crackers that he had begged Roz to bring out early.

The chicken caught in his throat again. "This has stringy bits in it," he complained.

"It's overcooked," Roz murmured, but Liam could

tell she didn't really care, even though she wasn't eating it, either. He felt sad. He'd made place cards and everything, and no one had even noticed.

"I can't eat it." Liam made a gagging sound and pushed his plate away.

Uncle Jack said quietly. "Now's not the time to act up."

Liam's throat tightened, this time with tears. He was tired of being the only one Uncle Jack didn't like. And he couldn't pretend he wanted a dumb old machine to throw him the ball. Baseball was something people did together. Furiously blinking back tears, he pushed the peas around his plate with the fork.

"Liam," Roz said gently, and he looked up. Her smile made him feel better. "Help me clear the table?" There was a conspirator's note in her voice that reminded him about the birthday cake.

Grievances forgotten, he scrambled off his chair and carried plates to the kitchen, where the cake sat in the pantry. Chocolate with chocolate frosting—Sam's favorite—and Liam had measured the ingredients. They put sixteen birthday candles in, and his eyes widened when Roz lit them because it seemed the whole cake was on fire.

Grinning, he pushed open the saloon doors and started singing at the top of his voice. "Happy birthday to you.... Happ—"

"Stop," shouted Sam, "I can't stand it. It's corny and phony and wrong!"

"I know that none of us is really in the mood for this," Auntie Roz said, "but it's still your birth—"

"You just don't get it," he yelled. "Why'd you have to make Mum's cake, huh? Tell me why?"

The candles were burning down, dripping wax into the icing.

"Liam said you always have chocolate cake on your—"

"You're not my mother, so stop trying to take her place!"

Auntie Roz whispered, "Oh, God, is that what all this hostility's been about?"

"Liam," said Uncle Jack, "take Cassie upstairs and play with her until we calm things down here."

Liam stared at Sam, who was all wild-eyed, and reached for Cassie's hand. "Come with me."

"No!" She pulled free of his grasp, so he grabbed her new toy, taking pride of place beside her plate.

"I'm gonna play with this," he threatened, running out of the room.

With a squeal of outrage she chased after him. "Mine."

He didn't let her catch him until they were upstairs in his room, and by that time her face was a bright angry red. When Liam handed it over, she tried to hit him with the mallet, and he had to roll across the bed to get out of range. "Okay, okay, it's yours. I was just tricking. I'm sorry."

"Don't like you," she spat, and plonked herself down on the floor, cradling her toy like a baby. Normally that would have made Liam smile, but he was too worried about what was going on downstairs.

Through the floorboards he could still hear Sam's voice raised in anger, like the rumble of a train coming through a tunnel, getting louder and louder. Liam lay on his bed, jammed the pillow over his head and started singing "Silent Night," the Christmas carol they'd been practicing at assembly.

"'Si…lent night, ho…uh…ly night…'"

Cassie started hammering in the pegs. Bang, bang bang clunk.

"'All is calm.'" Liam's voice quivered, and the tears were hot under his lids.

Bang, bang went Cassie's hammer.

"'All is bright. Round yon verssssion, mother and child.'" He remembered he wanted to ask Roz what a version was. "'Sleep in heavenly pee…eece.'" Bang, bang.

Liam lifted a corner of the pillow. Over Cassie's hammering, Sam was still yelling, so he replaced it.

"'Slee…eep in heavenly peace.'"

CHAPTER NINETEEN

ROZ STOOD QUIETLY under Sam's verbal attack, telling herself not to take it personally, but she had to clench her jaw to stop her mouth trembling. Jack had tried to intervene, but she'd caught his arm and said, "Let him finish." Jack stood beside her now, his shoulder a comforting weight touching hers.

"You may have suckered Liam and Cassie into thinking you're shit-hot," Sam yelled, "but you don't fool me. You're just some sad-ass who hasn't got a life and is taking over Mum's."

"Enough." This time Jack moved so fast Roz couldn't stop him. He pinned Sam against the wall, applying just enough pressure to hold him. "Don't you know what Roz sacrificed to keep you here? Her job—"

"Jack," she interrupted, "I don't consider it a sacrifice. By keeping to your parents' routines and rituals," she explained to Sam, "I was hoping to make the transition easier—particularly for Cassie and Liam. That's all, I promise. I never meant to take anyone's place."

Jack shifted his hand to Sam's shoulder, and his voice was deep and resonant with emotion. "You think if you act like a hard-ass no one will figure out how scared you are…how lost and alone you feel. We understand that.

But lashing out at the people trying to help you isn't acceptable. How do you think your father would feel about this behavior? Your mother?"

Sam shoved free. "Don't tell me what Mum and Dad think...you hardly ever saw them! I'm sixteen, and I don't have to do what you say anymore." He stormed out of the room and up the stairs. Then his door crashed shut.

In the resulting silence, Roz looked at Jack. "Welcome home."

He smiled and it comforted her like balm, soothing every ragged edge of her nerves. "Come here." He opened his arms, and Roz wondered how she'd ever thought she didn't need him. She walked into them, felt them close around her like a warm blanket on a cold, cold night.

"Are you sure you still want to do this?" she joked, because if she didn't she'd cry.

"Yes." One word—so much conviction.

His response gave her courage. "If Sam really does hate me, then maybe he would be better off with Fee. Which means that Liam and Cassie would have to go, too, because we can't separate the kids."

Jack drew her down to the couch. "Sam doesn't hate you," he said gently. "I think he's grappling with the opposite problem. You and Julia both have the gift of making people feel loved."

For a minute she couldn't speak. "Thank you."

"By letting you in, Sam thinks he's being disloyal. We'll talk to him again when the little ones are in bed. Now tell me what Grimble said before we call Liam and Cassie down."

She took a deep breath. "The first step is informal

mediation with a judge acting as facilitator. If we reach a consensus with Fee, it doesn't go any further."

"And if we don't?"

"Lawyers get involved, the case goes to Family Court, where apparently both sides try and present themselves in the best light by discrediting the other. And a third party—the judge—decides who gets custody."

"Mediation it is, then."

"Jack, I think we should leave lawyers out of this as long as possible."

"I agree. Fee's had a shock. When she sees we're back together and very serious about our responsibilities, she'll come around. I'll tell her that we're willing to send the kids over to England at least once a year, or bring her family over here—at my expense. I'm sure once we reassure her that she'll see plenty of them there'll be no problem."

Did he know how tightly his fingers gripped hers? "You're overdoing the calm, soothing tone."

He grimaced and let go. "I do believe we'll sort this out amicably, but…"

"But you're emotionally involved. That's okay, I get it." She touched his cheek and he caught her fingers, turning his head to kiss the palm.

"Roz, let's get married again." Her heart leaped. "Legalize your connection to them, show the judge and Fiona we're committed. It will carry a lot more weight."

The first time he'd proposed marriage he'd told her he was crazy in love with her. Couldn't live without her. "It's something to think about," she said, managing a half smile.

There was a basket of washing on the table beside

them, ready to be folded. She got up, retrieved a queen-size sheet and smoothed out the white cotton.

"You're not keen." His voice was suddenly flat.

"No, it's a good idea. Why not?" She shook it out, ready for folding, and he caught the other side, started tugging her closer.

"Talk to me."

Cassie trotted into the room, saw the sheet stretched out and threw herself into the middle. They tightened their grip just in time to break her fall. "Swing," she demanded, "give me a swing." Obediently, they swung the little body from side to side in the sheet, and her giggles drew Liam downstairs.

"Is Sam okay?"

"He's still mad at us," Roz said honestly, "but we'll fix it."

Liam looked wistfully at Cassie tumbling and laughing in the sheet. "Hop on," said Jack. When the two kids were noisily enjoying themselves, he said, "Tell me what you want, Roz."

Why was she making such a fuss about this? She looked across the sheet to Jack. "Sure," she said briskly. "We'll get married again." *For the kids' sake.*

It was naive to expect the passionate commitment of their first marriage. Not after all that had happened. Not with all these new responsibilities. Still, there was sadness in her, a very different feeling from the fizzing excitement with which she'd awaited Jack's homecoming earlier.

Later, watching him cradle Cass as he read her a story, Roz told herself not to be ridiculous. They needed some time alone together, that was all. Of course they'd go back to the way they were.

As she tidied the toys with Liam, Jack lifted his gaze without skipping a beat in the story, and smiled at her, reinforcing her confidence. "'So Pinky, that intrepid mouse, went back to his home at the dump, wiser and a whole lot smarter about seagulls….' Is it bedtime yet?" The inquiry was completely innocent, but the intent in his eyes caused Roz to drop Mr. Potato Head, who hit the floor and scattered in all directions.

Wise guy. He knew full well that they wouldn't be sharing a bed for a while. Sex before marriage got complicated with a teenager in the house. Still, she sent him a sultry smile as she and Liam collected the remains of Mr. Potato Head. No harm in flirting.

"You know," said Jack, his tone no longer innocent. "I think my next repair is the trellis outside your bedroom window."

Liam crawled from under the couch holding the toy's mustache. "Yeah! Then we can climb it again."

"I never thought of that," said Jack.

Excited by the idea, Liam scampered out to have a look at the trellis.

As soon as he'd gone, Jack murmured, "Kiss me."

Cassie hauled herself up on his lap and planted a wet one on his cheek. "Read the book again."

"When your aunt stops laughing at me." Ruefully, Jack wiped the drool off his cheek. "Can't we have a different book?"

Cassie opened *Pinky* at page one and put it under his nose.

"Maybe our next child will be open to more variety," Roz said to console him.

The smile went out of Jack's eyes, like a cloud covering the sun. She shivered. "You don't want another baby?"

"Let's talk about that when things settle down. We've got enough on our plates at the moment."

As though a child was another burden.

And she had her answer. Things were never going to be the same.

While Jack put the younger kids to bed, Roz drove back to her apartment to pick some of the legal documents they would need for the mediation in two days' time.

"I'm a glass-half-full kind of girl," she told herself, trying to rationalize her devastating disappointment. "I'll have the man I love, the kids I adore, and if Jack doesn't want to have another child together, well, that's understandable. I'll lavish love on other people's babies."

Still, she had a quiet cry in front of Thomas's picture before she locked up and drove back.

With a huge effort of will, Roz concentrated on their immediate priorities. Sam should have cooled down by now and be ready to talk, and they needed to explain about the custody issue. Through her lawyer, Fee had requested no contact with either Roz or Jack until mediation. She wanted to see Sam tomorrow, but was insistent the younger children remain ignorant of the dispute as long as possible.

The common sense in that steadied Roz. Fee's heart was in the right place; of course she'd realize that the kids needed to stay in New Zealand with Jack and her.

She was at the traffic lights waiting to turn right into their neighborhood when a youth holding a duffel bag loped around the corner and headed west. His hoodie obscured his features, but Roz knew that gait.

Where on earth was he going?

With one eye on the red light, she opened the window. "Sam!" Her call was drowned out by the squeal of brakes and tires as a Nissan Skyline accelerated from the opposite direction and pulled up beside him. The throbbing bass of a boom box vibrated across the road in waves of sound when Sam opened the passenger door of the Nissan and jumped in.

Wait just a darn minute, mister. "Sam!"

A car honked impatiently behind her, so Roz drove through the lights, then pulled over. She reached the corner at a half run, and thank God, the Nissan was still there. "Sam!"

But he still couldn't hear her over the music. The interior lamp illuminated the driver's features as he leaned across the car to light Sam's cigarette. Roz gasped and broke into a sprint.

Dirk must have spent enough time with Sam at the funeral to swap mobile phone numbers.

Dirk glanced in the rearview mirror and said something to Sam, who twisted his head to look. Roz expected horror, guilt…. What she saw was narrow-eyed defiance.

She marched up to the car and tried to open the passenger door, but he was ahead of her, locking it and opening the window halfway.

For a moment they stared at each other, and she saw immediately that anger would get her nowhere. He didn't even bother hiding the cigarette in his hand. In a low, steady voice, she said, "Sam, please get out of the car."

Dirk leaned forward, all smiles and hostile civility. "You know, it's not polite to ignore people."

Roz kept her attention on her nephew. "Come home with me, now."

"Sheesh, she's doing it again, bro." Dirk slung one muscled arm across the back of his seat. The barbed-wire tattoo encircling his biceps was the color of a cheap blue pen. He released the handbrake, gave the engine a rev. "Don't you sweat, baby doll, I'll make sure he's tucked in at night." He laughed at his own wit.

"What does he mean?" Roz said sharply.

Sam shared a grin with the young man beside him. "I'm quitting school, getting a job and staying in New Zealand—living with Dirk. You and Jack can send me my money when you sell the house."

The situation was reaching nightmarish proportions. "That's not happening, Sam." She glared at Dirk. "Jack and I are applying for permanent custody, so you don't have to go anywhere."

"You want the house, you mean," Dirk said.

"Stay out of it," she snapped at him.

"Shit, you're right, bro," Dirk said to Sam. "She is one uptight bitch."

Sam squirmed, glanced at Roz. "I didn't say it like that."

"Let's discuss this at home," she said quietly, trying to hide her increasing desperation. Dirk's eyes were clear, but he had the sweaty, sharp tang of a chronic drinker. "Please, Sam, unlock the door."

Hesitantly, the teenager lifted the lock mechanism; they were both surprised when the button clicked down again. Roz saw Dirk was using the driver's controls to override Sam's action.

"Please, Sam," he mimicked, and their nephew looked

at him uncertainly. "You wanna be pussy-whipped for the rest of your life?"

Sam's jaw tightened and he lowered his hand. "You still wouldn't let me quit school, though, would you? I'm going with Dirk."

Roz jiggled the door handle. "As your guardian, I'm ordering you to open the door."

Dirk's eyes were flat and hard as he glanced across Sam. "My man's sixteen now, doesn't have to do what you say."

"What would *you* know about the law? Open the damn door."

Dirk smirked at her. "If there's one thing Evanses understand, sweet cheeks, it's how the law works. Otherwise how can you get around it?" The window whined shut.

Roz banged on the glass. "Sam, get out of the car *now!*"

Arms folded, he kept staring straight ahead. The blue Nissan accelerated away from the curb with a squeal of tires and disappeared around the corner, its taillights flashing, leaving her standing in an acrid cloud of exhaust fumes.

CHAPTER TWENTY

THOUGH HE'D NEVER BEEN near the neighborhood before, Jack recognized the place as soon as he saw it. The overgrown lawn, the sagging chain-link fence, the peeling paint on the wooden window frames, the old sofa on the porch that obviously did duty as outdoor furniture. The young guys sitting on it, half-drunk in the late morning sun, feet up on the porch rail, countering their hangovers with a cold beer. He'd crashed in places like this through his late teens.

There would be beer in the fridge and not much else, sheets that needed washing, dirty towels and a lot of bravado masking the fact that no one really gave a shit about them.

Some things never changed.

Jack jumped the gate, having seen at a glance it was rusted shut. He ignored the Doberman tied in the yard next door, barking furiously as it pulled on its chain.

Sam straightened as he approached; the others watched him through listless eyes, yawning and staying where they were. Dirk wasn't in sight…probably still in bed, which was just as well, because right now Jack wanted to beat him senseless. But violence wasn't his objective this morning.

He and Roz had stayed up half the night trying to track Sam down. The police hadn't been helpful. Sam could indeed leave home at sixteen unless Child, Youth and Family Services thought he was at risk. Jack could go through the application process. Neither he nor Roz was prepared to wait.

Ignoring the others, he said to Sam, "Is there somewhere private we can talk?"

His nephew lounged back in the chair, an old car seat with loose springs. "There's no point. You're not going to change my mind."

Jack waited.

"I don't see why you have to interfere when you don't care," Sam muttered, getting up.

"If I didn't care I'd leave you to learn the hard way."

Sam led him into the dim interior, damp and dark because of too-small windows. The teenager's royal-blue sleeping bag, incongruous in its newness, lay on the worn couch in the lounge. He pulled it aside so Jack could sit down, moving cans and magazines off the floor to make room for their feet. "We had a party last night," he said awkwardly.

"They spend all your money yet?"

"I had to pay a bond," he said defensively, "contribute to the rent and food kitty."

Jack looked at the beer cans. "Yeah, I can see that. So you want to quit school and get a job?"

"Already got one." Sam gave a cocky grin. "Dirk has a mate who's a builder. He needs a laborer."

"You gave up school to slave ten-hour days for minimum wage?"

"You left school at my age and did okay without qualifications."

"No, I didn't do okay. I went back to night school and got them, realizing I'd made a big mistake," Jack said grimly. "I only left home at sixteen because my father didn't give a shit about me."

Sam stuck out his chin. "There's no one left to give a shit about me, now Mum and Dad are dead."

"You know that's not true. I admit I haven't been the great guardian Roz has, but that's changing as of now. I'm taking you home."

"No, you're not." Sam backed away, his eyes hostile. "I'm sixteen and I don't have to do what you say anymore."

"That's where you're wrong." Jack picked up Sam's sleeping bag and repacked it. "Ants and Ju live on through the charge they placed in me, and I'm not letting them down again." He glanced at his nephew's face and his tone softened. "I'll always regret that I missed my brother's last years because I shut out the people I loved while I was grieving…. Like you're doing now, Sammy."

His nephew folded his arms. "What? You think you can *force* me to go with you?" he jeered.

Jack smiled. "I grew up with a man who washed his hands of me as soon as it got hard, and I'm not doing the same to you. So yes, if I have to pick you up and carry you out kicking and screaming, then I'll do it." He retrieved the rucksack beside the couch. "Until the Family Court says otherwise, you're living with us and abiding by our rules. And that means exams next week."

"I hate you!" Sam started to sob with impotent rage. "You don't understand *anything*."

"Son, it's because I understand," said Jack, "that I'm

doing this." Knowing better than to offer comfort, he handed Sam his sleeping bag, and watched the teenager unconsciously hug it.

Bleary-eyed, jeans hanging around his lean hips, Dirk appeared from the bedroom, scratching his chest. "What's up, bro?"

Jack said pleasantly, "What's up, *bro*, is that I'm taking our nephew home, and if I ever see your skinny ass around the house again, I'll kick it all the way back here."

The younger man bristled. "You touch me and I'll sue you for assault."

"Do you think I'm stupid enough to do it in front of witnesses?" Jack said coldly. "It'll come down to your word against mine, which means the police will look at our records. Mine's clean. How about yours?"

FEE WATCHED HER OLDEST nephew drum his fingers nervously on a marble table in the foyer of Auckland's Grand Hotel, where Sunday afternoon tea was being served.

"You side with me," Sam said, "and I'll testify for you in any custody hearing so you get Cassie and Liam."

There was an aspect of this quid pro quo that she didn't like. But that wasn't her immediate concern. "Sam, you're too young to be on your own. Come back with me to England."

He snorted. "And do what?"

She pushed the three-tiered cake stand toward him. On it were cucumber and salmon club sandwiches, scones dripping with jam and piled with cream, and fat slices of Black Forest cake. "You can go to the same school as the boys. They absolutely love it at Harrow."

"Board," he said with a colonial's instinctive horror

of the British institution. "No way." He helped himself to a large piece of the cake and put it on the bone china plate. "School's bad enough without spending every waking hour there."

"Okay," she said, thinking hard. "I'll support your bid for independence if you go back to school here for another year—then we'll review it."

"I get to live alone though, right? With my share of the sale of Mum and Dad's house?"

Fee hesitated. He was too young to make adult choices, too young to have free access to money that should be securing his future. She began to see the problem in all its dimensions.

She'd thought she could persuade him to come home with her, if only to be with his brother and sister. "What about Liam and Cassandra?"

He'd picked up his fork; now he put it down again. "Don't you start on about family staying together and all that bull…. I've had enough of it from Jack and Roz."

"Have you?" Uneasiness snaked through her, as uncomfortable as guilt. "Well, they have a point, Sam."

"Why does everyone have to try and make me feel guilty all the time because I want my own life? I can visit once a year or something, can't I?"

"We're…" she caught herself aligning with Roz and Jack "…*I'm* just encouraging you to think things through properly. The decisions you make now will affect your whole life."

"I thought you'd understand," he accused, pushing his plate away. "I thought you'd be on my side. Otherwise what's the point of…"

"Supporting me?" Fee finished. Now she was really

worried. "I thought it was because Jack and Roz were doing a terrible job?" He'd told her some truly horrific stories over the past thirty minutes.

"Of course it is," he mumbled, but he looked down at his trainers and her uneasiness grew. What kind of Faustian bargain was she making here? This boy needed care, boundaries....

"I can't let you live alone," she said, "or have free access to your inheritance. That would make me derelict in my duty to your parents."

She ignored his exclamation of impatience. "But I'm sure we can come to some arrangement—for you to board with a friend's family, for example, and come over to England for holidays. At least that would free you of Jack and Roz's influence on a day-to-day basis...if that's what you really want, Sam. Is it?"

His blue eyes were so filled with pain, it hurt her to look at him, and Fee made some instinctive gesture to touch. Sam moved, very slightly, so he was out of reach. "Yes," he said. "That's what I want."

Two lawyers flanked Fiona.

Out of the corner of her eye, Roz saw Jack give the same start of surprise as they entered the mediation room at the Family Court with Sam.

Jack reached for her hand and gave it a reassuring squeeze, which tightened when their nephew went to the other side of the circular maple table and pulled up a chair next to Fee. Sam shot them a quick glance that was half sheepish, half defiant. Fee patted his hand, then gave them a cool nod that had nothing concilia-tory about it.

Oh, God, thought Roz with a growing dismay, *we're in trouble.*

Sam had come back from his meeting with Fiona very quiet, and had slipped into his room straight after dinner, simply saying he'd told his aunt he wanted to stay in New Zealand. Given the events of the last twenty-four hours, Roz and Jack had let him be. Right now it was enough that he was prepared to go back to school when his suspension ended next week.

"What's going on?" she whispered to Jack as they took their seats.

"I suspect we'll find out," he murmured back.

Judge Sawyer was a man in his late sixties with a genial, weathered face and the kind of haircut that suggested a wife's inexpert hand. His wiry brows were equally in need of a professional trimming, jutting out over intelligent, deep-set hazel eyes.

He vigorously shook everyone's hand, then told Fiona's lawyers he expected them to behave themselves. Roz relaxed slightly.

"We're here to discuss who has permanent custody of Liam and Cassandra Galloway," Judge Sawyer began, glancing at his notes, "who have been in the interim custody of their appointed guardians, Jack Galloway and Rosalind Valentine, following their parents' deaths just over five weeks ago. Mr. Galloway and Ms. Valentine now wish to claim permanent custody of the children, as does the children's maternal aunt, Fiona Montgomery of England."

His gaze darted to all parties, seeking assent, and everybody nodded.

"During the period of temporary custody, Sam Evans

has turned sixteen. Ms. Valentine and Mr. Galloway, citing the special circumstances of his parents' recent death, are asking for an extension of custody until he is seventeen. Sam is requesting, with Mrs. Montgomery's support, that he be exempt from any final parenting order." Roz gasped. "Instead, he's asked that Mrs. Montgomery take responsibility for his well-being, though I understand relocation isn't on the cards. So this would be an advisory and support role only."

Roz couldn't stop a murmur of protest.

The judge raised his head. "This seems to be news to you, Ms. Valentine. Weren't you and Mr. Galloway informed of this in advance of mediation?"

"No," Jack answered grimly, "we were not."

Judge Sawyer frowned at Fee's lawyers and the elder of the two men cleared his throat. "The matters pertaining to day-to-day custody of Samuel Evans were only resolved between the parties, Sam Lucas Evans and Fiona Elizabeth Montgom—"

"This is an informal mediation, Bryce," the judge reminded him. "Let's leave the legalese outside the door and let the people involved speak for themselves, as much as possible. We are here to reach an amicable agreement, after all." He smiled at Sam. "And in this forum, everybody, I prefer to be called Horace."

I like him, thought Roz.

As though sensing her approval, he smiled at her. "Given the unique nature of these circumstances, all parties, including my own department, are seeking a quick resolution, which is why proceedings have been expedited."

Horace sat back and selected a mint from the bowl

in front of him. "Each of you will speak, but only I—" he looked pointedly at the lawyers "—may interrupt. Ms. Valentine, we'll begin with you."

Roz opened the folder she and Jack had sat up half the night preparing. Cassie had found it this morning, and a trail of pink marker squiggled across the page. In some strange way Cassie's handiwork steadied her.

She and Jack had agreed that honesty was the best policy, so she talked frankly about the challenges of the last five weeks, then summarized their case for keeping the children—all the arguments she'd honed on Jack.

When she'd finished, she addressed Sam directly, though he wouldn't look at her. "It's tempting to let you do what you want, so you'll like me," she admitted. "But every time my resolve wavers, I hear your mum's voice in my head, telling me to get with the program. I can't pretend I don't know what they wanted for you, Sam. And it doesn't include being separated from your little brother and sister, or living away from home before you're ready." Her throat closed up.

"The bottom line is that we're doing this because we love you, Sam," Jack finished for her. "And whatever happens here won't change that."

"Lovely sentiments," said Fiona crisply. "Now let's look at the facts. May I ask some questions?"

"Of course," said Horace. He reached for another mint, tossing one across the table to Sam, who instinctively caught it and grinned.

Frowning, Fiona nodded to her lawyers. What followed was nothing less than a mauling.

Hadn't Jack promised Fee custody? In fact, hadn't he resisted even temporary guardianship?

If the kids meant so much to him, why had his visits been almost nonexistent over the previous six years?

Oh, yes, their personal tragedy. Shouldn't they have informed Mrs. Montgomery—and social services—that their baby had died of crib death while under Jack's care?

Not that anyone was intimating neglect—the autopsy had said otherwise. They simply wondered why he'd never had counseling. Ms. Valentine had needed *lots* of it.

"For God's sake, who wouldn't?" Horace growled. A pile of cellophane mint wrappings littered the desk in front of him.

"That's our point, sir."

"And a good one," Jack acknowledged. "Roz made a faster recovery than I did as a result. But I've made my peace with our son's death."

After he answered he jotted something on a piece of paper and pushed it to Roz. *Stop gnashing your teeth. Better to know everything they've got in case this goes to court.*

Looking as sane as she could manage, she wrote back, *Then I get to kill them, right?*

Jack glanced at her note and bit back a smile. It took the edge off the dread growing inside her.

"You know," said Fee tartly, "with one divorce already behind you—two in Roz's case—I don't see your remarriage as any guarantee of security."

Sam spoke for the first time. "You guys are getting remarried?" During the discussion of Thomas's death he'd been shooting them anxious glances from under his hoodie. Now he smiled at Roz. "That's gr—"

Fiona put a restraining hand on his arm. Her nails were the palest mauve, exactly the color of her lipstick. "Roz, Sam told me you hit Jack and that Liam witnessed it." Sam dropped his head in confusion. "How does that constitute good parenting?"

"It doesn't," she replied, trying to catch Sam's eye again to reassure him. "But I immediately apologized and—"

"I provoked her," said Jack.

"And what happens when the kids provoke her? Will she hit them and then immediately apologize?"

"Don't be ridiculous," said Jack. "With that single exception, Roz has never—"

Again Fee interrupted. "What about you dragging Sam home against his will? Was that good parenting?"

"Actually," Roz answered, "it was. Dirk Evans has a criminal record."

Fee didn't know that; Roz could tell by the way her eyes widened in shock. "Of course I knew the father was bad news, but—"

Her lawyer, Bryce, cut her short with professional ease. "And what about when Mr. Galloway allowed a six-year-old to attend his parents' funeral against *your* advice, Ms. Valentine? And against my client's? I understand the child became hysterical and had to be carried out of the church. Was *that* good parenting?"

"No," said Jack, "but I've learned—"

"Learned," said Bryce. "Really? Didn't your niece nearly die under your care a week ago because neither of you bothered to find out the family's medical history?"

"Jack saved Cassie's life," said Roz hotly. Under the

table his hand came down on hers, warm and encompassing.

"*We* saved her life," he corrected. "Fiona, you've made mistakes, too, but undermining each other is not the way forward. Get rid of these guys and let's talk sensibly."

Fiona stood up and nodded to her lawyers, who did the same. "Unless you're prepared to hand over the children, there's nothing further to say. For me, it comes down to this. If you two are so wonderful with Cassie and Liam, then why is their older brother supporting me?"

CHAPTER TWENTY-ONE

SAM ASKED TO STAY with Fee and, reluctantly bowing to Roz's judgment, Jack gave permission. His nephew had a hangdog expression and was obviously feeling guilty about taking sides.

Roz saw the teenager's unhappiness, too. "You'll always be able to change your mind, Sam," she told him as they left the mediation chamber. "Like Jack said, we love you."

For a moment Sam hesitated, then, shaking his head miserably, walked outside with Fee's lawyers and Judge Sawyer, who'd also despaired of making ground today.

"Go back to your hotel," he'd told Fee sternly when he'd dismissed them, "and think very seriously about the consequences of taking an adversarial approach."

As his sister-in-law passed, Jack blocked her exit. "If we can't reach an agreement here, it will go to a defended court hearing, and the decision will be taken out of our hands. Is that what you want, Fiona? Strangers deciding what's best for the kids?"

She lifted her chin. "So let me have them."

Jack shook his head.

"I'll guarantee access." She added bitterly, "*This* time we'll put the arrangement on paper."

He met her gaze squarely. "I'm sorry for going back on my word, Fiona, but we didn't have any right to make custody decisions without Roz. And at the time I didn't think I had anything to offer these kids. I do now and, more importantly, so do they."

"Sam doesn't."

"Sam was angry at us when he talked to you. For pity's sake, you must see how conflicted the poor kid is."

She avoided his gaze. "We're all conflicted, Jack."

"I know what you're feeling guilty about," Roz said quietly.

Fiona lost her poise. "I…d-don't know what you mean."

Neither did Jack. But he trusted Roz's instincts. "What is it?"

"Ju and Ants died on the way to something Fee arranged for them. Liam mentioned it once." She turned back to Fiona, and the movement released the faint scent of her apple blossom perfume. "But until today I'd never made the connection with your need for custody. You're looking to salve a guilty conscience, aren't you?"

"That's ridiculous," Fiona snapped. But her strained expression said otherwise.

Jack suddenly felt immense sympathy for her. "Fiona," he said gently, "guilt is a corrosive emotion that skews your judgment and ruins your life. Believe me, I know. After Thomas's death, I lived with it for six years."

Until Roz dragged him kicking and screaming back into life. Thank God for her. On a surge of emotion he watched his ex-wife touch his sister-in-law's hand, concern in her blue eyes.

"Come and stay with us," Roz suggested. "See for yourself how the kids are with us."

"My lawyers have advised me—"

"Screw the lawyers," Jack interjected. "We can solve this as a family."

She shook her head and her mouth set in a stubborn line. "I want my sister's children."

Jack's sympathy evaporated and he put a hand under Roz's elbow. "Then we'll see you in court."

JACK WATCHED AS Roz filled the kettle at the kitchen sink, her head bowed. Under the shiny black ponytail, her neck seemed unbearably fragile.

He came up behind her and enfolded her in his arms, resting his chin on her hair. "We need to talk about the worst-case scenario."

"If Fee wins," she said steadily, "I don't want to appeal, drag this out for months, years.... It will be too hard on them, Jack."

He'd been thinking the same thing. "She hasn't won yet."

"But she has a good case."

"Yes." Still holding her, he took the kettle out of Roz's hand and set it on the counter. "Go sit on the porch where the kids won't overhear us." Cassie and Liam were in bed, but it was safer to take no chances. "I'll finish making the drinks, then we'll talk for five minutes about losing, before strategizing for a win. Agreed?"

He could feel her shoulders relax a little. "Agreed."

When he followed ten minutes later, Roz was so still in the shadows, sitting in a cane chair, that Jack thought she must still be inside. Then Thomas's bracelet glimmered as she moved her hand.

Tea slopped out of the mugs as Jack placed them unsteadily on the table.

Roz began speaking in a rush. "Once I'm working again, I figure I should be able to save enough to go see them once a year. And if we keep this whole court thing civilized, maybe Fee will let them come to New Zealand for a holiday…in a year or two when they're older. By then I should be able to afford a bigger apartment."

"What the hell are you talking about?"

She started twisting the bracelet again, around and around her wrist. "There's no hurry to get remarried if we lose custody, is there? If you want more time to think about that kind of commitment."

His astonishment gave way to a gut swoop of fear. "Are the kids the only reason you agreed to remarry me?"

"Aren't they the reason you suggested it?"

"Hell, no!" How could she even think such a thing? His gaze fell on the bracelet. *She thinks I'm going to leave. Because that's what I do when things get bad.*

"I want to marry you because from the minute I saw you I loved you," he said passionately, "and I'll love you until the day I die."

Her eyes widened; she swallowed.

Jack caught her wrist and dropped to his knees in front of her. Under his fingers, the metal was smooth and warm from her skin. He lifted it to his lips, kissed Thomas's name, then the jumping pulse point underneath it. "In my heart, you never stopped being my wife."

"Then why," she cried, "did you give up on us?"

"Because…" he forced himself to expose his deepest shame "…because I couldn't fix it for you."

"Some things can't be fixed, Jack, and…" her hand crept back to the bracelet "…love doesn't conquer all. Our divorce proved that."

"You're right," he said simply. "It doesn't." Pulling her out of the chair, Jack took her place, then gathered her onto his lap. "My love couldn't save Thomas. Your love couldn't stop me self-destructing." His gaze stayed unwavering on hers. "But you've made me believe that love's still worth everything you have to suffer for it. And if the worst happens, and we lose custody of these kids, then I'll pay that price again, willingly. And if you want another baby, then we'll have another baby, because life with you is all about courage."

Tears filled her eyes; she buried her face in his shoulder and said in a muffled voice, "I love you so much, Jack."

He lifted her face, holding it between his hands, and his voice was unsteady as he told her, "Whatever happens with custody, I'm not going anywhere. We're getting remarried and I'm going to wake up beside you every morning for the next fifty or sixty years, until one day, Roz, you forget I ever left."

The last strain on her face relaxed into a tremulous smile. "How about I just remember you came back?"

His throat tightened. "That will work."

LIAM KNEW EXACTLY WHERE the courthouse was because his class had been on a tour there once. Molly's mum, who could type in stuff as fast as people talked, worked there part-time, and his class had been learning about how laws worked so they could make some up for the school. He'd come up with "No borrowing other people's rulers without permission."

Cassie started whining as they got to Dunlop Street, but he'd put some shortbread in his pocket. She quietened when he handed over a biscuit. He figured they had to keep moving because he didn't want to leave the babysitter locked in the bedroom for too long in case she ran out of oxygen.

He would tell the people at court to go and let her out. Maybe they'd put him in jail, but this was too important, and Liam felt very strongly that he had to go by himself to show he wasn't being made to do anything he didn't want to.

Seemed people worried about that a lot.

In the last few days he'd been asked a lot of questions 'bout stuff by strangers, and he'd answered truthfully, like Auntie Roz and Uncle Jack had told him. "I want to live here with them." He even told about the deal he'd offered Uncle Jack, to show how serious he and Cassie were about staying.

"And what did he say, son?" said Ellie Walters. She was the only one of the social services people he knew, so Liam turned to her with relief.

"He said he'd think about it, but I haven't had time to ask him since then." The way she'd looked at the others gave Liam a bad feeling in his tummy.

Yesterday he'd remembered again to ask Uncle Jack about the deal, but he'd only laughed and ruffled Liam's hair. "I'd never take your money, mate. Incidentally, I couldn't get batteries for that baseball pitching set I bought you. Is it okay if I just throw the ball to you instead?"

"Yeah!" said Liam.

On their way out he'd seen an album opened at a picture of Dad pitching to Liam in the yard. "That's my favorite," Liam had exclaimed.

"Mine, too," said Uncle Jack. "You know, the clues were always there. I just wasn't ready to see them."

"Huh?" said Liam.

"It doesn't matter. Let's play ball."

Now Liam wanted to tell those people what Uncle Jack had said about not taking the money. He'd overheard Uncle Jack say that the court made the decision about who got to take care of him and his sister, so he and Cassie had to go speak to the people there.

Cassie started whining and dragging on his hand again, and Liam gave her another biscuit. "Nearly there," he coaxed, because he could see the big redbrick building at the end of the street. As they trotted closer, a meter maid stopped him.

"Hey, there, dude. Where's your mummy?"

"In heaven."

Cassie nodded solemnly. "Heaven."

The woman looked startled. "Well, who's looking after you and your sister? You're too small to be out walking by yourself."

"I'm sorry," he said politely, tugging on Cassie's hand, "but we're not s'posed to talk to strangers."

"Little boy, wait a minute."

"Run," he whispered to Cass, and she did, shrieking with joyous terror. At the courthouse, they had to slow down because Cassie needed to plant both feet on each broad step before tackling the next one. Glancing over his shoulder, Liam saw the meter maid still watching them. With a faint frown, she started to follow.

So now he had no time to stop at the big doors leading to the dark interior, which he wanted to do, because he was a teeny bit scared.

A Maori lady in a uniform sat at a desk inside the door. She peeked at him over her reading glasses, then looked around for a grown-up. Liam stood up straighter when her attention came back to him, curious now. "Yes, young man?"

"I have to speak to somebody," he said, "about a cus…a cust…" He racked his brains. "A custard issue." *Issue* was an easier word to remember because it reminded him of a sneeze.

"I see." Wrinkles folded into deep creases at the sides of her brown eyes as she smiled. "Your name?"

"Liam Jack Galloway."

She wrote it down, then took off her glasses and regarded Cassie, who was sucking her thumb. "And who is this with you?"

Liam yanked on his sister's arm and her thumb came out of her mouth with a soft popping sound. "My witness."

FEE AND SAM WERE DRIVING to her lawyers' office when her nephew's cell phone rang.

"Tell whoever it is you can't chat now, Sam," she said impatiently. "We've got too much to do." She hoped to talk him into a haircut and some new clothes after the appointment, get rid of that neglected look that Sam seemed to think was so cool.

Over the couple of days he'd been staying in the hotel with her, she'd grown increasingly worried about him. He was sullen, uncommunicative…even depressed, a far cry from the staunch, convincing ally who'd bolstered her conviction that she was doing the right thing in pursuing custody.

Last night she'd steeled herself to ask him if there was something he'd like to tell her. It was the closest she could come to asking if he'd had a change of heart, because the thought of not getting the children was too painful to contemplate.

"No," he'd snapped, and gone back to watching TV. A few minutes later he'd added moodily, "What good would it do now, anyway? Roz and Jack hate me."

He seemed to have tuned out what Fee grudgingly admitted was a surprising maturity on his guardians' part in handling his defection. But it wasn't in her interests to remind him, and self-preservation won. Although her conscience still prickled her.

In the passenger seat beside her now, Sam jerked upright and gripped his cell phone. "You're *where?* Yeah, sure I'll come get you. Um…" Out of the corner of her eye she saw him dart her a worried glance. "I'll get there as soon as I can."

Fee shifted down a gear as the city traffic started to thicken. "Is something wrong?"

"Yeah. A friend of mine's got an emergency and I said I'd help him out. Can you drop me at Main Street as you drive past?"

She tried to keep the exasperation out of her voice. "Sam, we're due at the lawyers for an important meeting! Ring him back and tell him you can't make it."

"I don't care about the lawyers! Lia...my friend needs me."

Fee wasn't the wife of a barrister for nothing and she had the truth out of him in five minutes. Liam and Cassie had run away from their babysitter and were at the courthouse. Liam had called Sam in a naive belief that their big brother could prevent Roz and Jack from finding out. Fee took great pleasure in calling them at *their* lawyer's office and telling them to go rescue their elderly babysitter while she collected the children with Sam.

"This is one more example," she fumed thirty minutes later as she buckled the young offenders into the backseat, "of totally inadequate supervision."

Cassie growled.

"I'm never gonna tell you anything again, Sam," Liam said hotly to the back of his brother's head. "You're the meanest, horrible-ist bum-bum and I hate you!"

Sam said nothing and, glancing up, Fee saw he was hunched in the front passenger seat. "Liam, don't talk to your brother like that. He's doing what he thinks is best."

"So was we," Liam said sullenly. "We want to stay with Auntie Roz and Uncle Jack, but no one will listen to us 'cause we're little."

In the process of getting into the driver's seat, Fee bumped her head when she raised it in shock. "Oh, my God, they've turned you against me."

"No, they haven't!" Sam snapped. "They always say nice things about you...and Roz makes us phone you even when we don't want to. You're the one who made a war out of this." His Adam's apple bobbed as he swallowed. "And now I can never go home."

Fee took her hand off the ignition key. "Is that how you really feel?"

Liam misinterpreted her. "We do want to talk to you sometimes," he said, "only not when you're trying to make us do stuff we don't want to—like you did when we were on holiday. Mum said you can't help it and—"

"Shut up, Liam," Sam interrupted savagely. "You're hurting her feelings."

"Sorry, Auntie Fee," Liam mumbled.

She made a massive effort and smiled. Because Julia was wrong. Fee could help it. She started the car.

"Where are we going?" Liam asked warily. "To your hotel?"

"No," said Fee. "I'm taking you home."

Liam and Cassie tumbled out of the car as soon as she parked in the driveway, but Sam balked when she told him to join them. "What will I say to Jack and Roz?"

"'Sorry' is always a good start. Then tell them you'll accept an extension of the parenting order. And that I'm letting them have custody."

"Will you come in with me?"

I've done enough damage. "Darling, some things a man has to do on his own, and making amends is one of them. But they love you. It'll be fine."

To her surprise, he leaned over and gave her a fierce hug. "Thank you."

Fee fumbled for her sunglasses, her composure starting to unravel. "All right, off you go."

Still, she waited until the front door opened. Jack caught the younger ones up in his arms, and she could hear him doing the relieved rant of a father. Climbing up on the porch, Sam started to stammer something about giving up smoking, and Roz cut him off with a fierce hug.

"So," said Fee, "that's that." She started the engine and began backing down the drive, her eyes so full of tears she nearly ran Jack over when he suddenly blocked her route. Slamming on the brakes, she steeled herself for a verbal onslaught as he came around to the driver's window.

His eyes were moist. "Thank you."

"I'm sorry," she croaked, "that it ever came to this. I won't bother you again."

He reached through the open window and took her car keys. "You're not leaving, Fiona. You're staying with us until you fly home, and while you're here we're going to organize when your family next sees the kids."

She couldn't bear his kindness. "Jack, you don't understand. Their death *was* my fault."

Instead of stepping back in horror, he opened her door and guided her out of the car with a firm hand under her elbow. "I doubt that, but talk to me."

"I kept telling them that they should go out for a romantic dinner and spend some time on their own.... I all but pushed them out the door. 'Go and have a good time,' I said, 'and I'll look after the children.'" Her voice dropped to a whisper. "It was the last thing I said to them. 'I'll look after the children.'" Blindly, she groped for the door handle, and instead found herself enfolded in her brother-in-law's arms.

He held her very tightly, but his voice was calm and sure. "It's only takeaways for dinner tonight," he said, "but I know you won't mind the informality—being family."

CHAPTER TWENTY-TWO

ROZ WOKE FROM a lovely dream about Thomas, and thought she was still in one. Jack lay beside her, his shoulder a broad cliff in the dark, rising and falling with his deep, even breathing.

In the hall a night-light glowed a pale blue, and downstairs she could hear the sporadic hum of the refrigerator, the fall of ice in the icemaker. Beside the bed, the cat stopped licking its paws and stared at her for a moment before returning to the task.

It was instinctive to turn, still half-asleep, and slide her hand down the slope of Jack's shoulder and back lower to the swell of tight buttock. *Mine.*

Waking, he flung a protective arm across her upper body. "I love you," said her new husband.

Burying her nose in his shoulder, Roz breathed in the clean scent of him and the fainter saltiness of hot sex and crisp, cool cotton. "'Behold, thou art fair, my beloved,'" she murmured, "'yea, pleasant: also our bed is green. The beams of our house are cedar, and our rafters of fir.'"

"Acutally," Jack said sleepily, "the beams are kauri and the rafters are macrocarpa."

Roz grinned. "'For, lo,'" she continued, "'the winter is past, the rain is over and gone.'" Now she knew why the verse had come into her head. Because of its joy. "'The flowers appear on the earth, the time of the singing of birds is come, and the voice of the turtle is heard in our land.'"

There was a croak from under the bed and they both laughed. "That bloody frog," said Jack. Wide-awake now, he asked curiously, "What was that?"

"Song of Solomon. I learned it by heart when I was twelve for a bible class speech competition. It was *so* romantic... 'Many waters cannot quench love, neither can the floods drown it: if a man would give all the substance of his house for love, it would utterly be condemned.'"

"I would give all for love," said Jack, "particularly this house."

"Quit teasing your wife." Roz picked up his hand and kissed the warm knuckles, suddenly deeply, intensely grateful. "'Set me as a seal upon thine heart,'" she finished, "'for love is strong as death.'"

Jack was silent a moment, then cradled her against his chest. "No," he corrected gently. "Stronger."

Twelve months later

IT WAS CHRISTMAS EVE and the arrival hall at Auckland International Airport was packed. People jostled and queued and griped amid the decorations and tinny carols played over the loudspeaker between flight announcements.

It was also raining as Jack strode out of the entrance's double doors with his suitcase. "Guess we won't be having Christmas at the beach this year," said his companion.

They'd sat next to each other in business class on the flight home from Tokyo, and Jack wished he'd lost Damien Stanhope in customs because the guy was a card-carrying grinch.

"Actually, I will be at the beach," he replied. "We're driving down to Beacon Bay to spend Christmas with my foster brother and his family."

Damien shuddered. "So you've still got a three-hour drive ahead of you. Rather you than me."

The two men moved out of the human tide, staying under the shelter of the building's overhang.

"Well, I guess this is where we part ways," said Jack. "Merry Christmas."

They shook hands. "Don't talk to me about Christmas," Damien started, then his eyes fixed on something over Jack's shoulder. "Bloody hell, will you look at that menagerie!"

Jack turned and grinned.

Six months pregnant, Roz—his wife of seven months—came toward him pushing Cassie in a luggage trolley. Cass was dressed like a Christmas fairy and held a sign: Welcome Home, Uncle Jack. Where's My Present? Beside her Liam hung on to the trolley, being dragged along on his skateboard.

Sam walked behind, in full Goth regalia wearing a Christmas tree ornament in his left ear and bright red nail polish. He was hand in hand with a very pretty girl also dressed all in black.

Jack saw a condom talk looming in his near future, but even that couldn't stop a surge of pure unadulterated happiness. "That's not a menagerie," he said, "that's my family."

* * * * *

Here is a sneak preview of
A STONE CREEK CHRISTMAS,
the latest in Linda Lael Miller's acclaimed
MᴄKETTRICK *series.*

A lonely horse brought vet Olivia O'Ballivan to
Tanner Quinn's farm, but it's the rancher's love
that might cause her to stay.

A STONE CREEK CHRISTMAS
Available December 2008
from Silhouette Special Edition

Tanner heard the rig roll in around sunset. Smiling, he wandered to the window. Watched as Olivia O'Ballivan climbed out of her Suburban, flung one defiant glance toward the house and started for the barn, the golden retriever trotting along behind her.

Taking his coat and hat down from the peg next to the back door, he put them on and went outside. He was used to being alone, even liked it, but keeping company with Doc O'Ballivan, bristly though she sometimes was, would provide a welcome diversion.

He gave her time to reach the horse Butterpie's stall, then walked into the barn.

The golden retriever came to greet him, all wagging tail and melting brown eyes, and he bent to stroke her soft, sturdy back. "Hey, there, dog," he said.

Sure enough, Olivia was in the stall, brushing Butterpie down and talking to her in a soft, soothing voice that touched something private inside Tanner and made him want to turn on one heel and beat it back to the house.

He'd be damned if he'd do it, though.

This was *his* ranch, *his* barn. Well-intentioned as she was, *Olivia* was the trespasser here, not him.

"She's still very upset," Olivia told him, without turning to look at him or slowing down with the brush.

Shiloh, always an easy horse to get along with, stood contentedly in his own stall, munching away on the feed Tanner had given him earlier. Butterpie, he noted, hadn't touched her supper as far as he could tell.

"Do you know anything at all about horses, Mr. Quinn?" Olivia asked.

He leaned against the stall door, the way he had the day before, and grinned. He'd practically been raised on horseback; he and Tessa had grown up on their grandmother's farm in the Texas hill country, after their folks divorced and went their separate ways, both of them too busy to bother with a couple of kids. "A few things," he said. "And I mean to call you Olivia, so you might as well return the favor and address me by my first name."

He watched as she took that in, dealt with it, decided on an approach. He'd have to wait and see what that turned out to be, but he didn't mind. It was a pleasure just watching Olivia O'Ballivan grooming a horse.

"All right, *Tanner,*" she said. "This barn is a disgrace. When are you going to have the roof fixed? If it snows again, the hay will get wet and probably mold…"

He chuckled, shifted a little. He'd have a crew out there the following Monday morning to replace the roof and shore up the walls—he'd made the arrangements over a week before—but he felt no particular compunction to explain that. He was enjoying her ire too much; it made her color rise and her hair fly when she turned her head, and the faster breathing made her perfect breasts go up and down in an enticing rhythm. "What makes you so sure I'm a greenhorn?" he asked mildly, still leaning on the gate.

At last she looked straight at him, but she didn't move from Butterpie's side. "Your hat, your boots—that fancy red truck you drive. I'll bet it's customized."

Tanner grinned. Adjusted his hat. "Are you telling me real cowboys don't drive red trucks?"

"There are lots of trucks around here," she said. "Some of them are red, and some of them are new. And *all* of them are splattered with mud or manure or both."

"Maybe I ought to put in a car wash, then," he teased. "Sounds like there's a market for one. Might be a good investment."

She softened, though not significantly, and spared him a cautious half smile, full of questions she probably wouldn't ask. "There's a good car wash in Indian Rock," she informed him. "People go there. It's only forty miles."

"Oh," he said with just a hint of mockery. "*Only* forty miles. Well, then. Guess I'd better dirty up my truck if I want to be taken seriously in these here parts. Scuff up my boots a bit, too, and maybe stomp on my hat a couple of times."

Her cheeks went a fetching shade of pink. "You are twisting what I said," she told him, brushing Butterpie again, her touch gentle but sure. "I meant…"

Tanner envied that little horse. Wished he had a furry hide, so he'd need brushing, too.

"You *meant* that I'm not a real cowboy," he said. "And you could be right. I've spent a lot of time on construction sites over the last few years, or in meetings where a hat and boots wouldn't be appropriate. Instead of digging out my old gear, once I decided to take this job, I just bought new."

"I bet you don't even *have* any old gear," she challenged, but she was smiling, albeit cautiously, as though she might withdraw into a disapproving frown at any second.

He took off his hat, extended it to her. "Here," he teased. "Rub that around in the muck until it suits you."

She laughed, and the sound—well, it caused a powerful and wholly unexpected shift inside him. Scared the hell out of him and, paradoxically, made him yearn to hear it again.

* * * * *

Discover how this rugged rancher's wanderlust is tamed in time for a merry Christmas, in A STONE CREEK CHRISTMAS. In stores December 2008.

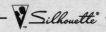
Silhouette®

SPECIAL EDITION™

**FROM *NEW YORK TIMES*
BESTSELLING AUTHOR**

LINDA LAEL MILLER

A STONE CREEK CHRISTMAS

Veterinarian Olivia O'Ballivan finds the animals
in Stone Creek playing Cupid between her and
Tanner Quinn. Even Tanner's daughter, Sophie,
is eager to play matchmaker. With everyone
conspiring against them and the holiday season
fast approaching, Tanner and Olivia may just get
everything they want for Christmas after all!

*Available December 2008
wherever books are sold.*

Visit Silhouette Books at www.eHarlequin.com LLMNYTBPA

HARLEQUIN Romance

Marry-Me Christmas

by *USA TODAY* bestselling author

SHIRLEY JUMP

A *Bride* FOR ALL *Seasons*

Ruthless and successful journalist Flynn never mixes business with pleasure. But when he's sent to write a scathing review of Samantha's bakery, her beauty and innocence catches him off guard. Has this small-town girl unlocked the city slicker's heart?

Available December 2008.

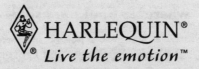

HARLEQUIN®
Live the emotion™

www.eHarlequin.com   HR17557

REQUEST YOUR FREE BOOKS!

2 FREE NOVELS PLUS 2 FREE GIFTS!

HARLEQUIN®

Super Romance®

Exciting, emotional, unexpected!

YES! Please send me 2 FREE Harlequin Superromance® novels and my 2 FREE gifts (gifts are worth about $10). After receiving them, if I don't wish to receive any more books, I can return the shipping statement marked "cancel." If I don't cancel, I will receive 6 brand-new novels every month and be billed just $4.69 per book in the U.S. or $5.24 per book in Canada, plus 25¢ shipping and handling per book and applicable taxes, if any*. That's a savings of close to 15% off the cover price! I understand that accepting the 2 free books and gifts places me under no obligation to buy anything. I can always return a shipment and cancel at any time. Even if I never buy another book from Harlequin, the two free books and gifts are mine to keep forever.

135 HDN EEX7   336 HDN EEYK

Name	(PLEASE PRINT)	
Address		Apt. #
City	State/Prov.	Zip/Postal Code

Signature (if under 18, a parent or guardian must sign)

Mail to the **Harlequin Reader Service:**
IN U.S.A.: P.O. Box 1867, Buffalo, NY 14240-1867
IN CANADA: P.O. Box 609, Fort Erie, Ontario L2A 5X3

Not valid to current subscribers of Harlequin Superromance books.

Want to try two free books from another line?
Call 1-800-873-8635 or visit www.morefreebooks.com.

* Terms and prices subject to change without notice. N.Y. residents add applicable sales tax. Canadian residents will be charged applicable provincial taxes and GST. Offer not valid in Quebec. This offer is limited to one order per household. All orders subject to approval. Credit or debit balances in a customer's account(s) may be offset by any other outstanding balance owed by or to the customer. Please allow 4 to 6 weeks for delivery. Offer available while quantities last.

Your Privacy: Harlequin is committed to protecting your privacy. Our Privacy Policy is available online at www.eHarlequin.com or upon request from the Reader Service. From time to time we make our lists of customers available to reputable third parties who may have a product or service of interest to you. If you would prefer we not share your name and address, please check here. ☐

HSR08R

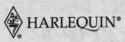

HARLEQUIN®

American ★ Romance®

HOLLY JACOBS
Once Upon a Christmas

Daniel McLean is thrilled to learn he
may be the father of Michelle Hamilton's
nephew. When Daniel starts to spend
time with Brandon and help her organize
Erie Elementary's big Christmas Fair, the
three discover a paternity test won't make
them a family, but the love they discover
just might....

**Available December 2008
wherever books are sold.**

LOVE, HOME & HAPPINESS

www.eHarlequin.com   HAR75242

HARLEQUIN
Super Romance®

COMING NEXT MONTH

#1530 A MAN TO RELY ON • Cindi Myers
Going Back

Scandal seems to follow Marisol Luna. And this trip home is no exception.
She's not staying long in this town that can't forget who she was. Then she
falls for Scott Redmond. Suddenly he's making her forget the gossip and
rethink her exit plan.

#1531 NO PLACE LIKE HOME • Margaret Watson
The McInnes Triplets

All Bree McInnes has to do is make it through the summer without anyone
discovering her secrets. But keeping a low profile turns out to be harder than
the single mom thought—especially when her sexy professor-boss begins to
fall in love. With her!

#1532 HIS ONLY DEFENSE • Carolyn McSparren
Count on a Cop

Cop rule number one: don't fall in love with a perp. Too bad Liz Gibson forgot
that one. Except unlike everybody else, she doesn't believe Jud Slaughter
killed his wife. Now she has to prove his innocence or lose him forever.

#1533 FOR THE SAKE OF THE CHILDREN • Cynthia Reese
You, Me & the Kids

Dana Wilson is *exactly* what Lissa thinks her single father needs. Dana is a
single mom *and* the new school nurse. Lissa's dad, Patrick Connor, is chair of
the board of education! Perfect? Well, there may be a few wrinkles that need
ironing out....

#1534 THE SON BETWEEN THEM • Molly O'Keefe
A Little Secret

Samantha Riggins keeps pulling J. D. Kronos back. With her he is a better
man and can forget his P.I. world. But when he discovers the secret she's been
hiding, nothing is the same. And now J.D. must choose between his former
life and a new one with Samantha.

#1535 MEANT FOR EACH OTHER • Lee Duran
Everlasting Love

Since the moment they met, Frankie has loved Johnny Davis. Yet their love
hasn't always been enough to make things work. Then Johnny is injured and
needs her. As she rushes to his side, Frankie discovers the true value of being
meant for each other.

Khalil Gibran

EL PROFETA

Copyright © EDIMAT LIBROS, S. A.
C/ Primavera, 35
Polígono Industrial El Malvar
28500 Arganda del Rey
MADRID-ESPAÑA
www.edimat.es

ISBN: 978-84-9764-346-7
Depósito legal: CO-833-2007

Colección: Clásicos de la literatura
Título: El Profeta
Autor: Khalil Gibran
Introducción: Amalia Navarro Mateo
Diseño de cubierta: Juan Manuel Domínguez
Impreso en: Taller de libros, S.L.

IMPRESO EN ESPAÑA – *PRINTED IN SPAIN*

KHALIL GIBRAN

EL PROFETA

Por Amalia Navarro Mateo

PRÓLOGO

I

El Líbano ha sido llamado con razón «Puerta de Oriente». Es una tierra en la que el espiritualismo al que fuerza la reseca soledad del desierto se mezcla con el humanismo indolentemente vitalista al que impele el azul intenso del Mediterráneo. Con sus famosos cedros —símbolo en el centro de la bandera nacional—, fenicios, griegos y romanos construyeron sus naves, los egipcios fabricaron sus sarcófagos y todos los pueblos de los alrededores labraron las vigas de sus templos, y dejaron a cambio las huellas de sus raíces impregnadas de sus concepciones particulares del hombre y del mundo. Cruce, pues, de culturas y, en consecuencia, tierra fecunda para que crezca la tolerancia, el respeto hacia lo que merece ser conservado y ese sano escepticismo liberador que permite romper con la cerrazón de la creencia presuntamente inamovible y abrir de par en par todos los poros de la sensibilidad a la naturaleza y a los afectos humanos.

Gibran Khalil Gibran nació el 6 de diciembre de 1883 en Bcherri, la ciudad típicamente libanesa que se levanta sobre una pequeña meseta, junto a uno de los acantilados de Wadi-Quadisha (Valle Sagrado). Durante dos décadas atrás, el país había obtenido una cierta autonomía, apuntalada en buena medida por su larga tradición católica maronita, que le había mantenido aislado durante siglos frente al dominio oscurantista y cerril del imperio turco. Los años de la infancia de Gibran son los mismos en que surge una nueva clase dirigente de influencia francesa, proyectada hacia Europa, mediadora comercial e intelectual entre el sector sometido a la opresión turca y las nuevas corrientes de opinión que soplan hacia el Mediterráneo, desde Londres, Viena o París.

Gibran, nieto de un sacerdote maronita, hijo de un pequeño propietario de ganado, es un símbolo vivo de ese cruce de culturas que es su país de origen. Con sólo trece años marcha con su madre y sus hermanos a Boston, atraídos por las oportunidades que parece ofrecer el Nuevo Mundo, mientras su padre permanece en el Líbano, manteniendo su pobre propiedad. El adolescente Gibran entra en una escuela privada donde se educan americanos de adopción procedentes de diversas naciones. Más tarde, por consejo de su hermanastro, regresa a Beirut, donde se matricula en la Escuela Maronita para estudiar árabe y francés. Durante las vacaciones, redescubre con su padre las montañas, los bosquecillos umbríos, las venerables ruinas que dejara la antigüedad y los parajes pedregosos de su tierra natal. En el abandonado monasterio de Mar-Sarkis, su espíritu ya cultivado despierta a una intensa sensibilidad sazonada de sabiduría popular que, acrisolada tras siglos de cultura, se halla impregnada de un naturalismo soberbio y triunfante. Nuestro autor sueña, empero, con volver a América, etapa imprescindible para conseguir fama y dinero, y poder regresar definitivamente al Líbano.

Mas a su retorno a América, la desgracia, revestida de enfermedad incurable, se cierne sobre su madre y sus hermanos. Con su hermana superviviente, Mariana, trata de abrirse camino. Se siente responsable del sacrificio de su familia para que él triunfara en el difícil mundo del arte. A la sombra de los rascacielos americanos —indignos sustitutos de los milenarios cedros de su patria—, empieza a escribir para los periódicos árabes de Nueva York. Simultanea la pluma con los pinceles, y en ambas artes su exquisita sensibilidad pugna por superar una técnica todavía no dominada. En los albores de su producción pictórica, expone sus obras en un estudio de Boston, pero un voraz incendio arrasa su colección, y le niega al artista la gloria y el beneficio. Años después, Gibran se alegraría del accidente que puso fin a su etapa todavía inmadura, lo que le permitiría mejorar una obra pictórica que hoy se halla diseminada por todo Oriente Medio, Europa y América.

Breves libros, poemas y artículos en árabe marcan el inicio de su carrera literaria. Fue en esta época cuando conoció a Mary Haskell, mujer de extraordinaria sensibilidad, que supo intuir el genio de Gibran; le animó a que estudiara en el extranjero y a que escribiera en inglés, tras dominar mejor este idioma, para llegar a un público más numeroso. De 1908 a 1910 estudia arte en París, luego regresa a Boston y finalmente se instala en Nueva York. Treinta y cinco años tiene cuando resume sus pensamientos y su filosofía en *La Procesión,* escrita en forma de versos árabes. Dos años después, da a conocer su obra más madura: *El Profeta,* convertido en «best-seller» internacional durante cuarenta años. Las opiniones de los críticos son contradictorias. Mientras unos consideran sus pensamientos «nocivos, revolucionarios y peligrosos para las mentes juveniles», otros juzgan que en ellos «coexisten resonancias de Jesucristo y de los Evangelios».

Gibran, que nunca había sido fuerte ni física ni psíquicamente, se halló siempre expuesto con facilidad al dolor desde su más temprana niñez. Su gigantismo se debe, pues, al esfuerzo sobrehumano de su voluntad, empeñada en una actividad casi compulsiva, por depurar técnicas, combinar estilos, dominar idiomas y servir de vehículo de emociones universales entre pueblos de distintas culturas. Durante los cinco años que siguieron a la publicación de *El Profeta,* Gibran alcanza el pináculo de su fama y de su productividad. Su obra es conocida tanto en el mundo árabe como en los sectores más cultos de habla inglesa. *El Loco* había sido precisamente su primer libro en esta lengua. Gibran ponía en boca de un demente una serie de lúcidos discursos que recuerdan los del Zaratustra nietzscheano. *La Procesión,* su obra principal de poesía arábiga, es un diálogo entre un sabio y un joven, en el que uno expresa su irritación ante la vida, el mal y la represión, y acusa al hombre de ser una simple marioneta manejada por la ambición (es el aspecto crítico y negativo del poema), y el otro alaba la vida sencilla del campesino, en la que no existen dolores, castigos ni opresiones.

La Tempestad, aparecida en 1920, es una obra con ecos de Valéry y de Nietzsche, en la que se ensalza a los fuertes y se ofrecen técnicas para endurecer la voluntad de los débiles. *El Precursor,* editada el mismo año, es el libro que Gibran dedicó a exponer su antidogmatismo, y a ridiculizar a los que se creen en posesión de una única verdad. Tres años más tarde, nuestro autor da a conocer la obra en la que había estado trabajando durante largo tiempo: *El Profeta*. El amor, el matrimonio, la ambición de poder y de dinero son los temas fundamentales que Gibran desarrolla en este libro, traducido a más de veinte idiomas. Su obra editada a título póstumo es *El jardín del profeta* (1933), y en ella describe nuestro autor la relación íntima entre el hombre y la naturaleza. Hacia el fin de su vida, Gibran escribió *Jesús, el Hijo del Hombre,* interpretación muy personal de la figura de Cristo, presentado como el hombre que vivió plenamente la vida con todo lo que ella contiene de dolores y alegrías. Pese a que el autor niega en ella la divinidad de Cristo, Arnold Bennett señaló que los árabes deberían sentirse orgullosos de que Gibran hiciera recordar la Torah, los salmos y las enseñanzas de Jesús al pueblo materialista de los Estados Unidos.

Aquejado de una terrible enfermedad, Gibran se esfuerza en donar a la humanidad lo mejor de sí mismo, y en cristianizarlo en literatura y en pintura. El 9 de abril de 1931, un amigo le encuentra sumido en el dolor y pálido por la enfermedad, pese a que continúa sonriendo con valentía. Se niega a que le lleven a un hospital; quiere vivir sus últimos días entre sus dibujos y los esbozos de sus obras. Al día siguiente, muere en el hospital neoyorquino de San Vicente. Sólo tiene cuarenta y ocho años de edad; su período de madurez se trunca inexorablemente, en un momento en que tanto cabía esperar de su talento artístico.

Tras haber sido honrados sus restos en Estados Unidos, el cadáver de Gibran, acompañado de su fiel hermana Mariana, es transportado a su tierra natal en el barco «Providence», envuelto en la banderas norteamericana y libanesa. Nunca el pueblo de Beirut había presenciado una congregación tan numerosa de personas, apiñadas para recibir el cortejo fúnebre. El artista pertenecía al pueblo, y éste se volcó para recibir a quien consideraba su poeta nacional, por encima de todo su cosmopolitismo. Sus restos descansan en la capilla de piedra del monasterio de Mar-Sarkis, donde Gibran había querido morar el resto de su vida. Su buena amiga Mary Haskell envió allí una buena parte de la producción del escritor y pintor, así como el mobiliario de su estudio, para formar con todo ello un museo donde se rindieran honores perpetuos a su genio y a su personalidad indiscutibles. Hoy en día, su tumba es lugar de peregrinación de todos los que aún creen posible la realización de la utopía de una sociedad pacífica e idílica, plena de amor y transida de una perpetua felicidad.

II

El Profeta es, en realidad, un enorme poema; un poema intemporal y eterno pleno de una sabiduría que resiste el paso de los siglos y las barreras lingüísticas y culturales. Leyéndolo podemos estar en condiciones de rebatir cualquier tipo de relativismo. El lenguaje usado por Gibran, pese a tener evidentes resonancias árabes, es el lenguaje del Hombre, con mayúscula y sin adjetivos. ¿Debe a esto su aceptación a un tiempo por el ajetreado neoyorquino, el campesino libanés y por esa nueva «clase social» que es la juventud de hoy, cuya sensibilidad pacifista y planetaria tanto se acomoda a la expresada por Gibran?

Obra de madurez, pero pletórica de fuerza y de energía: imaginativa y realista, poética y práctica, *El Profeta* es la cristalización de las experiencias vitales de un hombre que llegó a ser ciudadano del mundo. G. Kheirallah, traductor de este libro al inglés, emitió el siguiente juicio: «El poema es la autobiografía inconsciente de Gibran: Gibran el sabio, suavizado por los años, y Gibran el rebelde, quien vino a creer en la Unidad y la Universalidad de toda existencia y quien anheló la libertad simple e impersonal, difundida armoniosamente en todas las cosas.»

Gibran sigue aquí una técnica muy conocida en la historia de la literatura universal: proyectar sus enseñanzas vitales en la persona de un profeta «elegido y bien amado». ¿No es este el juego de Nietzsche hablando por boca del legendario Zaratustra? ¿No se oculta Platón tras la máscara de Sócrates, el maestro divinizado por la autoinmolación de su vida?

El poema se inicia con una metáfora también universal: la del hombre que tiene que emprender un viaje por mar hacia su isla natal —símbolo de la hora de la muerte, retorno a los orígenes—. Hasta los dolores sufridos en la ciudad de Orfalese se han vinculado tanto a la persona del profeta que éste no puede emprender el viaje sin aflicción. Es la resistencia a desasirse de lo habitual y cotidiano lo que se enfrenta a la llamada irresistible del mar sin orillas.

De los campos cercanos a la costa acuden hombres a despedir a Almustafá, y éste se ve obligado a transmitirles el saber adquirido tras muchos días de silencio y soledad. A la manera de Cristo en la última cena con sus discípulos, el profeta siente la necesidad de comunicar sus consignas definitivas, de legar el testamento de sus enseñanzas. Los habitantes de Orfalese

11

ruegan a Almustafá que se quede con ellos. Él ha sido la luz de sus vidas y el objeto de su más entrañable cariño. Nada han expresado hasta este momento, pero «el amor no conoce su hondura hasta el instante de la separación».

Almitra, la profetisa que primero creyó en Almustafá, le pide que comunique a los hombres congregados en la plaza «lo que le ha sido mostrado entre el nacimiento y la muerte». Ella es la que abre el círculo de las preguntas al pedir al maestro que hable sobre el amor y el matrimonio. Acto seguido, los presentes interrogan al profeta sobre los niños, el dar, el comer y beber, el trabajo, la alegría y la tristeza, las casas, el vestir, el comprar y el vender, el crimen y el castigo, las leyes vigentes, la libertad, la razón y la pasión, el dolor, el conocimiento interior, el enseñar, la amistad, el hablar, el tiempo, lo bueno y lo malo, el orar, el placer, la belleza, la religión y, por último, la muerte. Éstos son los temas en torno a los cuales se articula la predicación de Almustafá. Cada uno de ellos constituye una breve pero enjundiosa consideración que divide las diferentes partes del poema. No deja de ser significativo que el poeta empiece hablando del amor y termine hablando de la muerte.

Se trata, en suma, de interrogantes, de problemas que inquietan al hombre desde que éste fue capaz de reflexionar. El lector se extrañará quizá de que entre estos temas eternos no figure el problema de Dios. Gibran se refiere a la divinidad sólo de pasada y siguiendo la indicación que hizo en otro de sus libros: «Sería más prudente no hablar tanto de Dios, a quien no podemos comprender, y pensar más en nosotros, a quienes sí podemos comprender.»

En todo caso, el Dios de Gibran se parece mucho más al de ese otro gran poeta oriental que es Tagore, que al Dios de los teólogos y de los metafísicos. La religión se naturaliza aquí, pierde su carácter trascendente, pasa de ser una actividad específicamente separada de la vida cotidiana para identificarse con el trabajo, el descanso y los sentimientos más humanos. «Vuestra vida de todos los días es vuestro templo y vuestra religión», dice el profeta.

Respecto a Dios, éste no es objeto de especulación teórica, ni se halla ubicado en un mundo inaccesible para el hombre. Si queremos hablar en términos filosóficos, habría que decir que Gibran está más cerca de los inmanentistas que de quienes subrayan el carácter trascendente de la divinidad y se esfuerzan en separar a ésta del mundo. Nuestro autor es claro en este sentido: «Si llegáis a conocer a Dios, no os convirtáis en explicadores de enigmas. Mirad más bien a vuestro alrededor y lo veréis jugando con vuestros hijos. Y mirad hacia lo alto; lo veréis caminando en la nube, desplegando sus brazos en el rayo y descendiendo en la lluvia. Lo veréis sintiendo en las flores y elevándose luego para agitar sus manos desde los árboles.» ¡Cuántas frases similares a ésta podríamos encontrar en Tagore!

En pleno siglo XII el gran filósofo árabe Averroes escribió que un creyente ingenuo diría: «Dios está en el cielo.» Y añadió: «Un observador agudo, sabiendo que Dios no puede ser representado en el espacio como una entidad física, diría: "Dios está en todas partes y no solamente en el cielo."» En suma, hay una línea tradicional árabe para la que «el espacio y la materia están en Dios»; que diviniza al hombre, que utiliza el concepto ancestral de divinidad para elevar al ser humano y rechaza esa otra corriente que le convierte en mero esclavo de un despótico señor. De este modo, para Gibran, es Dios quien ora a través de los labios del hombre, quien quiere a través de nuestra voluntad... En última instancia, Dios se identifica con lo mejor del hombre, y su templo es el templo invisible que abarca a la naturaleza entera.

En *El jardín del profeta* —obra que en cierto modo es una continuación de la que ahora prologo—, dice Gibran: «Piensa ahora, amado mío, en un corazón que contenga a todos los corazones, en un amor que rodee a todos los amores, en un amor que rodee a todos los amores, en un espíritu que contenga a todos los espíritus, en una voz que envuelva a todas las voces y en un silencio más profundo e intemporal que todos los silencios.» ¿No quiere decir esto sino que Dios es la comunidad de todos los seres humanos, por encima de las diferencias religiosas y culturales que se empeñan en trazar barreras en el seno de lo que es uno e indivisible?

Paralelamente a este esfuerzo por introducir la idea de Dios en el plano de una naturaleza infinitamente plural y cambiante, se halla la divinización de la Vida —así, con mayúsculas—, concebida como una fuerza expansiva que supera la limitación de sus manifestaciones en individualidades concretas. En este tema, Gibran ofrece resonancias nietzscheanas. Su postura resulta especialmente clara cuando habla de los hijos: «Vuestros hijos no son vuestros hijos. Son los hijos y las hijas de la Vida, deseosa de perpetuarse.» Y cuando habla de la comida y de la bebida, observe el lector con qué delicadeza trata la cuestión del sacrificio de animales e incluso de frutos para que sirvan de alimento al hombre. Lo ideal para el profeta sería que el hombre se alimentara de la luz, como las plantas en el aire. Pero, ya que esto no es posible, aconseja que «nuestra mesa sea un altar en el que lo limpio y lo inocente, el mar y la pradera, sean sacrificados a aquello que es más limpio y aún inocente en el hombre».

Como resultado de este pensamiento, el saber acerca del hombre, en orden a su dignificación y exaltación, ocupa el primer lugar de las reflexiones del profeta. Ante todo, este conocimiento es —siguiendo la máxima del oráculo de Delfos que Sócrates hizo suya— autoconocimiento. «Conócete a ti mismo» representa el primer imperativo. El pedagogo puede ofrecer la fe que tiene en su sabiduría y el afecto que profesa al discípulo. Igualmente, el astrónomo, el músico y el matemático pueden hablar de la forma como entienden sus respectivos objetos de conocimiento; pero su misión no tiene otro sentido que el de enseñar a los demás a pensar, a oír, a medir y, en una palabra, a sentir por sí mismos. En último término, cada individuo debe «estar solo en su comprensión de Dios y en su conocimiento de la tierra». Gibran hace, pues, hincapié en la importancia radical del conocimiento interior.

Ahora bien, esta vía interiorista, que llega a Gibran desde Platón a través del misticismo naturalista de Avicena, y que genera el auténtico conocimiento, no desemboca en un individualismo. Como «el yo es un mar inconmensurable», el sujeto que se autoconoce descubre el valor de su perspectiva, pero a la vez atisba la pluriformidad del espíritu, de un espíritu que es «peregrino de todas las sendas», que «se despliega como un loto de pétalos innumerables».

Al igual también que Nietzsche, y como todos los místicos, Gibran desconfía de la palabra que puede matar el espíritu. Y es que el hombre recurre al lenguaje cuando deja de estar en paz con las vivencias e ideas que acuden a él en el silencio de la soledad. El miedo a un yo empobrecido y raquítico que tal vez se nos revela en medio de la soledad puede impedirnos el hablar con otros como forma de escapar de nuestra más íntima realidad. El lenguaje sólo adquiere un valor cuando es palabra entre amigos y es el espíritu el que mueve los labios de ambos y guía sus lenguas.

Nadie sino uno mismo puede pacificar su alma. La razón y la pasión humanas no son enemigas irreconciliables, sino que están llamadas a entenderse si cada una desempeña su papel. El procedimiento exclusivista de la razón torna al hombre frío y calculador; la pasión desencadenada y sin frenos que le guíen «es una llama que se quema hasta su propia destrucción». La primera ha de gobernar a la segunda, pero ésta ha de vivificar a la primera, transmitirle su ímpetu y su energía. El profeta aconseja, entonces, «descansar en la razón y moverse en la pasión».

Hallar la libertad es algo mucho más profundo que romper ataduras externas, abolir leyes injustas y destronar tiranos. Si los hombres no empiezan por borrar las huellas que tales ataduras, leyes y tiranos dejaron en sus almas, no alcanzarán la auténtica libertad. Bien es cierto que a quienes, como Gibran, han puesto de relieve la importancia de la libertad interior se les ha criticado históricamente por defender una concepción espiritualista de la libertad y admitir que el hombre es libre aun cuando se halle sometido a explotación y dominios ajenos.

No es, empero, este el caso de Gibran. Nuestro autor va mucho más allá en el tratamiento del tema en cuestión. Pone el dedo en la llaga cuando plantea si las leyes injustas y los tiranos no habrán sido erigidos por quienes —por decirlo con palabras de Erich Fromm— tienen «miedo a la libertad». A nadie se le priva de la libertad si antes no busca en lo más íntimo de su corazón que se le despoje de ella. Por ello sólo la liberación interior, esto es, la pérdida del temor de ser libres, puede eliminar leyes injustas y tiranos arbitrarios.

También se muestra Gibran como un «maestro de la sospecha» —en la línea de un Nietzsche, un Marx y un Freud— cuando interrogan al profeta los habitantes de Orfalese sobre las leyes de la ciudad. Dictar leyes hace felices a los ciudadanos —señala Almustafá—, pero todavía sienten más gozo al transgredirlas. Con una serie de atinadas metáforas, el profeta denuncia a los legalistas que son incapaces de vivir sin normas, que ocultan bajo el cumplimiento de la ley sus personales incapacidades, que critican a quienes siguen antes al espíritu que a la letra, que ponen en solfa a quienes violan la moral tras haberla quebrantado ellos. Frente a tales legalistas, «a quien camina mirando el sol ninguna imagen dibujada en la tierra será capaz de contenerle».

Desde esta perspectiva, sólo se puede hablar del bien, no del mal. Y el profeta advierte que bueno no es el que se debilita voluntariamente ante el débil, ni el que agudiza la necesidad y la carencia de quien no tiene lo que él. No ser bueno no significa ser malo. En la medida en que es el anhelo de que el propio yo se agitante quien determina el criterio de bondad, no se puede condenar a nadie por el hecho de que ese ansia se dé en su persona de una forma poco intensa.

Especial interés merece la posición de Gibran ante el amor. Destaca en él el dolor que esconde, aunque ello no es una objeción para que nos resistamos al mismo. Constituye una prueba para el hombre, que éste no puede evadir. Respecto al matrimonio, denuncia la depen-

17

dencia que suele generar entre sus miembros, el ansia de dominar al otro que suscita. «Permaneced juntos —aconseja el profeta a los esposos—, pero no demasiado juntos.» «Amaos con devoción, pero no hagáis del amor una atadura.»

Frente a estos dolores y pérdidas de la propia independencia que puede producir el amor, Gibran canta las excelencias de la amistad. El amigo es presentado como la respuesta a nuestras necesidades, «nuestra mesa y nuestro hogar», porque «cuando hay amistad, todos los pensamientos, todos los deseos todas las esperanzas nacen y se comparten en espontánea alegría».

Amigo no es aquel a quien sólo buscamos para entretener nuestros ratos de ocio, sino el que buscamos para vivir con él todas las horas. Gibran parece dar a entender que la auténtica relación humana no es la marcada por el sexo, que fácilmente esclaviza, y por las leyes que regulan una vinculación como la del matrimonio. La comunicación humana sólo puede darse de una forma libre, espontánea, sincera, no sujeta a normas ni a instituciones. Y ello sólo puede encontrarse en el seno de la amistad.

Pese a todo lo dicho, el pensamiento de Gibran es tan rico en matices y sugerencias, que resulta imposible extractarlo en unas pocas páginas. *El Profeta* es uno de esos libros que se cree haber ya leído, pero que siempre nos descubre nuevas cosas al volverlo a leer. Obra breve en su extensión, pero profunda y rica en su contenido, un lector perspicaz tardará mucho en empaparse de sus enseñanzas, aunque sus páginas sean reducidas. Se trata, pues, de un libro de pensamientos: esto es, de un libro que incita a pensar; que nos obliga a interrumpir su lectura constantemente para que sus palabras extiendan su fragancia por los recovecos de nuestra intimidad.

No de otra forma merece ser leído Gibran; no otra es la respuesta que espera del lector un poeta-filósofo que «ha puesto a menudo su dedo en su propia llaga para poder creer más en quien lo lea y conocerle mejor».

AMALIA NAVARRO MATEO

EL PROFETA

ALMUSTAFÁ, el elegido y bien amado, el que era un amanecer en su propio día, aguardó durante doce años en la ciudad de Orfalese la vuelta del barco que debía devolverlo a su isla natal. Y a los doce años, en el séptimo día de Yeleol, el mes de las cosechas, subió a la colina, más allá de los mu-ros de la ciudad, y miró hacia el mar. Y vio su barco emergiendo de la bruma.

Se abrieron, entonces, de par en par las puertas de su corazón y su júbilo voló sobre el océano. Cerró los ojos y meditó en los silencios de su alma.

Sin embargo, cuando descendía de la colina, cayó sobre él una tristeza honda y pensó en su corazón: ¿Cómo partir en paz y sin pena? No; no abandonaré esta ciudad sin una grieta en el alma.

Interminables fueron los días de dolor que pasé entre sus muros e interminables fueron las noches de soledad y, ¿quién puede separarse sin pena de su soledad y de su dolor?

Demasiados fragmentos de mí espíritu he dejado en estas calles y son muchos los hijos de mi anhelo que corren desnudos entre las colinas. No puedo dejarlo sin aflicción y sin pena.

No es una túnica la que hoy me saco, sino mi propia piel, que desgarro entre mis manos.

Y no es un pensamiento el que dejo, sino un corazón, endulzado por el hambre y la sed.

Sin embargo, no puedo detenerme más.

El mar, que lleva todas las cosas hacia su seno, me llama y debo embarcarme.

Porque quedarse, aunque las horas palpiten en la noche, es congelarse y cristalizarse, y ser ceñido por un molde.

Desearía llevar conmigo todo lo de aquí, pero, ¿cómo hacerlo?

Una voz no puede llevarse la lengua y los labios que le dieran un sonido. Sola debe buscar el éter.

Y sola, sin su nido, volará el águila cruzando el sol.

Entonces, cuando llegó al pie de la colina, miró al mar otra vez y vio a su barco acercándose al puerto y, sobre la proa, los marineros, los hombres de su propia tierra.

Y su alama los llamó diciendo:

Hijos de mi anciana madre, jinetes de las mareas: ¡cuántas veces habéis surcado mis sueños! Y ahora venís en mi vigilia, que es mi sueño más profundo.

Estoy preparado para partir y mis ansias, con las velas desplegadas, aguardan el viento.

Respiraré una vez más este aire quieto, miraré sólo una vez hacia atrás, amorosamente.

Y luego estaré junto a vosotros, marino entre marinos.

Y tú, inmenso mar, madre sin sueño.

Tú que eres la paz y la libertad para el río y el arroyo. Permite un rodeo más a esta corriente, un murmullo más a esta cañada.

Y luego iré a tu encuentro, como una gota sin límites a un océano sin límites.

Así, caminando, vio a lo lejos que hombres abandonaban sus campos y sus viñas y se encaminaban apresuradamente hacia la ciudad.

Y oyó sus voces que gritaban su nombre de lugar a lugar, y se contaban el uno al otro que su barco había llegado.

Y se dijo a sí mismo:

¿Será el día de la partida el día del encuentro?

¿Y será mi crepúsculo mi verdadero amanecer?

¿Y qué ofreceré al que dejó su arado en la mitad del surco, o al que ha detenido la rueda de su lagar?

¿Se volverá mi corazón un árbol cargado de frutos que yo recoja para regalárselos?

¿Fluirán mis deseos como una fuente para colmar sus copas?

¿Será un arpa bajo los dedos del Poderoso o una flauta a través de la cual fluya su aliento?

He buscado el silencio, ¿qué tesoros he hallado en él que pueda ofrecer sin desconfianza?

Si este es mi día de cosecha, ¿en qué campos sembré la semilla y en qué estaciones, mi cosecha?

Si esta es, en verdad, la hora en que he de levantar mi antorcha, no es mi llama la que arderá en ella.

Oscura y vacía levantaré mi antorcha.

Y el guardián de la noche la llenará de aceite y la encenderá.

En palabras decía estas cosas. Pero mucho quedaba sin decir en su corazón. Porque él no podía expresar su más profundo secreto.

Y cuando entró en la ciudad, toda la gente vino a él, y lo aclamó a una voz.

Y los viejos se adelantaron y dijeron:

No nos abandones.

Tú has sido un mediodía en nuestro crepúsculo y tu juventud nos ha dado sueños para soñar.

Tú no eres un extranjero entre nosotros; no eres un huésped, sino nuestro hijo bien amado.

Que no sufran nuestros ojos la sed de su rostro.

Y los sacerdotes y las sacerdotisas le dijeron:

No permitas que la olas del mar nos separen, ni que los años que pasaste aquí se conviertan en un recuerdo.

Tú caminaste como un espíritu entre nosotros y tu sombra ha sido una luz sobre nuestros rostros.

Te hemos amado mucho. Nuestro amor fue sin palabras y muchos velos lo han cubierto.

Pero ahora clama en voz alta por ti y ante ti se descubren. Y es verdad que el amor no conoce su hondura hasta el momento de la separación.

Y vinieron también a suplicarle. Pero él no les respondió. Inclinó la cabeza y aquellos que estaban a su lado vieron caer lágrimas sobre su pecho.

Él y la gente se dirigieron, entonces, hacia la gran plaza, frente a la cual estaba situado el templo.

Y salió del santuario una mujer llamada Almitra. Era una profetisa.

Y él la miró con indecible ternura, porque fue la primera que lo buscó y creyó en él cuando apenas si había estado un día en la ciudad.

Y ella le saludó, diciendo:

Profeta de Dios, buscador de lo supremo; largamente has hurgado las distancias buscando tu barco.

Y ahora tu barco ha llegado y debes marcharte.

Profundo es tu anhelo por la tierra de tus recuerdos y por el lugar de tus mayores deseos. Pero nuestro amor no te atará y nuestras necesidades no detendrán tu paso.

Pero sí te pedimos que, antes de que nos dejes, nos hables y nos ofrezcas tu verdad.

Y nosotros la daremos a nuestros hijos y a los hijos de nuestros hijos, y ella no morirá.

En tu soledad, has velado durante nuestros días, y en tu vigilia has sido el llanto y la risa de nuestro sueño.

Descúbrenos ahora ante nosotros mismos y dinos todo lo que te ha sido mostrado entre el nacimiento y la muerte.

Y él respondió:

Pueblo de Orfalese, ¿de qué puedo yo hablar sino de lo que en cada momento se agita en vuestras almas?

Dɪᴊᴏ Almitra: Háblanos del Amor.

Y él alzó su cabeza, miró a la gente y la quietud descendió sobre todos. Entonces, con fuerte voz, dijo:

Cuando el amor os llame, seguidlo.
Aunque su camino sea duro y penoso.
Y entregaos a sus alas que os envuelven.
Aunque la espada escondida entre ellas os hiera.
Y creed en él cuando os hable.
Aunque su voz aplaste vuestros sueños, como hace el viento del Norte, el viento que arrasa los jardines.

Porque así como el amor os da gloria, así os crucifica.
Así como os da abundancia, así os poda.
Así como se remonta a lo más alto y acaricia vuestras ramas más débiles, que se estremecen bajo el sol.
Así caerá hasta vuestras raíces y las sacudirá en un abrazo con la tierra.

Como a gavillas de trigo él os une a vosotros mismos.
Os desgarra para desnudaros.
Os cierne, para libraros de los pliegues que cubren vuestra figura.

Os pulveriza hasta volveros blancos.

Os amasa, para que lo dócil y lo flexible renazca de vuestra dureza.

Y os destina luego a su fuego sagrado, para que podáis ser sagrado pan en la sagrada fiesta de Dios.

Todo esto hará el amor en vosotros para acercaros al conocimiento de vuestro corazón y convertiros, por ese conocimiento, en fragmento del corazón de la Vida.

Pero si vuestro miedo os hace buscar solamente la paz y el placer del amor...

... Entonces sería mejor que cubrierais vuestra desnudez y os alejarais de sus umbrales.

Hacia un mundo sin primavera donde reiréis, pero no con toda vuestra risa, y lloraréis, pero no con todas vuestras lágrimas.

El amor no da más que de sí mismo y no toma nada más que de sí mismo.

El amor no posee ni es poseído.

Porque el amor es todo para el amor.

Cuando améis no digáis: «Dios está en mi corazón», sino más bien: «Yo estoy en el corazón de Dios.»

Y no penséis en dirigir el curso del amor porque será él, si os halla dignos, quien dirija vuestro curso.

El amor no tiene otro deseo que el de realizarse.

Pero si amáis y no podéis evitar tener deseos, que vuestros deseos sean éstos:

Fundirse y ser como el arroyo, que murmura su melodía en la noche.

Saber del dolor del exceso de ternura.

Ser herido por nuestro propio conocimiento del amor.

Y sangrar voluntaria y alegremente.

Despertar al alba con un alado corazón y dar gracias por otro día de amor.

Despertar al mediodía y meditar el éxtasis amoroso.

Volver al hogar cuando la tarde cae, volver con gratitud.

Y dormir con una plegaria por el amado en el corazón y una canción de alabanza en los labios.

ENTONCES, Almitra habló otra vez:

¿Qué nos diréis sobre el Matrimonio, Maestro?

Y esta fue su respuesta:
Nacisteis juntos y juntos permaneceréis para siempre.

Estaréis juntos cuando las blancas alas de la muerte esparzan vuestros días.

Y también en la memoria silenciosa de Dios estaréis entre vosotros.

Amaos con devoción, pero no hagáis del amor una atadura.

Haced del amor un mar móvil entre las orillas de vuestras almas.

Llenaos uno al otro vuestras copas, pero no bebáis de una misma copa.

Compartid vuestro pan, pero no comáis del mismo trozo.

Cantad y bailad juntos, y estad alegres, pero que cada uno de vosotros sea independiente.

Las cuerdas de un laúd están separadas aunque vibren con la misma música.

Dad vuestro corazón, pero no para que vuestro compañero se adueñe de él.

Porque sólo la mano de la Vida puede contener los corazones.

Y permaneced juntos, pero no demasiado juntos.

Porque los pilares sostienen el templo, pero están separados.

Y ni el roble crece bajo la sombra del ciprés ni el ciprés bajo la del roble.

Y UNA MUJER, que sostenía un niño contra su seno, dijo: Háblanos de los Niños.

Y él dijo:

Vuestros hijos no son vuestros hijos.
Son los hijos y las hijas de la Vida, deseosa de perpetuarse.
Vienen a través de vuestros, pero no vienen de vosotros.

Y aunque están a vuestro lado, no os pertenecen.
Podéis darles vuestro amor, pero no vuestros pensamientos.
Porque ellos tienen sus propios pensamientos.
Podéis cobijar sus cuerpos, pero no sus almas.
Porque sus almas viven en la casa del porvenir, que está cerrada para vosotros, aun para vuestros sueños.
Podéis esforzaros en ser parecidos a ellos, pero no busquéis hacerlos a vuestra semejanza.
Porque la vida no se detiene ni se distrae con el ayer.
Vosotros sois el arco desde el que vuestros hijos, como flechas vivientes, son impulsados hacia lo lejos.

El Arquero es quien ve el blanco en la senda del infinito y os doblega con Su poder para que Su flecha vaya veloz y lejana.

Dejad, alegremente, que la mano del Arquero os doblegue.

Porque, así como Él ama la flecha que vuela, ama también la estabilidad del arco y su constancia.

ENTONCES, un hombre rico dijo: Háblanos del Dar.

Y él respondió:

Dais muy poco cuando dais lo que es vuestro como patrimonio.

Cuando dais algo de vuestro interior es cuando realmente dais.

¿Qué son vuestras posesiones sino cosas que atesoráis por temor a necesitarlas mañana?

Y mañana, ¿qué traerá el mañana al perro que, demasiado previsor, entierra huesos en la arena sin huellas mientras sigue a los peregrinos hacia la ciudad santa? ¿Y qué es el temor a la necesidad, sino la necesidad misma?

¿No es, en realidad, el miedo a la sed, cuando el manantial está lleno, la sed inextinguible?

Hay quienes dan poco de lo mucho que tienen y lo dan buscando el reconocimiento, y su deseo oculto daña sus regalos.

Y hay quienes tienen poco y lo dan todo.

Son éstos los creyentes en la vida y en la magnificencia de la vida y su cofre nunca estará vacío.

Hay quienes dan con alegría y esa alegría es su fortuna.

Y hay quienes dan con dolor y ese dolor es su bautismo.

Y hay quienes dan y no saben del dolor de dar, ni buscan la alegría de dar, ni dan conscientes de la virtud de dar.

Dan como el mirto, que en el hondo valle ofrece su fragancia a los aires.

A través de las manos de los que como ésos son, Dios habla y desde el fondo de sus ojos Él sonríe sobre el mundo.

Es bueno dar algo cuando ha sido pedido, pero es mejor dar sin demanda, comprendiendo.

Y, para la mano abierta, la búsqueda de aquel que recibirá es mayor alegría que el dar mismo.

¿Y hay algo, acaso, que pueda guardarse?

Todo lo que tenéis será entregado algún día:

Dad, pues, ahora que la estación de dar es vuestra y no de vuestros herederos.

Decís a menudo: «Daría, pero sólo a quien lo mereciera.»

Los árboles en vuestro huerto no hablan de ese modo, ni los rebaños en vuestra pradera.

Ellos dan para vivir, ya que guardar es perecer.

Todo aquel que merece recibir sus días y sus noches, merece de vosotros todo lo demás.

Y aquel que mereció beber el océano de la vida, merece llenar su copa en vuestra pequeña fuente.

¿Habrá un mérito mayor que el de aquel que da el valor y la confianza —no la caridad— del recibir?

¿Y quiénes sois vosotros para que los hombres os muestren su seno y os descubran su soberbia, para atreveros a ver desnudos sus merecimientos y sin vacilaciones su soberbia?

Mirad primero si vosotros mismos merecéis dar y ser el instrumento de dar.

Porque, a la verdad, es la vida la que da la vida, mientras que vosotros, que os creéis dadores, no sois más que testigos.

Y vosotros, los que recibís —y todos vosotros sois de ellos— no asumáis el peso de la gratitud, si no queréis colocar un yugo sobre vosotros y sobre quien os da.

Elevaos, más bien, con el dador en su dar como en unas alas.

Porque exagerar vuestra deuda es no comprender su generosidad, que tiene el libre corazón de la tierra como su madre y a Dios como su padre.

ENTONCES, un viejo que tenía una posada dijo: Háblanos del Comer y del Beber.

Y él respondió:

¡Si pudierais vivir de la fragancia de la tierra y, como las plantas en el aire, ser alimentados por la luz!

Pero, ya que es necesario matar para comer y robar al recién nacido la leche de su madre para saciar vuestra sed, haced de ello un acto de adoración.

Y haced que vuestra mesa sea un altar en el que lo limpio y lo inocente, el mar y la pradera, sean sacrificados a aquello que es más limpio y aún inocente en el hombre.

Cuando sacrifiquéis un animal, decidle en vuestro corazón: «El mismo poder que te sacrifica, me sacrifica también a mí; yo también seré destruido.

La misma ley que te entrega en mis manos me dejará a mí en manos más poderosas.

Tu sangre y mi sangre son la savia que alimenta el árbol del cielo.»

Y, cuando mordáis una manzana, decidle un vuestro corazón:
«Tu pulpa ha de vivir en mi cuerpo.

Y las semillas de tu mañana florecerán en mi corazón.

Y tu fragancia será mi aliento.

Y gozaremos juntos en las estaciones de la eternidad.»

Y, en el otoño, cuando reunáis las uvas de vuestras parras para el lagar, decid en vuestro corazón:

«Yo soy también una parra y mi fruto será pisoteado en el lagar.

Y como vino nuevo será guardado en vasos eternos.»

Y en el invierno, cuando sorbáis el vino, que haya en vuestro corazón un canto para cada copa.

Y que vibre en ese canto la memoria de los días otoñales y un recuerdo para la parra y para el lagar.

Luego, dijo el labrador: Háblanos del Trabajo.

Y el Maestro respondió, diciendo:

Trabajáis para acompañar el ritmo de la tierra y del alma de la tierra.

Quien está ocioso es un extraño en medio de las estaciones y un prófugo de la procesión de la vida, que marcha en amistad y sumisión orgullosa hacia el infinito.

Cuando trabajáis, sois una flauta a través de cuyo corazón el murmullo de las horas se convierte en melodía.

¿Quién de vosotros querrá ser una caña silenciosa y muda cuando todo canta al unísono?

Se os ha dicho siempre que el trabajo es una maldición y la labor una desgracia.

Pero yo os digo que, cuando trabajáis, realizáis una parte del más lejano sueño de la tierra, asignada a vosotros al nacer ese sueño.

Y trabajando estáis, en verdad, amando a la vida.

Y amarla a través del trabajo es estar muy cerca del más profundo secreto de la vida.

Pero si en vuestro dolor afirmáis que el nacer es un desgarramiento y sostener la carne una maldición escrita en vuestra frente, yo os respondo que sólo el sudor de vuestra frente lavará lo que está escrito.

Os han dicho también que la vida es oscuridad y, en vuestra fatiga, os hacéis eco del jadear del fatigado.

Pero yo os digo que la vida es oscuridad cuando no hay un impulso.

Y todo saber es inútil cuando no hay trabajo.

Y todo trabajo es vacío cuando no hay amor.

Porque cuando trabajáis con amor estáis en armonía con vosotros mismos, y con los otros, y con Dios.

¿Y qué es trabajar con amor?

Es tramar la tela con hilos extraídos de vuestro corazón, como si vuestro amado fuera a usar esa tela.

Es levantar una casa con cariño, como si con vuestra amada fuerais a habitar en ella.

Es sembrar con ternura y cosechar con gozo, como si con vuestra amada fuerais a gozar del fruto.

Es infundir en todas las cosas que hacéis el aliento de vuestro propio espíritu.

Es saber que todos los muertos benditos se hallan ante vosotros, observando.

A menudo he oído decir como si fuera en sueños: «El que trabaja en mármol y encuentra la forma de su propia alma en la piedra, es más noble que el que labra la tierra.»

«Y aquel que arrebata el arco iris para colocarlo en una tela transformada en la imagen de un hombre es más que el que hace las sandalias para nuestros pies.»

Pero yo os digo, no en sueños, sino en la vigilia del mediodía, que el viento habla con la misma dulzura a los robles gigantes que a la menor de las hojas de hierba.

41

Y que sólo es grande aquel que transforma la voz del viento en una melodía, hecha más dulce por la gravitación de su propio amor.

El trabajo es amor hecho visible.

Y si no podéis trabajar con amor, sino solamente con disgusto, es mejor que dejéis vuestra tarea y os sentéis a la puerta del templo y recibáis limosna de los que trabajan gozosamente.

Porque si horneáis el pan con indiferencia, estáis haciendo un pan amargo que no alcanza para mitigar el hambre.

Y si protestáis al pisar las uvas, vuestro murmurar destila veneno en el vino.

Y si cantáis, aunque fuera como los ángeles, pero no amáis el cantar, estáis entorpeciendo los oídos de los hombres para las voces del día y las voces de la noche.

ENTONCES pidió una mujer: Háblanos de la Alegría y de la Tristeza.

Y él respondió:

Vuestra alegría es vuestra tristeza sin máscara.
Y de un mismo manantial surgen vuestra risa y vuestras lágrimas.
No puede ser de otro modo.
Mientras más profundo cave el pesar en vuestro corazón, más espacio habrá para vuestra alegría.
¿No es la copa que contiene vuestro vino la misma que estuvo quemándose en el horno del alfarero?
¿Y no es el laúd que serena vuestro espíritu la misma madera que fue tallada con cuchillos?
Mirad en el fondo de vuestro corazón cuando estéis contentos: comprobaréis que sólo lo que os produjo tristeza os devuelve alegría.
Y mirad de nuevo en vuestro corazón cuando estéis tristes: comprobaréis que estáis llorando por lo que fue vuestro deleite.

Algunos de vosotros tenéis la costumbre de afirmar: «La alegría es mejor que la tristeza», y otros: «No, la tristeza es un sentimiento superior.»

Pero yo os digo que son inseparables.

Llegan juntos y cuando uno de ellos se sienta con vosotros a la mesa, el otro espera durmiendo en vuestro lecho.

En verdad, estáis suspensos, como fiel de balanza, entre vuestra alegría y vuestra tristeza.

Sólo cuando estáis vacíos vuestro peso permanece quieto y equilibrado.

Así, cuando el que cuida el tesoro os levante para pesar su oro y su plata, es necesario que vuestra alegría y vuestro pesar suban y bajen.

UN ALBAÑIL, entonces, se acercó y dijo: Háblanos de las Casas.

Y él respondió, diciendo:

Levantad con vuestra imaginación una enramada en el bosque antes que una casa dentro de las murallas de la ciudad.

Porque así como tendréis huéspedes en vuestro atardecer, así el peregrino que habita en vosotros huirá siempre hacia la distancia y la soledad.

Vuestra casa es vuestro cuerpo grande.

Crece en el sol y duerme en la quietud de la noche, y siempre sueña.

¿No es cierto que sueña? ¿Y que, al soñar, deja la ciudad por el bosque o la colina?

¡Ah, si pudiera juntar vuestras casas en mi mano y, como un sembrador, desparramarlas por el bosque y la llanura!

Los valles serían vuestras calles y los senderos verdes vuestras alamedas; os buscaríais el uno al otro en los viñedos; luego volveríais con la fragancia de la tierra adherida a vuestras vestiduras.

Pero todo eso aún está lejos.

En su miedo, vuestros antecesores os colocaron demasiado juntos. Y ese miedo aún ha de durar. Durante un tiempo los muros de vuestra ciudad separarán vuestro corazón de vuestros campos.

Y, decidme, pueblo de Orfalese, ¿qué tenéis en esas casas? ¿Y qué guardáis con puertas y candados?

¿Tenéis paz, el quieto empuje que revela vuestro poder?

¿Tenéis recuerdos, los arcos lucientes que unen las cimas del espíritu?

¿Tenéis ese fulgor que guía el corazón desde las casas hechas de madera y piedra hasta la montaña sagrada?

Decidme, ¿los tenéis en vuestras casas?

¿O tenéis solamente comodidad y el ansia de comodidad, esa cosa fugaz que entra en una casa como un huésped y luego se convierte en dueño y después en amo y señor?

¡Ay!, y termina siendo un domador, y con látigo y garfio juega con vuestros mayores deseos.

Aunque sus manos son sedosas, su corazón es de hierro.

Arrulla vuestro sueño y sólo para colocarse junto a vuestro lecho y escarnecer la dignidad del cuerpo.

Se burla de vuestros sentidos y los echa en el cardal como si fuesen frágiles vasos.

En verdad os digo que el ansia de comodidad seca la pasión del alma y luego camina haciendo muecas en el funeral.

Pero vosotros, criaturas del espacio, vosotros, apasionados en la quietud, no seréis atrapados o domados.

Vuestra casa no será un ancla, sino un mástil.

No será la cinta brillante que cubre una herida, sino el párpado que protege el ojo.

No plegaréis vuestras alas para atravesar sus puertas, ni inclinaréis la cabeza para que no toque su techo, ni temeréis respirar por miedo a que sus paredes se agrieten o se derrumben.

No viviréis en tumbas hechas por los muertos para los vivos y, aunque lujosa y magnificiente, vuestra casa no se apoderará de vuestro secreto, ni encerrará vuestro anhelo.

Porque lo que en vosotros es ilimitado habita en la casa del cielo, cuya puerta es la niebla de la mañana y cuyas ventanas son las canciones y los silencios de la noche.

Y UN TEJEDOR dijo: Háblanos del Vestir.

Y él habló, diciendo:

Vuestra ropa cubre mucho de vuestra belleza y, sin embargo, no cubre lo que no es bello.

Y aunque buscáis la ropa que os haga sentir libres en vuestra intimidad, es fácil que halléis en ella un arnés y una cadena.

¿Seríais capaces de enfrentar al sol y al viento con más de vuestra piel y menos de vuestra ropas?

Porque el aliento de la vida nos llega con la luz del sol y la mano de la vida con el viento.

Algunos de vosotros afirmáis: «Es el viento del Norte el que ha tejido las ropas que usamos.»

Y yo os digo: ¡Ay! Fue el viento del Norte.

Pero la vergüenza fue su telar y la debilidad de carácter dio sus hilos.

Y rió en el bosque cuando terminó su trabajo.

No olvidéis que el pudor no es protección contra los ojos del impuro.

Y cuando el impuro ya no exista, ¿qué será el pudor sino los grillos y la impureza de la mente?

Y no olvidéis que la tierra goza con vuestros pies desnudos y que los vientos anhelan jugar con vuestro pelo.

Y UN MERCADER pidió: Háblanos del Comprar y el Vender.

Y él respondió:

La tierra os ofrece sus frutos y vosotros no sufriréis necesidad si sólo aprendéis a colmar vuestras manos.

Es en el intercambio de los frutos de la tierra donde encontraréis abundancia y satisfacción.

Pero si ese intercambio no se lleva a cabo con amor y bondadosa justicia, algunos serán impulsados por la codicia y otros sufrirán hambre.

Así, cuando vosotros, trabajadores del mar, de los campos y los viñedos, encontréis a tejedores, alfareros y vendedores de especias en el mercado...

... Invocad al espíritu guía de la tierra para que os acompañe y santifique las medidas y para que pese al valor de acuerdo con el valor.

Y no toleréis que el de manos estériles, el que busca vender palabra al precio de vuestra labor, intervenga en vuestras transacciones.

A ese hombre habréis de decirle:

«Ven con nosotros a los campos o acompaña a nuestros hermanos al mar y arroja tu red.

Que la tierra y el mar serán generosos para ti como lo son para nosotros.»

Y si acudieran los cantores y los bailarines y los tocadores de flauta, no os olvidéis de comprar de sus dones.

Porque también ellos son cosechadores de frutos e incienso, y lo que ellos traen, aunque hecho de sueño, es abrigo y alimento para vuestro espíritu.

Y, antes de abandonar el mercado, comprobad que nadie se marche con las manos vacías.

Porque el espíritu señor de la tierra no descansará en paz sobre los vientos hasta que la necesidad del último de vosotros no haya sido satisfecha.

ENTONCES, uno de los magistrados de la ciudad se acercó y dijo: Háblanos del Crimen y el Castigo.

Y él respondió, diciendo:

Es el momento en el que vuestro espíritu vaga en el viento.

Que vosotros, solos y desamparados, cometéis una falta para con los demás y, por tanto, para con vosotros mismos.

Y a causa de esa falta cometida, debéis llamar a la puerta del bienaventurado y esperar algunos minutos.

Como el océano es el dios de vuestro yo:

No conoce los caminos del topo ni busca los orificios de la serpiente.

Pero el dios de vuestro yo no habita sólo en vuestro ser.

Mucho en vosotros es aún hombre y mucho en vosotros no es hombre todavía, sino una forma grotesca que camina dormida entre la niebla, en busca de su propio despertar.

Y del hombre que hay en vosotros quiero yo hablar ahora.

Porque es él y no el dios de vuestro yo, ni la forma grotesca que camina en la niebla, el que conoce el crimen y el castigo del crimen.

A menudo os he oído hablar de aquel que comete una falta como si no fuera uno de vosotros, sino un extraño y un intruso en vuestro mundo.

Pero yo os digo que, así como el piadoso y el honrado no pueden elevarse más allá de lo más sublime que existe en cada uno de vosotros.

Así el débil y el malvado no pueden caer más bajo que lo más bajo que existe también en cada uno de vosotros.

Y, así como una sola hoja no se vuelve amarilla sino con el invisible conocimiento del árbol todo...

... Así el que falta no puede hacerlo sin la voluntad secreta de todos vosotros.

Como una procesión marcháis juntos hacia el Dios de vuestro yo.

Sois el camino y sois sus peregrinos.

Y cuando uno de vosotros cae, cae para que quienes lo siguen no tropiecen con el mismo escollo.

¡Ay! Y cae por los que le precedieron, por aquellos que, siendo su andar más rápido y seguro, no removieron, sin embargo, el escollo del camino.

Os hablo con verdad, aunque las palabras pesen duramente sobre vuestros corazones.

El asesinado es también responsable de su propia muerte.

Y el robado es también culpable de ser robado.

El justo no es inocente de los hechos del malvado.

Y el de las manos limpias no es ajeno a lo que el felón hace.

Sí, muchas veces el reo es la víctima del injuriado. Pero, más a menudo, el condenado es el que lleva la carga del que no tiene culpa.

No podéis separar al justo del injusto ni al bueno del malvado.

Porque ellos permanecen juntos ante la faz del sol, así como el hilo blanco y el negro están juntos en la trama del tejido.

Y cuando el hilo negro se rompe, el tejedor debe revisar la tela entera y controlar también el telar.

Si alguno de vosotros trajera a juicio a la mujer infiel...

... Haced que pese también el corazón de su marido en la balanza y mida la verdad de su alma.

Y haced que aquel que ha de castigar al ofensor mire en el espíritu del ofendido.

Y si alguno de vosotros castigara en nombre de la justicia y descargara su hacha en el tronco malo, haced que recuerde sus raíces.

Y encontrará, en verdad, las raíces de lo bueno y lo malo, lo fructífero y lo estéril, juntas y entrelazadas en el silente corazón de la tierra.

Y, vosotros, magistrados, que tenéis la obligación de ser justos.

¿Qué juicio pronunciaríais sobre aquel que, aunque honesto en su conducta, fuera un ladrón de espíritu?

¿Qué pena impondríais al que mata la carne y es, él mismo, destruido en el espíritu?

¿Y cómo juzgaríais a aquellos cuyo remordimiento es mayor que su pecado?

¿No es el remordimiento la justicia administrada por la ley misma que desearíais servir?

Sin embargo, no podréis cargar al inocente de remordimiento, ni librar de remordimientos el corazón del culpable.

Y el remordimiento vendrá en la noche, espontáneamente, para que los hombres despierten y contemplen su propio corazón.

Y vosotros, que pretendéis legislar sobre lo que es justo o injusto, ¿cómo podréis hacerlo si no miráis todos los hechos en la plenitud de la luz?

Sólo así sabréis que el erecto y el caído no son sino un solo hombre, de pie en el crepúsculo, entre la noche de su yo deforme y el día de su dios interior.

Y que la torre del templo no es más alta que la piedra más humilde de sus cimientos.

ENTONCES, un abogado dijo: Pero, ¿qué nos decís de nuestras Leyes, maestro?

Y él respondió:

Os hace felices dictar leyes.
Y, no obstante, gozáis más al violarlas.
Como los niños que juegan a la orilla del océano y levantan, con obstinada paciencia, torres de arena y las destruyen luego entre risas.
Sin embargo, mientras construís vuestras torres, el océano deposita más arena en la playa.
Y, cuando las destruís, el océano ríe junto a vosotros.
En verdad, el océano ríe siempre con el inocente.
Pero, ¿y aquellos para quienes la vida no es un océano y las leyes de los hombres no son fugaces castillos de arena.
Aquellos para quienes la vida es una piedra y la ley un cincel con el que tallarían a su gusto?
¿Qué del lisiado que odia a los que danzan?
¿Qué del buey que ama su yugo y juzga al alce y al ciervo del bosque como vagabundos sin ley?
¿Y la vieja serpiente, incapaz de librarse de su piel, que llama a los demás desnudos y libertinos?
¿Y aquel que llegó temprano a la fiesta de bodas y, una vez que se cansó y hartó de comer y beber, se aleja

diciendo que todas las fiestas son inmorales y los concurrentes violadores de la ley?

¿Qué diré de ellos sino que también ellos están a la luz del sol, pero dándole la espalda?

Ven sólo sus sombras y sus sombras son sus leyes.

¿Y qué es el sol para ellos, sino algo que produce sombras?

¿Y qué es el acatar las leyes, sino el encorvarse y rastrear sus sombras sobre la tierra?

Pero a vosotros, que camináis mirando el sol, ¿qué imágenes dibujadas en la tierra serán capaces de conteneros?

Y si vosotros viajáis con el viento, ¿qué veleta dirigirá vuestro andar?

¿Qué ley humana os atará si rompéis vuestro yugo lejos de la puerta donde los hombres han construido sus prisiones?

¿Y quién es el que os llevará a juicio si desgarráis vuestra ropa, pero no la abandonáis en el camino?

Pueblo de Orfalese: podéis cubrir el tambor y podéis aflojar las cuerdas de la lira, pero: ¿quién impedirá a la alondra del cielo que deje de cantar?

Y UN ORADOR dijo: Háblanos de la Libertad.

Y él dijo:

A las puertas de la ciudad y a la lumbre de vuestros hogares os he visto hincados, adorando vuestra propia libertad.

Así como los esclavos se humillan ante un tirano y lo alaban aun cuando los martiriza.

¡Oh, sí! En el jardín del templo y a la sombra de la ciudadela he visto a los más libres de vosotros utilizar su libertad como un yugo y un dogal.

Y mi corazón sangró, porque sólo seréis libres cuando aun el deseo de perseguir la libertad sea un arnés para vosotros y cuando dejéis de hablar de la libertad como de una meta y una realización.

Seréis en verdad libres, no cuando vuestros días estén libres de cuidado y vuestras noches vacías de necesidad y pena.

Sino, más bien, cuando la necesidad y la angustia rodeen vuestra vida y, sin embargo, seáis capaces de elevaros sobre ellas desnudos y sin ataduras.

¿Y cómo haréis para elevaros más allá de vuestros días y vuestras noches sin romper las cadenas que atasteis alrededor de vuestro mediodía, en el amanecer de vuestro entendimiento?

En verdad, eso que llamáis libertad es la más peligrosa de vuestras cadenas, a pesar de que sus eslabones brillen al sol y deslumbren vuestros ojos.

¿Y qué sino fragmentos de vuestro propio yo desecharéis para poder ser libres?

Si lo que deseáis abolir es una ley injusta, debéis saber que esa ley fue escrita con vuestras propias manos sobre vuestras propias frentes.

No la borraréis quemando vuestros Códigos ni lavando la frente de vuestros jueces, aunque vaciéis todo un mar sobre ella.

Y si es un tirano el que queréis deponer, tratad primero que su trono, erigido en vuestro interior, sea destruido.

Porque, ¿cómo puede un tirano obligar a los libres y a los dignos sino a través de un sometimiento en su propia libertad y una vergüenza en su propio orgullo?

Y si es un dolor el que queréis borrar, ese dolor fue elegido por vosotros más que impuesto a vosotros.

Y si es un miedo el que queréis borrar, el lugar de ese miedo está en vuestro corazón y no en el puño del ser temido.

En verdad, todo lo que percibís se mueve en vosotros como luces y sombras apareadas.

Y cuando la sombra huye desvanecida para siempre, la luz que queda se convierte en sombra de otra luz.

Así, vuestra libertad, cuando pierde sus cadenas, se vuelve ella misma cadena de una libertad mayor.

Y LA SACERDOTISA volvió a tomar la palabra: Háblanos de la Razón y de la Pasión.

Y él respondió, diciendo:

Vuestra alma es, a veces, un campo de batalla sobre el que vuestra razón y vuestro juicio combaten contra vuestra pasión y vuestro apetito.

Desearía poder ser el pacificador de vuestra alma y cambiar la discordia y la rivalidad de vuestros elementos en unidad y armonía. Pero, ¿cómo hacerlo si vosotros mismos no sois los pacificadores y los amigos de todos vuestros elementos?

Vuestra razón y vuestra pasión son el timón y las velas de vuestra alma viajera.

Si vuestras velas o vuestro timón se rompieran, no podríais más que agitaros e ir a la deriva o permanecer inmóviles en medio del mar. Porque la razón, gobernando sola, es una fuerza limitadora, y la pasión, desgobernada, es una llama que se quema hasta su propia destrucción.

Por tanto, haced que vuestra alma exalte a vuestra razón a la altura de la pasión, para que sea capaz de cantar.

Y dirigid vuestra pasión con el razonamiento, para que pueda vivir a través de su diaria resurrección y, como el ave fénix, elevarse de sus propias cenizas.

Desearía que consideraseis vuestro propio juicio y vuestro apetito como dos huéspedes queridos.

No honraríais, con seguridad, a uno más que al otro, porque quien es más atento con uno de ellos pierde el amor y la fe de ambos.

Entre las colinas cuando os sentéis a la sombra fresca de los álamos, compartáis la paz y la serenidad de los campos y praderas distantes, dejad que vuestro corazón diga en silencio: «Dios descansa en la razón.»

Y cuando llegue la tormenta y el viento poderoso sacuda el bosque y los truenos y relámpagos proclamen la majestad del cielo, dejad a vuestro corazón decir sobrecogido: «Dios se mueve en la pasión.»

Y ya que sois un soplo en la esfera de Dios y una hoja en el bosque de Dios, deberíais descansar en la razón y moveros en la pasión.

Y UNA MUJER pidió: Háblanos del Dolor.

Y él dijo:

Vuestro dolor es la eclosión de la celda que encierra vuestro entendimiento.

Así como la semilla de la fruta debe romperse para que su corazón se ofrezca al sol, así debéis vosotros conocer el dolor.

Y si pudierais mantener vuestro corazón maravillado ante los diarios milagros de la vida, vuestro dolor no os parecería menos maravilloso que vuestra alegría.

Y aceptaríais las estaciones de vuestro corazón así como habéis aceptado siempre las estaciones que pasan sobre vuestros campos.

Y esperaríais serenamente los inviernos de vuestra pena.

Mucho de vuestro dolor es elección de vuestro espíritu.

Es el remedio amargo con el que el médico que hay dentro de vosotros cura vuestro ser enfermo.

Por tanto, tened confianza en el médico y bebed el remedio en silencio y tranquilidad.

Porque su mano, aunque dura y pesada, tiene como guía la tierna mano del Invisible.

Y el vaso con que brinda, aunque queme vuestros labios, ha sido moldeado con la arcilla que el Alfarero ha humedecido con sus propias lágrimas sagradas.

ENTONCES, un hombre se acercó y dijo: Háblanos del Conocimiento Interior.

Y él respondió:

Vuestros corazones saben, en silencio, los secretos de los días y las noches...

... Pero vuestros oídos sufren por el sonido del conocimiento de vuestro corazón.

Querríais saber en palabras, lo que siempre supisteis en espíritu.

Querríais tocar con vuestras manos el cuerpo desnudo de vuestros sueños.

Y sería bueno que así lo hicierais.

El manantial escogido en vuestra alma necesita brotar y correr murmurando hacia el mar.

Y el tesoro de vuestros infinitos secretos sería revelado a vuestros ojos.

Pero no pongáis balanzas para pesar vuestro desconocido tesoro.

Y no registréis los secretos de vuestro conocimiento con cuchillos y sondas.

Porque el yo es un mar inconmensurable.

No digáis: «He hallado la verdad», sino más bien: «He hallado una verdad.»

No digáis: «He hallado la senda del espíritu.» Decid más bien: «He encontrado al espíritu caminando en mi senda.»

Porque el espíritu es peregrino de todas las sendas.

El espíritu no camina en línea recta, ni crece como el bambú.

El alma se despliega como un loto de pétalos innumerables.

ENTONCES, un pedagogo, dijo: Háblanos del Enseñar.

Y él respondió:

Nadie puede descubrirnos más de lo que descansa dormido a medias en el amanecer de nuestro conocimiento.

El pedagogo que camina a la sombra del templo, en medio de sus discípulos, no les ofrece su sabiduría, sino, más bien, su fe y su afecto.

Si él es sabio de verdad, no os pedirá que entréis en la casa de su sabiduría, sino que os guiará hasta el umbral de vuestro propio espíritu.

El astrónomo puede hablaros de su comprensión del espacio, pero no puede daros ese conocimiento.

El músico puede describirlos el ritmo que existe en todo ámbito, pero no puede daros el oído que detiene el ritmo ni la voz que le sirve de eco.

Y el entendido en la ciencia de los números puede hablaros de los valores del peso y la medida, pero no puede conduciros a ellas.

La visión de un hombre no cede sus alas a otro hombre.

Y así como cada uno de vosotros se halla solo ante el conocimiento de Dios, así debe cada uno de vosotros estar solo en su comprensión de Dios y en su conocimiento de la tierra.

Un HOMBRE joven pidió: Háblanos de la Amistad.

Y él dijo:

Vuestro amigo es la respuesta a vuestras necesidades.
Él es el campo que sembráis con amor y cosecháis con agradecimiento.
Y él vuestra mesa y vuestro hogar.
Porque vosotros os precipitáis hacia él con vuestra hambre y lo buscáis sedientos de paz.

Cuando vuestro amigo os hable con sinceridad, no temáis vuestro propio «no», ni detengáis el «sí».
Y cuando él permanezca en silencio, que vuestro corazón no cese de oír su corazón.
Porque cuando hay amistad, todos los pensamientos, todos los deseos, todas las esperanzas nacen y se comparten en espontánea alegría.

Cuando os separéis de un amigo, no sufráis.
Porque lo que más amáis en él se volverá nítido en su ausencia, como la montaña es más clara desde el llano para el montañés.

Y no permitáis más propósito en la amistad que la consolidación del espíritu.

Porque el amor que no busca más que la dilucidación de su propio misterio, no es amor sino una red que, lanzada, sólo recoge lo inútil.

Que lo mejor de vosotros sea para vuestro amigo.

Si él ha de conocer el menguante de vuestra marea, que también conozca su creciente.

Porque, ¿qué amigo es el que buscáis para matar las horas?

Buscadlo siempre para vivir las horas.

Porque él existe para colmar vuestra necesidad, no vuestro vacío.

Y permitid que haya risa y placeres compartidos en la dulzura de la amistad.

Porque en el rocío de las pequeñas cosas el corazón encuentra su alborada y se refresca.

Y UN RETÓRICO dijo: Dinos del Hablar.

Y él respondió:

Habláis cuando cesáis de estar en paz con vuestros pensamientos.

Y cuando sois incapaces de habitar en la soledad de vuestro corazón, vivís en vuestros labios, y el sonido de vuestras palabras es diversión y pasatiempo.

Y en muchas de vuestras palabras el pensamiento es asesinado.

Porque el pensamiento es un pájaro del espacio que, en una jaula de palabras, puede, en verdad, abrir las alas, pero es incapaz de volar.

Algunos hay entre vosotros que buscan al hablador por miedo a estar solos.

El silencio de la soledad revela ante sus ojos un yo decrépito y ansía escapar.

Y hay quienes hablan y, sin conocimiento ni premeditación, revelan una verdad que ni ellos mismos comprenden.

Y hay quienes poseen la verdad, pero no la traducen en palabras.

Cuando encontréis a vuestro amigo a la vera del camino o en el mercado, dejad que el espíritu mueva vuestros labios y guíe vuestra lengua.

Que la voz en vuestra voz hable al oído en su oído. Porque su alma guardará la verdad de vuestro corazón, como el sabor del vino persiste en la memoria. Cuando el dolor está lejos y el vaso ya no existe.

Y UN ASTRÓNOMO dijo: Maestro, ¿y qué nos dices del Tiempo?

Y él respondió:

Mediríais el tiempo, lo infinito.

Ajustaríais vuestra conducta e incluso dirigiríais la ruta de vuestro espíritu de acuerdo con las horas y las estaciones.

Del tiempo haríais una corriente a cuya orilla os sentaríais a observarlo rodar.

Sin embargo, lo eterno en vosotros es consciente de la eternidad de la vida.

Y sabe que el ayer es sólo la memoria del hoy y el mañana es el ensueño del hoy.

Y que aquello que canta y piensa en vosotros habita aún los límites de aquel primer momento que sembró las estrellas en el espacio.

¿Quién de entre vosotros no siente que su capacidad de amar excede todos los límites?

Y, a pesar de ello, ¿quién no siente ese mismo amor, aunque sin límites, rodeado en el centro de su ser y no moviéndose sino de un pensamiento de amor a otro pensamiento de amor, ni de un acto de amor a otro acto de amor? ¿Y no es el tiempo, como el amor, indiviso y sin etapas?

Pero sí; en vuestro pensamiento, debéis medir el tiempo en períodos; que cada período encierre todos los restantes.

Y que el hoy abrace al pasado con remembranza y al futuro con deseo.

Y UNO DE LOS ANCIANOS de la ciudad dijo: Háblanos de lo Bueno y de lo Malo.

Y él dijo:

Puedo hablar de lo bueno, no de lo malo.

Porque, ¿qué es lo malo sino lo bueno torturado por su propia hambre y su propia sed?

En verdad, cuando lo bueno está hambriento, busca alimentarse en cavernas oscuras, y cuando está sediento, bebe hasta de las aguas estancadas.

Sois buenos cuando sois uno con vosotros mismos.

Sin embargo, cuando no lo sois, no sois malos.

Porque una casa desunida no es una cueva de ladrones; es sólo una casa desunida.

Y un barco sin timón puede vagar sin rumbo entre islotes peligrosos y no hundirse hasta el fondo.

Sois buenos cuando tratáis de dar de vosotros mismos.

Sin embargo, no sois malos cuando buscáis la ganancia que os enriquecerá.

Pero cuando lucháis por obtener, no sois más que una raíz que se prende a la tierra y succiona su seno.

Seguramente la fruta no puede decir a la raíz: «Sé como yo, madura y plena, y dando siempre de tu abundancia.»

Porque para la fruta el dar es una necesidad, como el recibir es una necesidad para la raíz.

Sois buenos cuando estáis completamente despiertos en vuestro discurso.

Sin embargo, no sois malos cuando dormís mientras vuestra lengua titubea sin propósito.

Y aun un vacilante hablar puede fortalecer una lengua débil.

Sois buenos cuando camináis hacia vuestra meta firmemente y con pasos audaces.

No sois, empero, malos cuando camináis cojeando hacia ella.

Aun aquellos que cojean no retroceden.

Pero vosotros que sois fuertes y briosos, cuidaos de no cojear delante del lisiado, imaginando que eso es bondad.

Sois buenos en incontables modos y no sois malos cuando no sois buenos.

Sois solamente perezosos y dejados.

Es una lástima que los ciervos no puedan enseñar su velocidad a las tortugas.

En vuestro anhelo por vuestro yo-gigante reposa vuestra grandeza y ese anhelo se encuentra en cada uno de vosotros.

Pero en algunos de vosotros ese ansia es un torrente que corre con fuerza hacia el mar, y se lleva los secretos de las colinas y las canciones de los bosques.

Y en otros es un hilo de agua que se pierde en ángulos y curvas, y se consume antes de alcanzar la playa.

Pero no dejemos que el que mucho anhela le diga al que anhela poco: «¿Por qué avanzas tan lentamente y te detienes tanto?»

Porque el que es verdaderamente bueno no pregunta al desnudo «¿Dónde están tus vestidos?», ni al vagabundo desamparado: «¿Qué le ha ocurrido a tu casa?»

Entonces, una sacerdotisa dijo: Háblanos del Orar.

Y él respondió:

Oráis en vuestra angustia y en vuestra necesidad; deberíais también hacerlo en la plenitud de vuestro júbilo y en vuestros días de abundancia.

Porque, ¿qué es la oración sino el expandirse de vuestro ser en el éter viviente?

Y es para vuestra paz que volcáis vuestra oscuridad en el espacio, es también para vuestro gozo que derramáis el amanecer de vuestro corazón.

Y si no podéis sino llorar cuando vuestra alma os llama a la oración, ella os enjugará una y otra vez hasta que encontréis la risa.

Cuando oráis, os eleváis para hallar en lo alto a los que en ese mismo momento están orando y a quienes sólo encontraríais en la oración.

Por tanto, que vuestra visita a ese invisible templo no sea más que éxtasis y dulce comunión.

Porque, si entrarais al templo solamente a pedir, no recibiréis.

Y si entrarais a pedir por el bien de los otros, no seréis oídos.

Basta con que entréis en el templo invisible.

No puedo enseñaros cómo orar con palabras.

Dios no oye vuestras palabras sino cuando Él Mismo las pronuncia a través de vuestros labios.

Y yo no puedo enseñaros la oración de los mares y los bosques y las montañas.

Pero vosotros, nacidos de las montañas, los bosques y los mares, podéis hallar su plegaria en vuestro corazón.

Y si solamente escucháis en la quietud de la noche, les oiréis decir, en silencio:

«Nuestro Señor, que eres nuestro ser alado, es Tu voluntad la que quiere en nosotros.

Es Tu anhelo, en nosotros, el que anhela.

Es Tu impulso el que, en nosotros, cambia nuestras noches, que son Tuyas; en días, que son también Tuyos.

No podemos pedirte nada porque Tú sabes cuáles son nuestras necesidades antes de que nazcan en nuestro ser:

Tú eres nuestra necesidad y dándonos más de ti, nos lo ofreces todo.»

Y UN ERMITAÑO que visitaba todos los años la ciudad, se adelantó y dijo: Háblanos del Placer.

Y él respondió, diciendo:

El placer es un canto de libertad, pero no es libertad.
Es el florecer de vuestros deseos, pero no su fruto.
Es una llamada de la profundidad a la altura, pero no es lo profundo ni lo alto.

Es lo aprisionado que toma alas, pero no es el espacio confirmado.
¡Ah! En verdad, el placer es una canción de libertad.
Y yo deseo que la cantéis con el corazón pleno, pero no que perdáis el corazón en el canto.
Algunos jóvenes entre vosotros buscan el placer como si lo fuese todo y son juzgados por ello y censurados.
Yo no los juzgaría ni censuraría. Les dejaría buscarlo.
Porque encontrarán el placer pero no lo encontrarán sólo...
... Siete son sus hermanas y la peor de ellas es más hermosa que el placer.
¿No habéis oído del hombre que escarbaba la tierra buscando raíces y encontró un tesoro?

Y algunos mayores entre vosotros recuerdan los placeres con arrepentimiento, como faltas cometidas en la embriaguez.

Pero el arrepentimiento es el nublarse de la mente y no su castigo.

Deberían ellos recordar sus placeres con gratitud como recordarían la cosecha de un verano.

Sin embargo, si los conforta el arrepentirse, dejad que se arrepientan.

Y algunos hay, entre vosotros, que no son ni jóvenes para buscar, ni viejos para recordar.

Y, en su miedo a buscar y recordar, huyen de todos los placeres para no olvidar el espíritu u ofenderlo.

Pero esa denuncia misma es su placer.

Y, así, ellos también encuentran un tesoro, escarbando con manos temblorosas para buscar raíces.

Pero, decidme: ¿quién es el que puede ofender al espíritu?

¿Ofende el ruiseñor la quietud de la noche? ¿Acaso la luciérnaga ofende a las estrellas?

¿Y molestan al viento vuestro fuego o vuestro humo?

¿Creéis que es el espíritu un estanque quieto que podéis enturbiar con un bastón?

A menudo, al negaros placer, no hacéis otra cosa que guardar el deseo en los reposos de vuestro ser.

¿Quién no sabe que lo que parece omitido aguarda el mañana?

Aun vuestro cuerpo sabe de su herencia y su justa necesidad, y no será engañado.

Y vuestro cuerpo es el arpa de vuestra alma.

Y sois vosotros los que podéis sacar de él dulce música o sonidos confusos.

Y ahora os estáis preguntando en vuestro corazón:

«¿Cómo distinguiremos lo que es bueno de lo que no es bueno en el placer?»

Id a vuestros campos y a vuestros jardines y aprenderéis que el placer de la abeja es reunir miel de las flores.

Pero es también placer de la flor el ceder su miel a la abeja.

Porque una flor es fuente de vida para la abeja.

Y una abeja es un mensajero de amor para la flor.

Y para ambos, abeja y flor, el dar y el recibir placer son una necesidad y un éxtasis.

Pueblo de Orfalese, sed en vuestros placeres como las abejas y las flores.

Y UN POETA pidió: Háblanos de la Belleza.

Y él dijo:

¿Dónde hallaréis la belleza y cómo haréis para encontrarla si ella misma no es vuestro camino y vuestro guía?
¿Y cómo hablaréis de ella si ella misma no enhebra vuestras palabras?

El agraviado y el injuriado dicen: «La belleza es amable y bondadosa.
Camina entre nosotros como una madre joven, casi avergonzada de su propia gloria.»
Y el apasionado dice: «No, la belleza debe infundir temor y contrición.
Como la tempestad que sacude la tierra bajo nuestros pies y el cielo sobre nuestros cabellos.»
El cansado y rendido dice: «La belleza es hecha de blandos murmullos. Habla en nuestro espíritu.
Su voz se rinde a nuestros silencios como una débil luz que se estremece por temor a las sombras.»
Pero el inquieto dice: «La hemos oído dar voces entre las montañas.
Y, con sus voces, se oyó rodar de cascos y batir de alas y rugir de fieras.»

Durante la noche, los serenos de la ciudad dicen: «La belleza vendrá del Este, con el alba.»

Y, al mediodía, los trabajadores y los viajeros dicen: «La hemos visto inclinarse sobre la tierra desde las ventanas del crepúsculo.»

En el invierno, el que se halla entre la nieve dice: «Vendrá con la primavera, saltando sobre las colinas.»

Y en el calor del verano, los cosechadores dicen: «La vimos danzando con las hojas de otoño y llevaba torbellinos de nieve sobre su pelo.»

Todas estas cosas habéis dicho de la belleza.

Pero, en verdad, hablasteis, no de ella, sino de vuestras necesidades insatisfechas.

Y la belleza no es una necesidad, sino un éxtasis.

No es una boca sedienta, ni una mano vacía que se extiende.

Sino, más bien, un corazón ardiente y un alma encantada.

No es la imagen que véis, ni la canción que escucháis.

Sino, más bien, una imagen que soñáis al cerrar los ojos y una canción que escucháis cuando os tapáis los oídos.

No es la savia que corre debajo de la rugosa corteza, ni el ala sometida por la garra.

Sino, más bien, un jardín eternamente en flor y una bandada de ángeles eternamente en vuelo.

Pueblo de Orfalese, la belleza es la vida, cuando la vida descubre su rostro esencial y sagrado.

Pero vosotros sois la vida y vosotros sois el velo.

La belleza es la eternidad que se contempla a sí misma en un espejo.

Pero vosotros sois la eternidad y vosotros sois el espejo.

Porque, ¿qué es morir sino erguirse desnudo?

¿Y qué es dejar de respirar, sino dejar el aliento libre de sus inquietos vaivenes para que pueda elevarse y expandirse y, ya sin trabas, buscar a Dios?

Sólo cuando bebáis en el río del silencio cantaréis de verdad.

Y sólo cuando hayáis alcanzado la cima de la montaña comenzará vuestro ascenso.

Y sólo cuando la tierra reclame vuestros miembros, bailaréis de verdad.

Y UN VIEJO SACERDOTE pidió: Háblanos de la Religión.

Y él dijo:

¿Acaso he hablado hoy de otra cosa?

¿No son todos los actos y todos los pensamientos religión?

¿Y aun aquello que no es acto ni pensamiento, sino un milagro y una sorpresa brotando siempre en el alma, aun cuando las manos pican la piedra o atienden el telar?

¿Quién puede separar su fe de sus acciones o sus creencias de sus trabajos?

¿Quién es capaz de desplegar sus horas ante sí mismo, y decir: Esto para Dios y esto para mí, esto para mi espíritu y esto para mi cuerpo?

Todas nuestras horas son alas que baten a través del espacio de persona a persona.

El que usa su moralidad como su más bella vestidura mejor andará desnudo.

El sol y el viento no agrietarán su piel.

Y aquel que define su conducta por medio de normas, apresará su pájaro-cantor en una jaula.

El canto más libre no surge detrás de las rejas ni dentro de las jaulas.

Y aquel para quien la adoración es una ventana que puede abrirse pero también cerrarse aún no conoce la mansión de su espíritu, que tiene ventanas que se extienden desde al alba hasta el alba.

Vuestra vida de todos los días es vuestro templo y vuestra religión.

Cada vez que en él entréis, llevad con vosotros todo lo que tenéis.

Llevad el arado y la fragua, el martillo y la guitarra.

Y todo lo que habéis hecho por gusto o por necesidad.

Porque en recuerdos, no podéis elevaros por encima de vuestras obras ni caer más bajo que vuestros fracasos.

Y llevad con vosotros a todos los hombres.

Porque, en la adoración, no podéis volar más lejos que sus esperanzas ni humillaros más bajo que sus angustias.

Y si llegáis a conocer a Dios, no os convirtáis en explicadores de enigmas.

Mirad más bien a vuestro alrededor y lo veréis jugando con vuestros hijos.

Y mirad hacia lo alto; lo veréis caminando en la nube, desplegando sus brazos en el rayo y descendiendo en la lluvia.

Lo veréis sonriendo en las flores y elevándose luego para agitar sus manos desde los árboles.

Y ENTONCES habló Almitra, diciendo: Queremos preguntarte ahora sobre la Muerte.

Y él respondió:

Queréis conocer el secreto de la muerte.

Pero, ¿cómo lo hallaréis si no lo buscáis en el corazón de la vida?

El búho, cuyos ojos atados a la noche son ciegos en el día, no puede descubrir el misterio de la luz.

Si en verdad queréis contemplar el espíritu de la muerte, abrid de par en par vuestro corazón en el cuerpo de la vida.

Porque la vida y la muerte son una, así como son uno el río y el mar.

En lo profundo de vuestras esperanzas y deseos descansa vuestro conocimiento del más allá.

Y como las semillas sueñan bajo la nieve, así vuestro corazón sueña con la primavera.

Confiad en vuestros sueños, porque en ellos está escondido el camino a la eternidad.

Vuestro miedo a la muerte no es más que el temblor del pastor cuando está en pie ante el rey, cuya mano va a posarse sobre él, como un honor.

¿No está contento el pastor, bajo su miedo, de llevar la marca del rey?

¿No le hace eso, sin embargo, más consciente de su temblor?

Y LLEGÓ la noche.

Y Almitra, la profetisa, dijo: Sea bendecido este día y este lugar y tu espíritu que se ha manifestado.

Y él respondió: ¿Fui yo el que habló? ¿No fui también uno de los que escucharon?

Descendió, entonces, las gradas del templo y todo el pueblo lo siguió. Y él subió a su barco y se irguió sobre el puente.

Y, mirando de nuevo a la gente, alzó la voz y dijo: Pueblo de Orfalese: el viento me obliga a marchar lejos.

No tengo la prisa del viento, pero debo irme.

Nosotros, los trotamundos, buscando siempre el camino más solitario, no comenzamos un día donde hemos terminado otro y no hay aurora que nos encuentre donde nos dejó el atardecer.

Aun cuando la tierra duerme, nosotros viajamos.

Somos las semillas de una planta tenaz y es en nuestra madurez y plenitud de corazón que somos entregados al viento y esparcidos por doquier.

Breves fueron mis días entre vosotros y aún más breves las palabras que he dicho.

Pero, si mi voz se hace débil en vuestros oídos y mi amor se desvanece en vuestro recuerdo, entonces volveré.

Y con un corazón más pleno y unos labios más dóciles al espíritu, hablaré.

Sí, he de volver con la marea.

Y aunque la muerte me esconda y el gran silencio me envuelva, buscaré, sin embargo, nuevamente vuestros espíritus.

Y mi búsqueda no será en vano.

Si algo de lo que he dicho es verdad, esa verdad se revelará en una voz más clara y en palabras más cercanas a vuestros pensamientos.

Me voy con el viento, pueblo de Orfalese, pero no hacia la nada.

Y, si este día no es la realización plena de vuestras necesidades y mi amor, que sea una promesa hasta que ese día llegue.

Las necesidades del hombre cambian, pero no su amor, ni su deseo de que este amor satisfaga sus necesidades.

Sabed, pues, que desde el silencio más grande he de volver.

La niebla que se aleja en el alba, y deja solamente el rocío sobre los campos, se eleva y se vuelve nube para caer después convertida en lluvia.

Y no he sido diferente de la niebla.

En la quietud de la noche he caminado por vuestras calles y mi espíritu habitó en vuestras casas.

Y los latidos de vuestro corazón estuvieron en mi corazón y vuestro aliento acarició mi cara.

Yo os conozco a todos.

¡Ay! Yo he sabido de vuestra alegría y de vuestro dolor, y, cuando dormíais, vuestros sueños florecían en mis sueños.

Y, a menudo, fui entre vosotros como un lago entre montañas.

Reflejé vuestras cumbres y vuestras laderas y aun el fluir de vuestros pensamientos y vuestros deseos, en manadas.

Y vino a mi silencio el torrente de risas de vuestros niños y los ríos anhelantes de vuestra juventud.

Y, cuando llegaron a lo más profundo de mi ser, los torrentes y los ríos no cesaron de cantar.

Pero algo más dulce que las risas y más febril que los anhelos vino hacia mí.

Fue lo infinito en vosotros.

El hombre inmenso del que sois apenas las células y nervios.

Aquél en cuyo canto todas vuestras canciones no son más que un latido apagado.

Es en el hombre inmenso en el que sois inmensos.

Y es al mirarlo que yo os vi y os amé.

Porque, ¿qué distancias puede alcanzar el amor que no participen de esa esfera inconmensurable?

¿Qué visiones, qué intuiciones podrán superar ese vuelo?

Como un roble gigante, cubierto de flores de manzano, es el hombre inmenso que habita en vosotros.

Su poder os ata a la tierra, su fragancia os eleva en el espacio y, en su durabilidad, sois inmortales.

Se os ha dicho que, como una cadena, sois tan partes como vuestro más débil eslabón.

Eso es sólo una parte de la verdad. Sois también tan fuertes como vuestro eslabón más fuerte.

Mediros por vuestra más pequeña acción es como calcular el poder del océano por lo instantáneo de su espuma.

Juzgaros por vuestras fallas es como culpar a las estaciones por su inconstancia.

¡Ay! Sois como un océano.

Y aunque barcos pesados esperan la marea en vuestras playas, vosotros, como el océano, no debéis apurar vuestras mareas.

Sois también como las estaciones.

Y aunque en vuestro invierno neguéis vuestra primavera.

La primavera, latiendo en vosotros, sonríe en su ensueño y no se ofende.

No penséis que yo os hablo de este modo para que vosotros os digáis: «No ha visto más que lo bueno que hay en nosotros.»

Yo sólo os digo en palabras lo que vosotros mismos sabéis en vuestro pensamiento.

Y, ¿qué es el conocimiento que dan las palabras sino una sombra del conocimiento inefable?

Vuestros pensamientos y mis palabras son ondas de una memoria sellada que protege el registro de nuestros ayeres.

Y de los antiguos días, cuando la tierra no nos conoció ni se conoció ella misma.

Y de las noches, cuando la tierra estuvo atormentada en confusión.

Sabios vinieron a vosotros a daros de su sabiduría. Yo he venido a tomar de vuestra sabiduría.

Y he aquí que he hallado lo que es más sublime que la sabiduría misma.

Es un espíritu ardiente en vosotros que junta cada vez más de sí mismo.

Mientras vosotros, ausentes de su expansión, lloráis el marchitarse de vuestros días.

Es la vida en busca de vida en los cuerpos amedrentados por la tumba.

No hay tumbas aquí.

Estas montañas y llanuras son una cuota y un peldaño.

Cada vez que paséis cerca del campo donde dejasteis a vuestros antecesores descansando, mirad bien y os veréis a vosotros mismos y veréis a vuestros hijos tomados de la mano.

En verdad, a menudo os divertís sin saberlo.

Otros han venido a quienes, por doradas promesas hechas a vuestra fe, habéis entregado riquezas, poder y gloria.

Menos que una promesa os he dado yo; sin embargo, habéis sido más generosos conmigo.

Me habéis dado la sed más profunda para mis años postreros.

No hay seguramente para un hombre regalo más grande que aquel que hace de todos su anhelos labios sedientos y de toda su vida un arroyo de agua fresca.

Y allí mi honor y mi premio:

Cada vez que voy al arroyo a beber, encuentro sedienta el agua viviente.

Y ella me bebe mientras yo la bebo.

Algunos de vosotros me habéis juzgado orgulloso y exacerbadamente esquivo cuando se trataba de aceptar regalos.

Soy, en verdad, demasiado orgulloso para recibir salario, pero no regalos.

Y aunque he comido bayas entre las colinas, cuando hubierais querido sentarme a vuestra mesa.

Y dormido en el pórtico del templo cuando me hubierais acogido alegremente.

¿No fue acaso vuestro cuidado, amante de mis días y mis noches, el que preparó la comida grata a mi boca y ciñó con visiones mi sueño?

Yo os bendigo aún más por esto:

Vosotros dais mucho y no sabéis que dais.

Verdaderamente, la bondad que se emula a sí misma en un espejo se convierte en piedra.

Y una buena acción que se califica a sí misma con nombres tiernos se vuelve pariente de una maldición.

Y algunos de vosotros me habéis llamado solitario y embriagado en mi propio aislamiento.

Y habéis dicho: «Se consulta con los árboles del boque, pero no con los hombres.

Se siente solitario en las cumbres de los montes, y mira nuestra ciudad a sus pies.»

Verdad es que he ascendido colinas y caminado por lugares remotos.

¿Cómo podría haberos visto sino desde una gran altura o desde una gran distancia?

¿Cómo se puede estar cerca de la verdad, a menos que se esté lejos?

Y otros, entre vosotros, me han llamado sin palabras, diciendo:

«Extranjero, extranjero; amante de cumbres inalcanzables, ¿por qué vives entre las cimas, donde las águilas hacen sus nidos?

¿Por qué buscas lo imposible?

¿Qué tormentas quieres atrapar en tu red?

¿Y qué vaporosos pájaros cazas en el cielo?

Ven y sé uno como nosotros.

Desciende y calma tu hambre con nuestro pan y apaga tu sed con nuestro vino.»

Y decían estas cosas en la soledad de sus almas.

Pero, si su soledad hubiera sido más profunda, hubieran sabido que lo que yo buscaba era el secreto de vuestra alegría y vuestro dolor.

Y que cazaba solamente lo mejor de vuestro ser, que divaga en las alturas.

Pero el cazador fue también el cazado.

Porque muchas de mis flechas sólo dejaron mi arco para hincarse en mi propio pecho.

Y el que volaba también se arrastró.

Porque, cuando mis alas se extendían al sol, su sombra sobre la tierra fue una tortuga.

Y el creyente fue también el escéptico.

Porque yo he puesto a menudo mi dedo en mi propia llaga para poder creer más en vosotros y conoceros mejor.

ÍNDICE

Introducción 5

El Profeta 21